SAWYER

TOREY HOPE: THE LATER YEARS

A.D. ELLIS

SAWYER
Torey Hope:
The Later Years

A.D. Ellis
www.facebook.com/adellisauthor
Copyright © 2015
Story Updated 2021

Cover by A.D. Ellis 2019

To Brett: From the moment we first spoke, I was inspired by you. Your sense of humor, your openness, your strength...all of these things allowed me to see your heart and I knew from the beginning what a special young man you truly are. Because of your honesty and willingness to answer my five thousand questions (I'm sure to you it seemed like more!), Sawyer's story has come to life. For that, and for just being you, Sawyer and I both say thank you.

To Renee.
Thank you for being generous enough to share him with me. He is an amazing man today because he had an amazing momma to learn from. Thank you both. I'm honored to call you both my friends.

QUOTES OF INSPIRATION

Let love in, let love win.

***

"You can't help who you love."
~Nicky Morgan

INTRODUCTION

Trigger Warning- this story contains scenes of homophobia, derogatory language, a hate crime, and sexual abuse.

Author's Note:

Sadly, I am very well aware, as I'm sure many readers are, that a large number of lesbian, gay, bisexual, and transgender individuals are not met with love, support, or acceptance. Sawyer, along with many of his gay friends, deal with discrimination, misconceptions, fear, and hatred throughout the book. The way this story played out came completely from Sawyer and the other characters, I just wrote the tale they wanted to tell. It may be a much rougher story than the ones some readers have heard or experienced; it may be a much happier version of what some readers have heard or lived through. But either way, it's a realistic story focusing on acceptance, hope, and love.

If you or someone you love need information or support in issues surrounding sexuality, please connect with one of the many organizations available to assist. Here are two such organizations:

PFLAG

http://community.pflag.org/getsupport

GLBT National Help Center

http://www.glbthotline.org/

A NOTE FROM THE AUTHOR

For those who like a little narrative along with a family tree. Here are the families of Torey Hope. Meet the Morgans, the Jordans, the Deckers, and the Martins.

John and Cindy Morgan have twin boys Nate and Nicky Morgan.

Nicky Morgan married Carly Malone and had children Zachary Malone Morgan and Alyson Elizabeth Morgan.

Nate Morgan married Libby Decker and had children Abigail Emerson Morgan and twins Decker Nathaniel and Sawyer Nicholas Morgan.

Libby Decker is sister to **Audrey Decker**, both are daughters of **Captain Robert Decker** and the late **Lois Decker**. Robert later married **Janie**.

Audrey Decker married **Jeremiah Jordan**. Jeremiah had a son, **Beckett**, from a previous marriage. Jeremiah and Audrey had **Megan Elise Jordan** and **Kendrick Robert Jordan**. Beckett got married in the first book of this series to a girl named Kenja.

Jeremiah is the son of **Jack and Judy Jordan**.

Captain Robert Decker had an estranged brother, Richard who was married to Corrine and they had a daughter named **Josie**. Josie married Jeremiah Jordan's best friend, **Kyle Martin** and they had children **Zoey Belle Martin** and **Asher Jeremiah Jordan**.

A NOTE FROM THE AUTHOR

For those who like a little narrative along with a family tree. Here are the families of Torey Hope. Meet the Morgans, the Jordans, the Deckers, and the Martins.

John and Cindy Morgan have twin boys Nate and Nicky Morgan.

Nicky Morgan married Carly Malone and had children Zachary Malone Morgan and Alyson Elizabeth Morgan.

Nate Morgan married Libby Decker and had children Abigail Emerson Morgan and twins Decker Nathaniel and Sawyer Nicholas Morgan.

Libby Decker is sister to **Audrey Decker**, both are daughters of **Captain Robert Decker** and the late **Lois Decker**. Robert later married **Janie**.

Audrey Decker married **Jeremiah Jordan**. Jeremiah had a son, **Beckett**, from a previous marriage. Jeremiah and Audrey had **Megan Elise Jordan** and **Kendrick Robert Jordan**. Beckett got married in the first book of this series to a girl named Kenja.

Jeremiah is the son of **Jack and Judy Jordan**.

Captain Robert Decker had an estranged brother, Richard who was married to Corrine and they had a daughter named **Josie**. Josie married Jeremiah Jordan's best friend, **Kyle Martin** and they had children **Zoey Belle Martin** and **Asher Jeremiah Jordan**.

The Families of Torey Hope

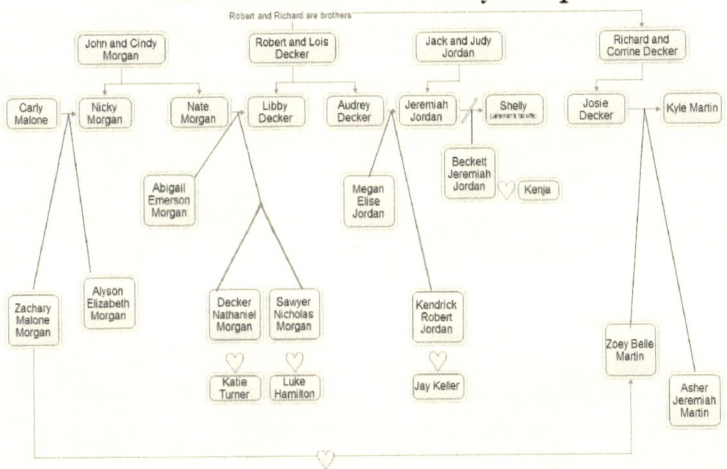

Real-life Contemporary Romance by A.D. Ellis

1

Sawyer, age 16

Shirts discarded and arms entangled around torsos, the young men rolled around the bed as if wrestling. Hidden, she watched from the doorway in fascination, not disgust or horror. Her mind struggled to make sense of something her heart had already accepted. As the boys' lips met in a sensual kiss, she brought her hand up to cover her surprise. She knew, instinctively, the act happening in front of her was what Sawyer had been missing, seeking, craving.

Knowing she should look away, afford them privacy, she couldn't unglue her eyes from the awkwardly arousing scene transpiring before her. Hands roamed, cupping ass cheeks; hips and tongues thrust in simultaneous dances. Red basketball shorts and tight gray boxer briefs slid down firm, muscular legs followed quickly by black shorts and black briefs moving down a second pair of toned legs. She'd seen the male anatomy in Health class, but the young men on the bed were aroused from their sensuous exploration and she felt her eyes widening in impressed awe at the size of their...male anatomy. Sawyer, the dark haired one, reached a hand down and grasped the other boy; the act was reciprocated and a delightful display began to play out before her. Mouths, teeth, and tongues clashed as hips thrust and fists pumped; rough breaths, sexually charged, resonated in the otherwise silent room.

She knew she should have left, should have allowed him this intimate moment, but it was too late; an ill-timed sneeze, obstructed by a quick pinch to the nose, but not thwarted completely, literally blew her cover.

She froze in the doorway as two heads, rosy-cheeked and breathing heavily, popped up and fists quickly abandoned that which they craved to hold tightly.

The lip she bit and the tears which sprang to her eyes weren't for herself; her heart broke for Sawyer. She knew he had worked to cover up the feelings and longings in his heart; she knew he strived for normal and easy and drama-free. Her heart was hurt for him, not because he was her boyfriend and had been caught making out with another guy, but because she knew he was already struggling and the challenging, uphill strife he faced would be a burden on his beautiful heart.

With shorts quickly replaced and shirts pulled over

heads, the two young men stood awkwardly in the middle of the room, warily observing her. She wondered who would speak first and what those infamous first words would be.

"So, um, Josh, this is Katie. My girlfriend. Katie, this is Josh." Sawyer had the decency to look embarrassed, but Katie wanted to ease his discomfort. She had fancied herself in love with him for a while, but in her heart she'd known there was something missing when they were together. Watching him at that moment, she knew she'd never seen her best friend look so alive, so interested, so radiant.

"Hi, Josh, it's nice to meet you." Katie smiled at Josh who seemed a bit more freaked out by the situation unfolding in front of him than Sawyer or Katie. Turning to her boyfriend, Katie spoke, "Hey, maybe you and I could have some time to talk and you could call Josh later?"

As if roused from a hypnotic state, Sawyer blushed and nodded. "Yeah, um, that would be good. So, I'll see you at school tomorrow, Josh. Um, maybe we could, um....yeah, bye." Sawyer's stumbled words were enough of a reason for Josh to hightail it from the room without a backward glance.

"Okay, so that was awkward all around. Want to get out of here and talk about what just went down?" Katie held her hand out to Sawyer and he knew in that exact moment that he would love her for the rest of his life; aside from his twin brother and cousins, she was his heart and best friend.

They left his house with him wondering in absolute horror what would have happened if his brother or parents had been the ones to walk in on him in bed with another guy. Reaching the main park in Torey Hope, they walked to the shelter house and perched themselves on top of a picnic table. Facing each other, sitting cross-legged, their knees touching, Katie reached for his hands.

"So, you know I love you, Sawyer, and that will never change. I think if I can witness what I just saw and still profess my love, I'm pretty solid in this relationship." He smirked and saw her smile at him in relief. "However, I think there are some things we need to get out in the open. First, I'm sure this is pretty obvious, I'm breaking up with you."

Sawyer threw his head back and laughed. Feeling the pent up frustration and anxiety leave his body calmed him. "Katie, I'm sorry for what you just saw...no, I'm not sorry you saw it, and I'm not sorry it happened; I'm sorry I didn't share my feelings with you before you had to walk in on it." He leaned in and kissed her gently. "I will forever love you, as my best friend, Katie. But you're right, we can't be together, not in *that* way; it wouldn't be fair to either of us."

They sat silently for a moment. Sawyer, deep in thought, his dark eyes focused on their hands. He appreciated Katie giving him the time he needed to gather his thoughts.

"So, I think I like guys; I think I'm gay, Katie-girl," he said it on a whoosh and then sat apprehensively as if the universe was going to strike him down. In a strangled whisper he repeated, "I think I'm gay."

She felt those words in her soul; the relief he felt in

speaking them, the fear he felt in admitting them. But the words from his mouth spoke of more to her heart; she heard his despair, his doubt, his dismay.

"Sawyer Morgan, look at me. You are gay. You're not a murderer or a pedophile or a thief; you have a great family and friends, they will support you no matter what. It will be harder for some of them at first, but they will come around. If they don't, you'll *always* have me."

She was taken aback at the vehement shaking of his head and his quick, "No! I'm not ready to tell anyone else."

She rubbed his hands in hers and raised an eyebrow. "Why not? Your family loves you like none other; they are one of the most loved families in Torey Hope. They would never not stand behind you."

"That's just it, Katie. I can't tell them right now. This is brand-new to me; I'm just admitting it and accepting it. If I tell them now, they will have to deal with the stress and possible embarrassment and drama it may bring; I can't do that to them right now. What if it causes problems at The Center? Let me figure this out within myself a little more first, then I can break it to them." His dark brown eyes pleaded with hers.

"Well, I want it stated on record that I think you're making a mistake, but I promise to support you; as long as you're not endangering yourself, I'll let you keep your secret. And it will be my secret, too." She squeezed his hand and felt his body relax. "So, how about you tell me about this revelation. How long have you known?"

"I think I started suspecting when I was about twelve. I remember seeing some guys at The Center who had taken their shirts off to play basketball, and I thought they were absolutely beautiful. I'd seen girls and women in swimsuits and felt nothing, but an attractive guy with his shirt off made my heart beat faster." Sawyer's eyes had a faraway look as he recalled the vast difference in feelings he'd had for males and females.

"Then, I met you and I wanted so badly to just fall in love and be normal. I'm so sorry, Katie, I really haven't been fair to you at all. It's not that kissing you isn't nice, but it doesn't light me on fire like kissing Josh does. I'm so very sorry you had to find out this way." Sawyer's head hung in shame.

"Sawyer, don't apologize." She felt tears build in her own eyes as the tears began to spill out of his. "I'll admit it was a bit of a shock to walk in and see that. But if I'm being honest with myself, I really wasn't that surprised. I love you and kissing you was nice, but I never felt all the butterflies and glitter that the girls talk about when they're gossiping about kissing boys. Seeing you with Josh, the way your body responded to his, knowing that our bodies had never responded to each other in that way, I knew in my heart that you were meant to just be my best friend." They dried their tears; they both erupted in laughter when Katie quipped, "At least you were gay before me; I'm not sure I could stand the social outcasting if the rumor started that I turned you gay."

Walking arm-in-arm, they headed back toward his house. "So, Josh, huh? Do you want him to be, like, your boyfriend?" Katie nudged Sawyer's hip in teasingly playful way.

"I like Josh, but I think I like him because he's the first guy I've kissed. I like his body next to mine; I like to have my hands on him; I like to kiss him. Do I like *him*? I don't know. I don't think he's any closer to admitting or accepting his sexuality than I am, so I don't see us becoming a couple and publicly outing ourselves. If anything, we'll spend time behind *closed* doors and try to figure things out for ourselves, individually."

Katie blushed at the mention of *closed* doors.

"Hey, bud, that door was practically wide open. I probably should have just walked away, but you two were astonishingly beautiful in your sexy little coupling, and I couldn't help myself. You should thank your lucky stars it was me and not your mom or dad or brother!" Katie wagged a finger sternly in front of his face.

Sawyer blanched yet again at the thought of his parents or twin brother, Decker, finding him in a compromising position with another man. He knew in his heart that his parents and brother would accept him no matter what, but he didn't want to bring undue stress or drama into their lives; for now, he'd keep it secret, but he'd tell them once he was a little more comfortable with it himself.

But the thing with keeping secrets and not being truthful with those who love you is that it gets harder and harder with each day. As the years passed, Sawyer realized he'd missed several prime opportunities to be upfront with his parents and Decker.

There were the numerous chances he had when he and Decker were alone. Playing video games, basketball, going for a run. He couldn't count the number of times he ended up with a bloody tongue from biting it so hard. The words were right there, he wanted so badly to say them, but his fear always got the best of him.

Helping his dad in the evenings or summers. He'd find himself painting a fence, cleaning out the garage, changing the oil in the car with his father.

"How's Kendrick and that girlfriend of his?" His dad would ask.

"Which one?" Sawyer and his father would laugh.

"What about you, you got your eye on anyone special?" Nate would give him the perfect opening, yet Sawyer would swig some water or get super busy in finding a rag to clean up the oil.

"Nah, no one in particular." The chance to tell the truth buzzed around his head like a bumblebee, but then it was gone, flying off to another flower.

The evenings in the kitchen helping his mom cook supper, setting the table, cleaning up the dishes. She'd lay down the cloth she was using to clean and cock her head in that special way that only she had. "Sawyer, you know we love you, right? Always."

Over the years he'd swallowed many baseball sized lumps trying to control his emotions. Fear, shame, guilt. It was like his mom knew he had a secret, but she didn't want to force it out of him.

He could picture himself telling her, "Mom, I'm gay."

But then he'd think of an analogy he'd once heard, *Words are like toothpaste. Once you squeeze the paste from the tube, you can't put it back in. Our words are like that, once we speak them, we can't take them back no matter how hard we try.*

Sawyer knew the analogy was meant for speaking harmful words, but he still couldn't get away from the hard truth, *Once you tell them, there's no taking it back. No matter what their reactions, you can't ever change things.*

He knew he wasn't ready to tell the entire family, but his brother and parents deserved to know the truth, he knew this. Yet he continued to keep it from them. After a while, it was a lie of omission which had been hidden so deep he feared Decker would be pissed that he'd kept it from him for so long. Would his parents be hurt that he'd lied to them on top of the disappointment in finding out their son was gay?

It all became too much. He'd dug himself so deep, he wasn't sure there was a shovel in the world that could save him. So Sawyer got by, he searched for himself, he longed for love, and he kept his secret hidden deep within.

2

*P*resent day, *Torey Hope*

Pensive brown eyes stared back at him as he regarded himself in the mirror. Part of him felt ready for this next step, another part of him wanted to keep plodding along, keeping his secret, hiding. He was so tired of hiding, but staying hidden brought him comfort. He was tired of secrets, but those secrets were his shield.

If he followed through with his plan, he would no longer be shielded, no longer able to protect himself and others from the truth. And that scared the fuck out of him. If he did this, he opened himself and his family up to ridicule, shame, embarrassment; the family business, The Center+, could suffer.

But if he didn't do this, he knew he'd sink back into the black hole he'd been in until recently. One person had known his secret for years, but that didn't save him from the derogatory names thrown at him in the halls and locker room when his brothers or cousins weren't around.

"Come on, man up, Morgan. The guys took it fine, Mom and Dad were supportive; it's time to let the rest of the family in on your secret." He smiled as he recalled the conversations he'd had not long ago with his twin brother and cousins. He'd assembled them all on a camping trip and broke the news, years after he should have opened up to them.

I'm gay.

His brother, Decker, had taken the news fairly well. He'd needed a solo walk through the woods to gather his thoughts; Sawyer suspected his always-in-control, serious, black and white brother also needed to come to grips with the fact that he'd never suspected his brother's sexuality was different than his own. How ironic that the one person Sawyer was the closest to in the whole world was the one person who was the most clueless.

Sawyer had held his breath practically the whole time Decker had been walking through the woods. A deluge of rain poured down as the dark sky broke open, yet Sawyer still sat alone at the campfire. His head had started playing tricks on him. *You disgust him...he can't stand the thought of having a gay brother...you've lost him...he's not coming back.* But Sawyer held out hope that Decker was just doing his usual thinking things through.

He had breathed a sigh of relief when Decker emerged,

soaking wet, from the woods. Walking towards him with purpose, his twin had stopped in front of him and spoke the most heartwarming, sincere words Sawyer had ever heard from him.

"You're my brother, always have been, always will be. I wish you could have told me sooner, but nothing has changed between us. I'll be there in any and every way that I can." Decker grabbed Sawyer and pulled him into a deep embrace, communicating his love and acceptance through his touch.

Telling his cousins, Zach and Kendrick, had been less emotional, and a lot more entertaining. Sawyer had to laugh at the questions his admission had stirred up.

"I'm gay." Two words that held such power. Would they laugh? Would they walk away in disgust? Would they be angry?

Zach smiled and nodded. "I think I've known that for a long time, man, but thanks for telling me."

"Wait, you knew? Why didn't you ever say something? Why did you joke with me about girls?"

"I don't know, I guess I figured you'd tell me when you were ready. I didn't want to bring it up if I was wrong and it offended you. I think I joked about girls thinking it would give you the opportunity to bring it up if you wanted to." Zach stood and walked to his cousin, reaching a hand down, he pulled the other man up into a hug. "Nothing changes, I've got your back, man."

Kendrick sat with his hand rubbing his chin. Would he be the one who couldn't accept it?

Eyes twinkling and a shit-eatin' grin on his face, he finally spoke. "What's it like to suck cock?"

The other three burst out laughing.

"Come on, I'm serious. Maybe I'm 'bi-curious,' who knows. I know I like burying myself deep in a girl, the tighter the better; I'm assuming being deep in a guy's ass has to feel pretty much like heaven on earth, right?"

Sawyer felt like he was having an out-of-body experience as he attempted to shake off his utter shock and awe at his cousin's words.

"Um, yeah, it's pretty close to heaven."

"See, I've always thought guys would probably suck cock better than girls; just like a girl could probably eat pussy better than most guys. Why? Well, as a guy, I know exactly what feels good, just like a girl knows exactly what feels good. I don't know if I'd ever actually do it, but I'd likely consider doing a guy; I don't know if I could let a guy fuck me though."

Kendrick paused in his musings and glanced at his cousins' open-mouthed expressions. "What? It's just stuff I've thought about before. Don't get me wrong, I love women, but being with a guy intrigues me a bit."

And with that, all the worries Sawyer had about telling his cousins he was gay floated off into the night air.

Later that night, they had settled in to their sleeping bags, relaxed and happy from the many beers they had consumed.

"So, really, what's it like?" Decker asked into the darkness.

"What? Sex with a guy?" Sawyer smiled as he spoke, finding it amusing that his brother and cousins were so interested.

"Yeah, man. I don't see myself or Zach ever sleeping with a guy; Kendrick, maybe. But, what's it like? How's it work?" At the snorts of laughter, Decker huffed, "I know how it works, I just wonder if it's that different from being with a girl."

"For me, it's different because it feels right. Being with girls felt wrong, awkward, strange. Being with a guy makes my heart flutter, my skin tingle, and my body grow warm." Sawyer began to get lost in thought, but he pulled himself back to the group.

"Kissing. Kissing is awesome. Soft lips, slick tongue, roaming hands, a little hair pulling, kissing is perfect." He closed his eyes and pictured the soft lips of a man who made his heart flutter.

Kendrick rolled to his back and propped his head on his bent elbows behind his head. "What about sex?"

"Depends on the person you're with and what you're both comfortable with. Oral, anal, jacking each other off, like I said, it just depends."

"Are you the one on top or the one on bottom?" Kendrick asked.

"Again, it depends. Some guys will only do top, some will only do bottom, some like to take turns. Some couples don't do anal, only oral and mutual masturbation. It's very much like sex with a woman, you have preferences; guys just have different options."

"Does it feel good? Top or bottom, does it feel good either way?" Zach cocked his head to the side and waited.

"If the guy is big, it can hurt at first; if he's rougher, it can be painful."

"Alright, enough gay sex talk tonight, boys. I'm beat." Kendrick laughed at his own words. "Can you imagine the earful someone would have gotten if they'd been outside the windows tonight?"

They all chuckled.

"Guys, thanks so much for being okay with this," Sawyer said. "Your reactions wouldn't have changed who I am, but it's good to know that I have you on my side."

His mouth curved into another soft smile as he replayed the conversation they'd had. He knew that not all people got such acceptance from family and friends when they came out; he was lucky his brother and cousins had taken it in stride.

Shortly thereafter, knowing he owed it to his parents and to himself to be honest after so many years of hiding, he had sat at the kitchen table with Decker there for support, and told his mom and dad his secret.

"I'm gay."

His mom, Libby, had cried, but quickly dried her tears and smiled at him.

"Momma, why don't you look shocked? Dad, why aren't

you surprised?" Sawyer had expected more of a reaction from them.

"Oh, baby boy, we've known for a while. Well, I wouldn't say we've known, but we've suspected for about 10-12 years now." Libby's smile was shaky, but she didn't appear devastated.

"Why didn't you say anything?" Sawyer questioned.

"Your mom brought it up to me several years ago. I think in the beginning we both hoped she was wrong, we didn't want you to have to suffer through the emotions and reactions. Then, when we were more sure about it, we talked and decided it was something you needed to come to on your own and all we could do was be here loving you until you were ready to talk to us." His dad, Nate, stood and walked to his son. "I love you no matter what. I don't like the idea of you being hurt or ridiculed, but nothing will ever change the fact that you're my son and I love you."

Libby sniffled and hugged Sawyer into her arms. "You'll always be my baby boy and I will love you until my dying breath. I hate that not everyone in your life and in this town will be as open about your sexuality, but you've got us on your side, no matter what."

He was two-for-two in the coming out department. Would his luck hold when he told the rest of his family? Eyeing his reflection in the mirror again, he sighed and leaned his hands on the bathroom counter. Apprehension bubbled inside mixing with fear and excitement. Telling the rest of his family held so much uncertainty. Knowing the numbers just weren't on his side, he knew in his heart he'd face objection and possible rejection from at least one, if not more, of his family members. Who would it be? Who would look at him with disgust or hatred?

Recently, years longer than it should have taken him, and as a promise kept to his college friend, he had admitted he was depressed and had started seeing a therapist. Dr. Parks specialized in counseling lesbian, gay, bisexual, and transgender patients. He had made Sawyer comb through memories, some that Sawyer would have rather kept buried. He detested the pain and hurt that came from sifting through the memories and feelings, but with the pain and hurt came realization that hiding and keeping secrets wasn't fair to himself or those around him.

He wanted to be free from it all. Admitting it only to Dr. Parks, there were times when he waffled between "freeing" himself by coming out to all the people in his life and living as an openly gay man, and "freeing" himself from the pain and heaviness of the burden by just ending it all. Dr. Parks made him talk more about that than he really wanted to.

"You're scared of rejection from your family. You're worried about causing them stress or embarrassment or shame. Speak to me about how you think they'd feel if you commit suicide." Dr. Parks was always very direct, never sugarcoating anything.

"Doc, I'd never do it; sometimes it's just nice to think

about what a relief it would be if none of this existed for me anymore." Sawyer had tried to avoid the question, but Dr. Parks hadn't let it go.

"So, how do you think your family would feel if you committed suicide?" He never strayed from the path he was on.

Head hanging and words whispered straight from his heart, Sawyer spoke, "They'd be devastated." Tears glistened in his eyes thinking of the pain his suicide would cause to those he loved.

"And what would that devastation be like for them if they later found out you're gay and you killed yourself rather than opening up to them?" Dr. Parks wasn't trying to cause more pain, but the question hurt.

Drawing a deep breath and closing his eyes, Sawyer tried to imagine how distraught his family would be if they found out he'd taken his own life because he felt like he couldn't be open with them. "It would absolutely destroy them."

He knew with certainty that he had to open up to them. He wanted to rid himself of the weight of this secret, he wanted love and support to help him navigate what had already proved to be rough waters. He feared rejection, but he knew he already had his parents and brother and cousins on his side, so he didn't fear absolute abandonment.

As he prepared to gather his family around to make his announcement, he allowed the past to play through his mind;

his journey to this point had been filled with family and friends, but the confusion, heartache, and uncertainty were never far away.

3

awyer, age 16

The ball swooshed through the hoop as the four young men played a game of basketball on the courts outside The Center after school. The rule in their family was homework could come after some downtime and physical activity as long as grades didn't falter.

"You going to the school dance this weekend?" Zach asked the question of all of his cousins.

"I wasn't planning on it; those things are always just couples practically having sex on the dance floor or groups of guys standing around shootin' the shit. I don't have a girl to kiss and no way I'm dancing, so I figured I'd get homework done so I'd be free the rest of the weekend." Decker dribbled around Sawyer and made an easy lay-up; he flashed a look of concern at his brother, knowing Sawyer was off his game.

"What about you, Kendrick? You've been in quite the funk since Jenny moved away; you going to the dance to find a new girl to make out with?" Zach laughed as his question threw Kendrick off long enough for his cousin to steal the ball from him and land a three-point shot.

"Fuck off, man. I don't want to talk about Jenny, and I don't need a dance to find girls to make out with." Kendrick wiped sweat from his brow, then grabbed his bag. "I gotta head out, guys; Mom is expecting me home to eat supper. Later." The slump of his shoulders and weariness in his voice as he walked off the court, gave away much more than his words.

Decker contemplated his cousin as he walked away. "What the hell is his problem lately? I know he and Jenny were pretty serious, and it sucks that she up and moved so suddenly, but he's never been this upset over a girl before."

"I don't know, man, but I'm ready for him to pull his head out of his ass and get over his pissy attitude; he's been a complete douche lately." With the game obviously wrapping up since one of the players had left, Zach stood at the free-throw line bouncing the ball. "What about you, Sawyer? You and Katie going to the dance? You guys have all the fancy moves since you've been practicing for that dance competition; you two could totally rule the dance floor. Get her all hot and sweaty and worked up and then take her back home for some hot and heavy makin' out." Zach waggled his eyebrows at Sawyer, always the tease and jokester.

"Nah, Katie and I broke up. We're just going to be friends." Sawyer tried to come across as nonchalant. Truth was, he wasn't hurting over losing Katie; they were great as best friends, even better than when they'd tried dating. His sadness and looming depression came from the war inside his head and heart.

He wanted to be honest with himself, his family, his friends. But he wasn't sure how everyone would react; he was more worried about the people around town causing issues for his parents, aunts and uncles, grandparents, and The Center.

Sawyer watched "normal" couples around school hold hands and kiss. He saw the love his parents shared; his entire family was one big happy love fest most of the time. His heart craved to find that, and his body longed for the physical touch of a man; instead, he hung out with Katie or his brother and cousins. It was safer this way, but it wasn't the way he wanted to live.

Maybe once he got out of Torey Hope for a while, went to college, he could explore and experiment more freely. He felt like he was Sawyer Morgan on the outside, but it was just a façade. The real Sawyer was gay, but he was being hidden away. He longed for the courage to be himself.

SAWYER, age 17

"Hey man, what was up with that guy? It looked like he was itching to fight; everything okay?" Decker's concern for him touched his heart and eased the pain from the ugly words he heard rattling in his brain.

"Faggot."

"You gay little fag."

"You really are a cocksucker."

"Fucking queer."

Aside from Katie and the few guys he'd messed around with over the past year, Sawyer had told no one about his sexuality. He knew Katie wasn't talking, and the guys weren't ready to out themselves as gay or even curious, so he figured they weren't spreading rumors. But the fact that he took Art, Theater, Music, and Choir classes in high school sort of attracted the local homophobic bullies to give him a rough time. He also participated in, and sometimes instructed, painting, pottery, dance, and acting classes at The Center in his free time. Close-minded, hateful people took that to mean it was open season on him.

Sawyer and Decker looked 100% exactly alike, but there was always something softer, more sensitive about Sawyer. Add that to the classes and hobbies he enjoyed, narrow-minded, fearful people were going to talk. Only two guys gave him a hard time at school; it wasn't unbearable, but it was enough to wear on him some days.

"Sawyer? Was that guy giving you a rough time?" Decker

pulled him from his thoughts. Decker didn't know Sawyer's secret, he was just always protective of his family.

Bringing himself back to the present, Sawyer shook his head and zipped up his bag. "Nah, man. Just a douche bag from one of my classes; he's mad because I won't give him my notes. He slept through most of the class and skipped it two days last week; expects me to just hand over my hard work because he screwed up. He's not a friend, so I don't feel like I owe him anything."

Passionate, sensitive, Sawyer would give a friend or family member the shirt off his back with no questions asked; leery, pained, jaded Sawyer wouldn't even give a second glance to someone who had hurt him or didn't deserve his kindness.

"Hell no, man. Don't give that dick anything." Decker, the protector, the serious one, clapped him on the back, and they headed toward home.

"Sawyer, why don't you invite a friend over for Taco Night? We haven't seen many of your friends around lately." His mother, Libby, kissed his cheek and hugged him.

His heart hurt; his head ached from holding back the tears he wanted to cry. "Sure Momma, I think I'll ask Katie to come over if you're okay with that." Libby's eyes stared sadly into his, as if she wanted to say more; he felt pulled to blurt out what had him so down and hurt, to tell her he was gay. Instead, he swallowed his pain again and called Katie.

She arrived long before Taco Night started at Grandma Cindy's, so they holed up in Sawyer's room. He knew Decker wouldn't be home; he was working on a business plan mock-up and would be at the library until late.

"Sawyer, what's wrong?" Katie pulled him into a warm embrace, and the tears he'd tried so valiantly to fight off began to fall. She let him cry on her shoulder for several moments, the dampness from the tears and his breath seeped through her shirt; she didn't mind, her friend was hurting, and she wanted to take away his pain.

"Remember Josh? We've hooked up a couple times." Sawyer's traitorous body recalled the intimate moments he'd shared with Josh as recently as last week.

"Sawyer, I know I've said this enough times to fill an entire book, but *please* be careful. By careful, I mean protection first and always. I want you to be happy and satisfied and fulfilled, but I can't stand the thought of you getting hurt if you aren't protected; that means making him be protected too. This is a conversation I never thought I'd be having, but if you're going to be intimate with guys, or girls for that matter, *please* protect yourself. I've read way too much about anal sex and oral anal sex; the diseases that can be spread are down-right terrifying. Second, by *be careful*, I mean with your heart." When Sawyer closed his eyes and sighed, Katie felt she'd hit a sore spot.

Rubbing her hands up and down his arms, she spoke softly. "Sawyer, I know you want love and acceptance and to find the same happiness your whole family seems to have, but you've got to be careful who you give your heart to. First, you're *young*; very few people find their happily ever after in high school. Maybe you'll find your happy-for-now, but don't get so down on yourself if you've not found *the one* yet; you've got so much time ahead of you for that. Second, I know you like Josh, but I feel like you just like him because he's willing to get physical with you. It's no secret I don't trust the guy. Neither of you are ready to go public yet, but I worry he's the type who would out you to save his own reputation or string you along, like a friend with benefits, while he fucks the popular girls to cover the fact that he likes dick."

Sawyer had to smile at how worked up Katie got when she talked about the topic. It wasn't the first time she'd voiced her concern about Josh; she really didn't trust him.

"Well, Katie-girl, I guess you can say 'I told you so' because Josh screwed me over today. The last time we were together, we talked about maybe making things a little more official between us; not coming out as a couple, but exclusively, albeit secretly, seeing each other." Sawyer laughed bitterly. "Well, I guess *I* talked about that." He got a faraway look in his eyes as he recalled their most recent night together.

"Bend over the arm of the couch." Josh smacked Sawyer's ass, and walked to get the lube from the drawer. Josh's parents were out as usual, so they had the house to themselves. Josh

wasn't a sensitive or caring lover; were any 17-year-old boys all that attuned to their partner's pleasure? Sawyer longed to be the top occasionally, and had voiced his desire often.

"Fuck that shit, man. I'm not gay, I'm not taking it up the ass." Josh answered the same way every time the subject was broached. Sawyer enjoyed the physical act, the intimacy; he wanted so badly for a real relationship to develop, so he let it go. He gave his body to Josh and wished for more.

"Spread your legs, Morgan." Dribbling the lube along his ass, Josh rubbed a finger around Sawyer's hole. Josh wasn't into foreplay, a few stretching movements with his finger was all Sawyer knew he'd get.

The first time they'd been together, Sawyer had convinced him to use a toy to prepare him. After a moment, Josh had ripped the toy out of Sawyer's ass, covered and lubed up, lined himself up and entered him with as much finesse as a rhino walking the runway. Sawyer had seen stars from the pain, but he was able to relax and enjoy the act eventually. Josh was too busy ramming into his ass, so Sawyer had jacked himself off, coming at the same time as Josh. It had been hot and sweaty and satisfying, but it hadn't been love. Maybe that would come?

Snapping out of his memory, Sawyer spread his legs and leaned farther over the arm of the couch. Reaching down, taking himself into his own hand, knowing he'd need to do his own work if he was going to get off, he groaned as the cool, wet liquid ran down his ass. Josh's hands spread his cheeks; using both thumbs, he massaged the hole and entered briefly.

Sawyer rocked his hips backwards, hoping to prolong the foreplay; he longed for the kisses and caresses they'd shared when they had first discovered their mutual attraction. He felt himself stiffen as he recalled the afternoons they'd jacked off together, both of their hands grasping their cocks as they rubbed together.

But now that Josh had consummated their relationship, they seldom made out or did anything else. Josh would call him, tell him he wanted to fuck him, and Sawyer would go running. In his mind, he convinced himself that Josh wanted him, they would eventually fall in love.

Releasing the breath he found he was holding, Sawyer bore down against Josh's advancing invasion. His body reacted; quickly tightening against the width of Josh's erection, then relaxing to allow him more entrance. Sawyer loved the moments when Josh entered him; he would grasp his hips and whisper in Sawyer's ear.

"God, yeah...Morgan, you're so fucking tight. Ahh, the way your ass grips my cock. Mmm, I love fucking your ass." Those moments were few and far between; Josh didn't whisper sweet nothings, he didn't compliment Sawyer, he never made mention of what they did together. Sawyer reveled in hearing his words during the few short moments it took him to reach his orgasm.

As they cleaned up, Sawyer brought up a subject he'd been

contemplating for a while. "Listen, I know neither of us is ready to go public with our relationship, but I wondered how you'd feel about making this exclusive, just us, no dating others."

In later moments, Sawyer would recognize the look of disgust and panic on Josh's face for what it was, but in that moment of vulnerability, he took it as nervousness on Josh's part. "I don't want to date anyone else, and I'd like it if you were only doing this with me."

Josh nodded, "Sure, sure man. That sounds good. Listen, I'll call you; my parents said they might come home early tonight, so you better split."

Sawyer paused in his deep recollections; rubbing his fingers roughly along his temples, he let his hands dig into his short, dark hair and grip fistfuls; the pulling pain helped to quiet the hurt in his heart.

"I was so stupid, Katie. I got to school today and found him kissing Amber, the head cheerleader. He didn't even look my way; I heard through the grapevine that they are an official couple now." Sawyer hung his head, trying to ward off the frustration, anger, and pain.

"He finally texted me this afternoon. *Sawyer, I'm not gay, please don't hit on me anymore. You're making me uncomfortable.*" Sawyer laughed bitterly. "I guess that's his way of threatening me not to mention what we were doing together to anyone. I wonder if he'll keep booty calling me and expect me to just come running?"

Katie hugged him close. "Sawyer, I'm so sorry. I'd never say, 'I told you so.' I'm just glad you're away from that jerk. He wasn't good for you; he used you for his own selfish needs. I don't mean to be harsh, but he was never going to come out or accept the fact that he liked fucking you. The only thing that would have been worse than what he did today is if he'd told others you were hitting on him and trying to get him to fuck you. If you don't want this secret out, you definitely need to be leery of being with guys who aren't ready to come out or aren't willing to keep your secret if you keep theirs." She rubbed her hands up and down his strong, muscular back and felt him shudder under her touch.

He brought his tear-stained face up to gaze into her beautiful eyes. Rubbing a soft finger along her bottom lip, he leaned in. His eyes clouded as his lips grazed hers. "I could do this, we could make this work. I love you, Katie, it wouldn't be a hardship to be with you." She allowed him to capture her lips in his, sighing into his touch. Gently pushing him away, she smiled sadly at him.

"Yes, we could make it work. We love each other dearly, and we'd have a nice life. But I'd always know what you long for, and you'd always know I was missing the passion, the spark, the heat. We're too good for that, Sawyer. I won't let you hide; one day, you're going to find a man who challenges you, makes your heart beat faster, and wants you for you. Until then, I'll stand by you as you work your way through the ass hats." She kissed him gently and held him quietly for a long time. "And I want it noted, your parents and brother would stand by your side as well." She felt him take a deep breath and knew it was a subject he wasn't ready to tackle.

When her belly growled, they both laughed.

"Come on, Katie-girl, I think it's time to get you some tacos." Sawyer held her hand as they made their way to Grandma Cindy's infamous Taco Night.

4

*S*awyer, college
College was good. Sawyer loved being out on his own, living with his brother and cousins. Classes were mostly fun and interesting; school had never been difficult for him. He and the guys were getting closer to their goal of graduating and returning to Torey Hope to expand The Center where many of his family worked or gave of their time, efforts, talents.

Sawyer never lacked for friends; he always had Decker, Zach, and Kendrick. He and Katie kept in touch, but he missed seeing her on a daily basis; he was sad to know that she wasn't planning to return to Torey Hope. He had male friends and female friends; he "dated" some women, but it never went further than recreational sex. Usually, Sawyer and the woman would hook up, and then she'd figure out he was gay. Some of the women stormed off, some of them stayed in the friend zone. Sawyer felt shame that he used women as substitutes; he wanted men, but having sex with women was expected and more accepted. He had slept with a few men since coming to college; none of those men were ones Sawyer was all that attracted to, but they provided him the connection and release he was longing for, even if just for a night.

Surrounded by his brother, cousins, friends, and lovers, Sawyer had never felt more alone.

Meeting Adam in his summer dance class opened Sawyer up to a completely new world. Adam was as obviously gay as a man could get; he was the epitome of the stereotype. He wasn't Sawyer's type and Sawyer wasn't his type, but they clicked as friends.

Kendrick had dubbed them "the odd couple." Adam was short and thin in stature, dark skinned, dark haired, and an absolute trope, which Sawyer had learned was slang for a stereotypical gay. He wore bright nail polish, tied most of his shirts at his waist, and walked around in shorter shorts than many women on campus wore. He was the exact opposite of Sawyer's tall, fit build. Sawyer was mostly comfortable in jeans, sweats, basketball shorts. But Adam was a lifeline for him; through Adam he found a world of gay men he'd known *had* to exist, but he had no clue how to go about discovering it.

"So, let me get this *straight*." Adam put a hand to his lips to suppress a smile about his little joke. "You've just been searching with no guidance? Sawyer, sugar, finding a gay in the wild is *tricky*. Sometimes I wish we had a hand sign or signal to alert gay men to other gay men, but until that happens, you've got to be careful. Oh, honey, I'm so glad you've found Adam. Adam is going to show you the way."

The first thing Adam did was set Sawyer up with gay dating apps on his phone. He used these to find anything from a random hook-up to dates to more serious relationships.

Adam introduced him to the best gay nightclubs. Sawyer didn't spend all of his time in these establishments, but it gave him somewhere to escape to when needed and a place to find people like him. Adam gave Sawyer the tools to find the freedom to be himself.

He didn't change who he was with his family and friends, but being able to act on the other side of himself was liberating.

"Sawyer, sugar, when are you going to let the gay side of yourself meet up and mingle with the other side of yourself?"

"I don't know, Adam; I'm not sure the two sides would like each other very much."

HE BATTLED DAILY with being true to himself and protecting his secret and his family. But with Adam guiding him, Sawyer enjoyed the last year of school more than he had the first three. He had random hook ups, dates, and some more serious relationships which lasted weeks into a couple months.

Sawyer spoke to Adam after a weekend hook up gone awry. Again.

"Dude, do you ever feel like a complete whore? Because sometimes I feel like a total whore."

"Sugar, I *am* a whore and proud of it. But Sawyer, *you* are not a whore. You average one to two hook ups a month; Kendrick averages one or two a weekend. Sweetie, I want you to continue with your random guys, being careful of course, and dating because you need the experience. But if there's one thing Adam knows, it's that you are *not* a whore. You enjoy the sex because, well, you're human and most of us enjoy the sex. But your heart is looking for love. Right now it may be looking in all the wrong places, but these experiences are preparing you for what comes next. You don't have it in you to be a lifetime player; I see it in your eyes every time you get ready for a new fling or a new date. You're always hoping this next guy will be the love of your life. I've met your cousins. I've heard all about your family. I know you come from a very happy and loving group of people; I understand what you're looking for and why. But sugar, sometimes we have to pick through a lot of garbage before we find that one special treasure." Adam paused in putting on his eyeliner.

"You're right, man, I *am* looking for love, but I'm *definitely* not having much luck with the guys I've been seeing. Some of those I blame on you; some were just pure bad luck."

Sawyer had to laugh when he thought of the long list of failed matches. It's not that he hadn't enjoyed some hot sex with several of them, most of them just weren't guys he'd be interested in introducing to his family.

"What? Who could you blame me for?" Adam feigned shock as a grin played on his lips.

"You know exactly the ones I'm talking about. First, there was Gregg, with 2 g's on the end. It's a good thing he had 2 g's on the end of his name because he was missing one testicle. I don't judge things like that, but the dude never stopped talking about it; he brought up his 'one nut' in every conversation with every person he talked to." Sawyer shook his head at the memory. Gregg had given a decent blow job, but they'd never made it to anything more because the man never stopped talking about his missing testicle.

"Okay, in my defense, I had heard rumors about it him being half nuts, but I didn't realize it was meant in the literal sense." Adam's laughter filled the room as he skillfully applied a bright turquoise hue along each finger nail.

"Man, that was so bad." Sawyer tried not to laugh, but couldn't help the snort that escaped his throat.

"Okay, so Half Nuts was my fault. But who else can you pin on me?" Adam challenged.

"How about William?" Sawyer raised his eyebrows in question. "Don't act like you don't remember him. William? He wanted me to call him Bubby and kept calling me Daddy?" When Adam busted out laughing, wiping away his mascara, Sawyer had to chuckle as well. "Damn, man, I couldn't even get it up around him. *'Oh, does Daddy like what Bubby has in his pants?'* I seriously wanted to puke. That was the longest two-hour date of my life. I'd owe you one for saving me from it if it wasn't your fault I was with him in the first place." Shaking his head and rolling his eyes at the memory, Sawyer stood from his perch on Adam's bed to stretch.

"Hey, I helped you figure out you weren't into the Daddy scene," he quipped. "Okay, so two were my fault. Surely you can't blame me for any more of them." Adam stood with his hands on his hips, waiting.

"How about the guy who wanted to collar me? What was his name? Dom N. Atrix? Where the hell did you even find that guy? You introduced him to me as Dom; leave it to you to conveniently forget the rest of his moniker. A freakin' collar, Ad! He wanted to walk me around like a damn dog."

"Now, wait just a darn minute, sweet cheeks. That one wasn't totally my fault. I hadn't known you long at that point; I'd heard Kendrick call you and your brother BDSM so I thought it meant you were into that kinky stuff." Adam had the decency to blush over setting him up with that catastrophe.

"Maybe next time you should ask first. BDSM is Kendrick's little joke with our names; Brothers Decker and Sawyer Morgan; neither Decker nor I are in to that type of stuff. Seriously man, can you see me with a dog collar on?"

Sawyer pretended to growl and bark, making Adam laugh out loud.

"Okay, so asking about the nickname would have helped in that situation. And actually, I *can* picture your sexy-as-sin ass with a dog collar on, but it's more in a grungy, black eyeliner, rock star type of way. Mmmmm, yeah, the image in my head is niiiice." Adam batted his lashes at Sawyer, making him smile and strike out with a teasing fist.

"Oww, careful Morgan, you know I'm sensitive and bruise easily." Rubbing his arm where Sawyer had landed the lightest of punches, Adam continued, "Okay, those three were my fault. No way you can saddle any more guilt on me."

"I'm sure I could think of some if you give me time. But no, the rest are pretty much just bad luck all around. Simon who was the most boring human being in the world, Alex who spent most of the night with his tongue stuck in my ear while breathing heavily, Kit the vegetarian who cried and had a public meltdown when I ordered a steak at dinner, Blake who was super-hot but spent the entire night watching himself in anything shiny he happened to find, and invited at least three girls and two guys to 'join the Blakenator later for a little fun.' And Conspiracy Theory Colin who was convinced I'd been sent on the date to spy on him for the Russians." Rubbing his hands through his short dark hair, Sawyer sighed. "Yeah, definitely no true love happening there."

"Now, now, now, sugar, let's not forget about the dates

that have gone well. If we're going to rehash the bad, we should pepper it with some good as well."

Leave it to Adam to always find the good in everything.

"Remember Brad? He was hot and sweet, and you said the sex was better than most. And what about Doug? You talked about that guy's cock for weeks; I almost started thinking he was King of Cocks. And let's not forget Alejandro. You're usually all about topping, but you gladly bottomed for him so he must have had *something* worthwhile." Adam waggled his eyebrows at Sawyer, trying his best to pull him from his funk.

"Yeah, the sex with those guys was out-of-this-world, but where are they now? Not here, not with me. Why? Sex was the only connection we had. We couldn't stay up late talking about art or music. We didn't go dancing together. None of them wanted to take the time to *know* me, they just wanted to fuck me or let me fuck them." Laying down heavily on Adam's bed, Sawyer sighed audibly. "I don't know man, I guess I'm just tired of it all. Tired of the random hook ups, tired of first dates leading nowhere other than the bedroom. Tired of having to go out of my way to keep all of this secret. The lack of connections and the living a double life so Decker, Zach, and Kendrick don't find out, those two things are exhausting me, man. I'm just done, over it. I'm out."

Adam looked at him sadly and shook his head. "That's the problem, darling boy. You're not *out*; you're still very much *in*. I know you have to come to this decision on your own, but I think coming out to your brother and cousins would open some doors for you. You could meet guys here on campus, you wouldn't have to hide and sneak around." Sawyer knew Adam only gave this lecture for his own good, but he got tired of hearing it. "At least consider, once you're home, living as a real-live adult, putting down roots, that you'll come clean to your family so you have their support and you can start living like the real you instead of this façade."

"No promises, man. I hear what you're saying, I do. I just don't know if I can bring all of that down on my family and open up that can of worms in Small Town, USA."

"Okay, then, what about this promise? Since you won't have me around to talk to; if you're not going to open up to at least Decker, would you promise me you'll start seeing a ther-apist once you're back in Torey Hope?" Adam spoke hopefully.

"Yeah, man, that part I *can* promise because I know I'll be lost without you to talk to." Sawyer stood and hugged his crazy friend to his chest. "Thanks, man, I know you're always just trying to help."

5

resent day

The couch welcomed Sawyer's weight as he sank onto it heavily. He had about an hour before he was scheduled to meet his family at his grandfather's house. The captain and Janie were having a get together and Sawyer had decided he would tell the rest of his family his secret.

The house was quiet. Decker and Katie were out running around before the family gathering; Kendrick was probably nursing a hangover in the bed of last night's conquest; Zach had left early to go help their cousin Zoey work in her garden. Sawyer appreciated the silence, but the stillness gave him too much time to overthink his decision.

A knock sounded at the door startling Sawyer from his thoughts. He pulled his 6'2" frame up from the brown suede sectional couch which took up two walls of their living room.

As he pulled opened the door, his face broke into a relieved smile; he hadn't realized he was longing for company, but seeing the man standing on his doorstep made him realize he needed a friend.

Did Hayden Marsten qualify as a friend or more? Now wasn't the time to evaluate their new relationship, he just knew he was grateful to have Hayden show up.

Stepping back from the door to allow Hayden room to enter, Sawyer offered a genuine smile to him. "Hey, man, what brings you by?" Sawyer knew the reason Hayden was there, but he decided to go with small talk first.

"As if you don't know why I'm here, Sawyer." The eye roll and head shake were subtle, but Sawyer caught them.

"You're right, I do. Thanks for coming to keep me company until I head over to the captain's house. I was feeling a little alone here with all of my thoughts." Sawyer stepped closer to Hayden and let the other man pull him into a comforting hug.

"Do you want something to drink? Have a seat, and I'll grab us something. I've got beer, water, pop, and juice." Sawyer longed for a beer to help with his nerves, but he wanted to have his faculties about him when he spoke to his family.

"I'll take whatever you're having, thanks." Hayden ambled to the living room and comfortably took a seat; he'd been over to the house enough times that he knew to just make himself at home.

Sawyer grabbed two water bottles out of the fridge setting them on the counter. Mechanically pulling two glasses out of the cabinet, the grinding of the ice maker as he filled the glasses didn't even faze him. Turning he stood at the sink as he poured water into the ice-filled glasses. Lost in thought, he gazed out the window.

He recalled the day Katie had first mentioned Hayden to him.

"Oh my goodness, Sawyer, I've found you a total hunk of a man."

"Really, Katie-girl? A total hunk, huh? And just where did you discover this total hunk?" Sawyer had smiled good-naturedly at his favorite girl.

"Well, I had gone to the bank on some business for The Center+. My friend from high school, Heather, works there. Anyway, she and I were chatting when this drop dead gorgeous man walked from one of the offices to get paper for his printer. She and I and every female in the place watched him as he walked back to his office, we probably had drool puddles that needed wiped up. Heather caught my eye, and we both started laughing. I whispered, 'Damn, I'm happily taken, but you should go after that one; he's HOT.' Heather sadly shook her head and whispered back, 'I totally would except he's 100% gay; I don't stand a chance with him.' So, I may have made it my mission to go to the bank as often as possible for the next couple weeks until I had met with this man and developed a friendship. During the small talk we made, I conveniently

found out that he's not married, not seeing anyone, AND he'd like to meet YOU."

"So this drop dead gorgeous man is living right here in Torey Hope, has no one in his life, and he just happens to want to meet me? What's the catch?" Sawyer had found it hard to believe.

"No catch, seriously. He is our age, moved here to take the branch manager job, hasn't met many people other than the employees at the bank, and knows the 'gay scene' in Torey Hope is pretty small; he is really a nice guy, even if you two don't hit it off romantically, wouldn't it be nice to have another friend?"

Sawyer had agreed to meet Hayden the next night. He wasn't willing to go so far as to call it a date, but he was happy to be meeting someone none the less.

He walked hesitantly towards the park bench. Katie had said Hayden was going to meet him at the park, but he wasn't sure if this man was who he was looking for. Sawyer took a moment to study the man as he walked in from the side. He had a strong profile, light brown hair that was long enough to need to be pushed out of his eyes, but it wasn't messy, in fact it was styled very neatly. The man wore a pair of khakis and a pale blue polo shirt. Sawyer immediately felt the contrast between his own jeans and button down; he'd dressed nicely, but this man definitely had more of a 'business' air about him.

When the man's eyes scanned the park and landed on him, Sawyer knew he'd lost his opportunity to check him out. Their eyes locked and the other man stood; walking towards each other, Sawyer felt an immediate kinship. It was as if, at the moment their eyes met, he knew he'd found a friend who would understand his struggles, even if nothing romantic ever blossomed between them.

"Sawyer?" The man's smile brightened his handsome face, and his pale blue eyes sparkled.

"Hayden, right? Good to meet you, man. Katie's told me a lot about you; thanks for agreeing to meet up with me." Sawyer stuck his hand out and quickly appreciated Hayden's firm grip. If he noticed the lack of heat or sparks as their flesh touched it was only fleetingly.

"Katie is a great girl. If I played for that team, I'd be pursuing her for sure." Hayden's flirty wink brought a smile to Sawyer's face.

"Yeah, well, I'm pretty sure my twin brother, Decker, would take issue with that." Sawyer let go of Hayden's hand and glanced around the park. "Would you like to sit or walk?"

"Damn, there's two men walking around Torey Hope with your looks? What are the odds?" Changing subjects abruptly, Hayden motioned toward the walking path, "Let's walk for a bit, it's a beautiful day; plus sitting to talk would seem too much like a job interview."

"So, Katie tells me you're the branch manager at Torey Hope First Financial? How did you get into banking?" Sawyer felt at ease with Hayden and found himself relaxing into a comfortable conversation.

"I had always planned on following in my father's foot-steps and taking over his position as bank president in my hometown of Chicago." Mentioning his father's lofty position didn't come across as bragging, just passing along information; Hayden seemed like a very down-to-earth guy. "But, when I graduated from college and started working for my dad in order to one day take over his position, I made the mistake of dating one of my coworkers - a male coworker." Hayden's eyes met Sawyer's with a mixture of regret and humor.

"Oh, wow; I take it dear old dad didn't realize you were gay? I bet that went over well." Sawyer pitied his new friend as he wondered about his own family's reaction; would they deny him his position at The Center+?

"That's putting it mildly. Dad flipped out, fired me, threw me out of the apartment he'd been paying for, and forbid my mother to contact me. He cut me off financially and severed all ties between me and my younger siblings." The deep sigh in Hayden's voice was the only clue that he was still affected by the events he was describing. "So, I stayed with a friend for a bit. Not the guy I'd been dating; he dumped me as soon as he got fired by my dad. I started applying anywhere and every-where I could find banking positions. Within three months, I landed the job here in Torey Hope, and I've been here about six months now."

Sawyer nodded his head as Hayden finished his explana-tion. "So, how do you like our little Torey Hope? I'm sure it doesn't exactly stack up to the big metropolis of Chicago."

Sawyer didn't mind visiting larger cities, but he'd never had an urge to live in one; he enjoyed the quieter small town life that he'd grown up with.

"Actually, I worried I'd be bored out of my mind, but it's not really that bad. I've made some friends. The restaurants are quaint and delicious. The town is gorgeous. There's shopping here and in nearby towns; overall, I think it's a great place." Hayden's words held a "but."

"I hear a 'but' that you're not speaking." Sawyer smiled. "Let me guess, the gay scene in Torey Hope isn't really as hoppin' as you're used to?"

"Bingo, we have a winner, give this man a prize." Hayden laughed and they stopped at the shelter house. Hayden sat down on the top of a picnic table and Sawyer mirrored his position on a table opposite him.

"I know exactly what you mean; I haven't done an official census, but I think the total number of gay men in Torey Hope is probably...um, two?" Hayden threw his head back and laughed at Sawyer's words.

"Tell me about it, man. I was so happy when Katie told me she had a gay friend; I thought 'even if he's butt-ugly, at least he could be a friend'." Hayden stood from the table and walked into the space between Sawyer's legs. "Imagine my delight when I found out that you aren't butt-ugly; in fact, you're one of the most attractive men I've ever seen."

Sawyer had to lean back on his hands to look up into Hayden's face. He didn't feel a spark or a heat with Hayden, *but his body reacted nonetheless; it had been a long time since he'd felt a man so close to him. "Good to know I'm not butt-ugly, thanks for that." Sawyer spoke sarcastically and pushed up off of his hands to bring his face closer to Hayden's.*

Hayden's groin intruded farther into his space and Sawyer felt the evidence of his interest pressing up against his own. Putting his feet down on the ground to allow his height to equal Hayden's, Sawyer let Hayden's hands pull his hips forward as soft, smooth lips came down on his mouth.

As his lips and tongue enjoyed the physical contact, his heart fought down the disappointment that he felt no real heat or desire with Hayden. He told himself he should be fair to Hayden and give him the 'just friends' speech, but he also knew how badly he wanted a friend, an equal, someone who understood, so he kept quiet.

He let the kiss go on longer than it should have; he agreed to another date; he added yet another secret to his treasury.

"Hey, man, did you travel to a freshwater spring to get that water? You've been in here forever." Hayden's voice behind him brought him from his thoughts.

Dripping with condensation from the glasses, he recognized how cold his fingertips were. "Sorry about that. I just got caught up in my thoughts for a bit."

"Oh, yeah, what were you thinking about?" Hayden's tone indicated he wondered if he himself were anywhere in those thoughts, but he had a way of teasing while also being sincere in his concern.

"Actually, I was just thinking about the day we met and how glad I am to have someone in town who I know 'gets it;' I love my brother and cousins and Katie, but they can't completely understand because they haven't lived it." Sawyer turned and stepped in closer to Hayden, effectively pinning him against the counter.

His heart and head told him to sit down with Hayden and talk about his plan to tell the rest of his family, but his body was yearning for physical contact; he wanted to *feel,* he did not want to be left alone with his thoughts and fears.

"So, I guess I should be saying 'thank you, Hayden;' but I think instead of saying the words, I'd rather show you." His fingers threaded through the hair just brushing Hayden's collar and applied just enough pressure to bring his mouth close enough to his that their breaths mingled.

Not waiting for more of an invitation, Hayden covered the last few centimeters and devoured Sawyer's mouth. Sawyer's body responded, he craved more, but deep inside he knew it wasn't Hayden he desired. *Don't be unfair to him, Sawyer. If you don't feel it with him, let him know.* Sawyer's head spoke harshly to him as his tongue slid along Hayden's bottom lip. At the nip and sting of Hayden's teeth on his own bottom lip, Sawyer's body spoke in a desire-laden voice. *You're not hurting anyone. Who knows, maybe Hayden is using you too. Just enjoy it while you can.*

Letting his body speak for him, Sawyer's hands traveled slowly down the sides of Hayden's torso and gripped the man's hips, pulling him forward so that their hard lengths collided.

"Oh, God, Sawyer; damn that feels good. Again." Hayden whispered hotly against Sawyer's ear and groaned appreciatively when Sawyer did as he was told.

Hot hands palmed, rubbed, gripped; lips, tongues, teeth clashed.

"Holy shit! What the fuck?" Hayden's hips bucked violently away from the counter. "Ahh, damn, that's cold!"

Sawyer's sex-filled mind took a moment to clear, but he quickly realized the glass of ice water had been knocked over on the counter and spilled on the back of Hayden's pants from his waist down.

Trying not to laugh, Sawyer grabbed a towel and tried to help Hayden sop up the worst of the spill before drying the pooling water from the counter.

"Laugh it up, Morgan. Shit, nothing like a bucket of ice water dumped down your pants to cool down the heat of making out. Sorry, bud, I think anything I was thinking about doing has now shriveled up and lost interest for the moment."

The men laughed and headed toward the front door.

"Thanks for coming over; you helped take my mind off today for at least a little while." Sawyer leaned in and kissed Hayden enjoying the sigh that escaped from the other man; Hayden was an attractive guy, he was fun to be around, Sawyer couldn't do much better. But would it just be settling on the one gay guy he knew in town? Would Sawyer be giving up passion and heat just to be comfortable and safe?

"No worries, man. I'm glad I could help. No matter how your talk with your family goes, feel free to come over later tonight. I'll be up late; I'd love to see you." Hayden gripped Sawyer's chin and guided brown eyes to meet blue. "We don't have to classify whatever this is between us; friendship, convenience, something more? There's no reason to worry about it right now; let's just see where it goes." Leaning in to feather a kiss against Sawyer's mouth, Hayden whispered, "Come over tonight, I want to be with you."

And with that, he walked out the door leaving Sawyer with a hot rock between his legs, guilt in his heart, and way too many thoughts bombarding his brain.

6

Sawyer's maternal grandfather, Robert Decker, otherwise known as the captain, had grilled a feast of steaks, chicken, and pork chops. Between the meat, baked potatoes, salad, and dessert, everyone was stuffed full. Dishes had been cleared, and the family was just milling about.

Sawyer had given his mom and dad a head's up that he was planning to tell the rest of the family, and Libby was already teary-eyed while Nate had his jaw clenched as if he wanted to protect his son from whatever was about to come.

"Hey, Deck? Can I talk to you for just a minute?" Sawyer headed out the back door and stood on the steps.

"What's up, man?" Decker stood beside him and glanced at his twin brother, the other half of his heart and soul.

Without needing words from Sawyer, Decker sensed his brother's apprehension. "Ahh, so tonight's the night, huh? No worries, man, you've got this. You know we're on your side, no matter what." His hand shot out and curled around Sawyer's; they stood hand-in-hand like they had when they were 5-years-old walking into Kindergarten for the first time.

"Yo, BDSM, you staying out here all night or what?" Kendrick stuck his head out the door; when he saw his cousins' hands joined, he stepped the rest of the way out while giving a silent nod to Zach who joined them immediately.

"What's going on? What's wrong?" Kendrick's usually joking eyes were as serious as Sawyer had seen them in a long time.

"You're telling them, aren't you? Now?" Understanding dawned on Zach and he reached a hand out, placing it on Sawyer's shoulder.

"Ah, shit man, okay, I got it. Don't sweat it, we're here for you." Kendrick's hand landed on Sawyer's other shoulder. In a swift action, he stretched his arms out to encompass all of his cousins, pulling them tight against his chest the best he could.

"We got this. There's never been anything the four of us couldn't face, together. Sawyer, man, I know the pressure is really on *you*, but you've got to know that none of us will ever turn our backs on you. Ever." Kendrick fell silent and just let the love between them fill the silence.

"Um, could I have everyone sit down in the living room for just a minute? I have something I need to talk to you all about." Sawyer's voice held a quiver, but only those who knew what was coming picked up on it.

As the family gathered in the spacious, comfortable living room, Sawyer pulled a chair in from the kitchen. Sitting front and center of the misshapen circle they had formed, he felt like the leader of a group therapy session.

"So...God, this is hard...um, first, I need you all to know just how very much I love you. And I'm so sorry I've kept this from you for so long. The last thing I ever wanted to do was hide or lie, but I also never wanted to bring stress or embarrassment or problems onto any of you." Sawyer took a deep breath and imagined the words tumbling from his lips. Once he said them, he could never take them back.

"What I'm going to say will be a big surprise to some of you. I know there will be a lot of different emotions, so if you have questions or want to talk to me alone, let me know."

With a deep breath, Sawyer glanced at his brother and cousins. Their nods of support and approval were all he needed.

"I wanted you all to know, I'm gay. I've known for quite some time, but it took a while for me to accept it myself, and I've just recently started telling a few people. I don't want to cause problems in the family, but I couldn't lie to you about who I am any longer."

A heavy silence echoed in the room. Sawyer's heartbeat

sounded in his ears, the blood roaring like waves against the shore. He lifted his head, not knowing when he had allowed it to drop in shame. Before him he saw a sea of faces painted with a mixed variety of reactions.

"Don't hang your head in shame, Sawyer." Kyle Martin, as close to a blood-related uncle as possible without being part of the actual bloodline, stood up and walked to where Sawyer was sitting. "Stand up."

When Sawyer stood, he came eye to eye with the man he'd called Uncle Kyle his entire life. Tattooed and pierced, Kyle wore his hair in outlandish styles and bright colors; he had always been the one to march to the beat of his own drummer.

"I'm proud of you for telling us. I'm sorry if any of us made you keep the secret longer than you wanted to. Don't you ever hang your head in shame in front of your family or anyone else. Stand strong and true to who you are. And if all else fails, use my motto, 'Fuck'em all.'"

With those words, Kyle drew Sawyer into a hug and the younger man felt a deep sense of relief that he at least had one more person on his side.

Chuckling at his uncle's words, Sawyer spoke quietly, "Thank you, Kyle. That means a lot, man."

As Kyle and Sawyer sat back down on their respective seats, a movement caught Sawyer's eye. Jeremiah Jordan, Kendrick's dad, stood up. His wife, Audrey, attempted to grab his hand, but he stalked to the doorway.

"Dad?" Kendrick's voice was strained as if he felt physical pain toward his father's reaction.

"Not now, Kendrick. I can't be here right now. I can't watch you all sit around and act like this is a good thing. I'm not sure I can ever do that." Jeremiah shook his head in what appeared to be disgust as he stormed through the kitchen and out the back door.

Audrey stood and walked to Sawyer. "I'm sorry, sweetie. He'll come around. I love you, always." The door slammed behind her as she headed out to find her husband.

"Fuck, man, I'm sorry. I never thought my dad would react that way." Kendrick's hand left a trail of destruction as it combed through his hair.

With a sinking feeling in his heart, he turned to observe the rest of this family. A few members weren't in attendance that night, he'd have to contact them and speak to them personally. Several of the younger members of the family didn't seemed fazed at all by his announcement, and that helped soothe his nerves slightly. As his eyes traveled around the group, he felt as much as he saw acceptance and support.

His uncle, Nicky, looked confused, but that was to be expected with Nicky's limited understanding of the world around him. Sawyer knew he'd have to talk privately to the man, and he knew his aunt Carly and his dad would also help to explain things to Nicky.

It wasn't until his eyes found his grandparents, John and

Cindy, and his grandpa, the captain, that he really felt betrayed and helpless. The people who had told him they loved him all of his life were now looking at him with contempt and disgust.

John's eyes shone with sorrow, as if he wanted to support Sawyer, but he had to side with his wife. Cindy spoke in disbelief and fear of what others would say, "Sawyer, this is not right, it's in the Bible for goodness sake. What will the people at church say? You can't like men, you just can't. You're a handsome, strong, smart young man. You've just not found the right girl yet. But, *she will* come along. This is just a phase." Her head shook more and more as she spoke, her distress evident.

"Grandma, this isn't a phase. I simply don't like girls, I find men attractive, and I want to spend my life with a man, not a woman." He knew his words were hurting her, but he knew they had to be said. He didn't want her having a false hope that he would grow out of his feelings.

"I won't stand for a queer to be in my house. It's not right, it goes against all that this family believes in." The captain's words cut harshly into Sawyer's heart. He had wondered which of his family would be the most hateful about it, but the betrayal he felt at his grandfather's words was more painful than he could have ever prepared for.

"Dad! I will not have you speak to my son that way. I know this has come as a shock to you, but you will not use derogatory words toward him. If you ban him from your home, you will lose me along with several others." Libby's voice was strong and confident as she issued her ultimatum.

"I just can't stand the thought of a fag...sorry, a *homo-sexual* being around my family. You telling me you're okay if he brings some guy here, and we have to watch them kissing? Don't even get me started on how sick I feel if I think about him being with another man *physically*. It's wrong; it's not natural. I can't do it." With that, the captain stood. "I need everyone to leave now."

The captain's wife, Janie, stood beside her husband, but her eyes were angry. "I'm sorry. Robert and I will have a talk and we can all regroup; we'll see everyone at Jack and Judy's later this week for dinner as usual. And you *all* are welcome here at any time, no questions asked." Her last words were directed at Sawyer, but her fiery eyes burned at her husband.

As the crew silently filed out of the house, it felt as if everything had just gone awry. These families had had several disagreements over the years, but they'd always stuck together. Having people divided against him, divided against each other, it all felt so wrong. And he was helpless to fix it.

"Sawyer, we're here for you, whatever you need." Nate hugged his son to him tightly. "I think they are all just surprised. I'll talk to my mom and dad. I think everyone will come around. But until then, don't feel like any of this is your fault."

7

*A*fter saying goodbye to the supportive members of his family, Sawyer wandered for a bit. He knew Decker and Katie would have gladly spent the evening with him, or Kendrick would have taken him out for drinks and laughs to keep his mind occupied, or Zach and Zoey would have kept him entertained, but as much as he fought against the suffocating feeling of being alone, right then all he wanted was to be away from his family.

His mind wasn't being fair to them, and he knew it. Only a few members of his family had let him down, betrayed him, hurt him. But he was lumping them all together in his heart and mind right now. Deep down he knew that he was blessed to have the support, but the bitter pain in his heart, as the words other family members spoke replayed in his head, was too much for him to deal with.

Without conscious thought, Sawyer found himself in his car, driving up the long driveway to Hayden's home. Sitting in a daze outside the spacious ranch-style dwelling, Sawyer fought his inner demons. He knew he was at Hayden's for the wrong reasons. He wasn't there because he loved Hayden; he wasn't there because he wanted a future with the man. Sure, looking at his friend's beautiful home, he could picture them cohabitating, raising their precious adopted children, having family and friends over for parties. But it was just a scripted fantasy in his mind, there was no real feeling to it, no passion.

So, going to Hayden's house, knowing what Hayden wanted from him, was wrong on many levels. His mind knew it; his heart knew it, but his body longed to be held, comforted, and loved on, even if just for a short time. For a couple hours, he would allow Hayden to help him escape, to stop feeling the pain and the hurt and the betrayal. Sawyer knew it would all come crashing down on him later, and he'd feel even worse for what he was going to let happen between them, but for the moment, escaping the pain would be worth it.

Lifting his head from the steering wheel, Sawyer glanced at the front door of Hayden's house to see the man he'd quickly come to consider a friend standing and watching him. He appreciated that Hayden hung back and gave him time. Their eyes met and Hayden's arm lifted in a slight wave. Sawyer's slight smile was rueful as he watched Hayden turn around and walk into his home, leaving the door open behind him. The invitation was clear; Hayden was offering tonight, tomorrow, forever. All Sawyer had to do was accept.

"Tonight. All I can offer is tonight, Hayden. I'm so sorry." His ragged whisper echoed in the silence of his car.

Walking to the door, Sawyer let all rational thought leave his mind. Hayden was his friend, he was offering to comfort him, no one was going to get hurt. "Yeah, keep telling yourself that, Morgan. He's going to get hurt. Eventually." He ground his teeth against the feeling of disgust he felt for himself.

He found Hayden in the living room, drinks poured and ready on the coffee table. Sawyer walked to the table, grabbed a shot glass, and downed the fiery liquid. Sawyer wasn't much of a drinker, and he appreciated that Hayden had provided just one shot a piece. He didn't want shit-faced to be added to his list of negatives when his world crashed around him in T minus two and a half hours.

"Want to talk about it?" Hayden wrapped his arms around Sawyer from behind, nuzzling his nose against Sawyer's muscular back.

Gritting his teeth, Sawyer spoke softly. "Most of them were fine with it. Grandpa John seemed to want to support me, but had to side with Grandma Cindy, and she was all worried about the Bible and what people would think. She's probably lining up females for me to date as we speak. My Uncle Jeremiah got up and left saying he couldn't be okay with it. The captain..." Sawyer's voice caught. The captain's response had been the most hurtful of all. "He called me a few choice words and banned me from his house."

Turning in Hayden's arms, Sawyer savored the welcoming warmth. This was what he needed, this human connection, this feeling of being accepted and wanted and desired. "Verdict tonight was to leave it, let things cool down, and see how it all plays out." Grasping the back of Hayden's head, he whispered against the other man's mouth, "I'm done talking now." He let his tongue explore Hayden's lips before plunging into his mouth.

Sawyer felt Hayden's length pressed hard against his own. He reached between them and palmed the other man. "Give me this. Make the hurt go away."

Within seconds, clothing was removed and Sawyer sighed as skin touched skin. When Hayden fisted their lengths in his hand and began to stroke, Sawyer swallowed a groan and stumbled backwards to the couch. Sitting down on the couch he quickly grasped Hayden's hips and pulled the man towards his face. The erection in front of him was impressive and Sawyer eagerly took it into the heat of his mouth. From the hiss which escaped Hayden's lips, Sawyer knew the man wasn't going to last long. Selfishly, he knew he needed more than a blowjob to erase the pain tonight. With a few more licks and sucks, he pulled off of Hayden and leaned back against the couch. Hayden dropped to his knees and Sawyer closed his eyes against the warmth of his mouth around him.

"God, that's good Hayden, but I need more." Sawyer reached for his pants and produced a condom as Hayden scrambled to the bathroom for the bottle of lubrication.

When Hayden made a move to sheath Sawyer's erection, Sawyer pulled back. "Not tonight, I need you tonight. Make me feel, take away the pain." A harsh kiss passed between them as Sawyer quickly rolled the condom down Hayden's length.

Sawyer sat on the couch and pulled his legs up to rest his feet on the cushions beside him. The cool liquid Hayden drizzled on his skin made Sawyer catch his breath. When Hayden began to prepare him with a finger, Sawyer grunted, "No, just get inside me. Now." If he let himself think about what was happening, the guilt would consume him.

A shadow of worry crossed Hayden's face, but he gave in to Sawyer's request.

Sawyer gritted his teeth and pushed against the invasion. The searing heat helped to numb the aching pain in his heart for a moment. As Hayden found a rhythm, Sawyer closed his eyes and focused only on the pleasure. There was no pain, no hateful words, no betrayal. He was loved, and cherished, and wanted. He gasped when Hayden gripped his cock in a strong fist and began to jack him off. "I knew we'd be so good together, Sawyer. God, it's so good."

Blocking the words Hayden whispered fervently in his ear, Sawyer concentrated only on the physical act between them. After they both found their release, Sawyer allowed his legs to relax and welcomed the kisses placed on his neck as Hayden snuggled into him.

"Let's go get cleaned up." Sawyer knew that a shower could lead to more, but he felt the need to escape any possible intimate conversations with Hayden.

AN HOUR LATER, the buzz of the shot he'd consumed was gone. He'd taken his hurt out on Hayden in the shower, and he was feeling the beginnings of a downward spiral growing and churning inside of him. He thanked a disappointed and confused Hayden, feathered a brief kiss against his lips, and drove off.

He knew there was only one place he could find complete solace to work out his emotions at this time of night. He headed to The Center+ knowing he could go a few rounds with the punching bag, throw a lump of clay on the pottery wheel, paint until his heart was numb to the pain, and run a thousand miles on a treadmill if it would get him away from the hurt.

He just hadn't planned on someone else being there.

8

He breathed deeply to center himself. Luke Hamilton had a war battling inside, and yoga was one of his preferred ways to fight back. Calming music soothed him while the darkness behind his closed eyelids allowed him to imagine a perfectly still, crystal clear lake at the base of a majestic mountain. Several deep breaths later as he reached the end of his yoga workout, Luke felt the anger and frustration which stemmed from a phone call with his father leave his body, and his soul felt at peace.

Allowing one last cleansing breath to fill his chest, he stood and walked from the yoga studio to the gym area. Knowing he'd fight with too much built-up anger if he didn't center himself, Luke had done his yoga first, but was itching to go a few rounds with the punching bag. As a student of both yoga and Pilates, Luke was a walking contradiction to also be involved in Mixed Martial Arts. All three practices had served him well and he felt grateful to have been hired at The Center+ to teach MMA style classes.

Luke approached MMA from the position of incorporating many styles of martial arts. The sensationalized cage fighting that most people thought of with MMA was not something he would be instructing at The Center+. His students would learn the basics of martial arts and how to use their skills to protect themselves, exercise their body, and enhance their inner well-being; Luke would not be instructing or promoting violent or dramatized methods. He had been very clear on that position when he interviewed for the job, and he felt that The Center+ hired him in part because of his stance.

He'd previously interviewed with Sawyer Morgan, but had been called in for a second interview. During that interview with Nathan Morgan, one of the higher-ups with The Center+, Luke had blushed when he spoke the cliché, "I'm a lover, not a fighter." Mr. Morgan had smirked and raised an eyebrow in question of Luke's passion for martial arts.

"What I mean is that I do several martial arts for exercise and well-being, but I don't use the methods to condone violence or harm anyone. I don't want to take this job if parents are going to be signing their kids up so they can kick someone's ass, or if adults are going to sign up in hopes of getting in some cage on a televised MMA show. I will teach the basic history, the art form, the benefits, but I won't teach it as a violent means to an end." He'd blushed a bit more and ducked his head as Nate had continued to watch him. "I guess you can just call me Mr. Miyagi."

Nate had thrown his head back in laughter and offered him the job on the spot. "I'll want you to set up a final meeting with my sons, Decker and Sawyer, but I have no doubt they will be as sold on you for this position as I am. Sawyer has already spoken very highly of you after his preliminary interview with you."

Luke had already met Decker Morgan who was the main manager of The Center+, and he liked the man immediately. He could tell that Decker was a no-nonsense type of guy and ran a tight ship. He had met with Sawyer a couple times to discuss the plans for the programs, and he had felt an immediate connection to Decker's twin. Sawyer was in charge of the Arts Program at The Center+. Sawyer and his cousin, Zach, were working together to combine Sawyer's art programs with Zach's physical fitness programs since Luke would be teaching several art forms through meditation, yoga, Pilates, and martial arts.

Luke couldn't lay a finger on exactly why he felt a connection to Sawyer Morgan, but he felt like he and Sawyer had been friends for a lifetime.

Now as he walked into the gym, he instinctively knew the man beating the shit out of a punching bag was Sawyer Morgan. He was an exact replica of Decker, but he appeared softer, more fragile, even as he was putting the hurt to the bag.

Halting at the doorway to the gym, Luke allowed a shadow to hide his lithe, athletic body so he could observe undetected. An unwanted, long-since-forgotten response shot through his body; his veins pumped with liquid heat as he watched Sawyer's muscular form pummel the stuffed leather swinging in front of him.

Closing his eyes, struggling to retrieve that sense of centeredness he'd achieved just moments before, Luke fought down the feeling of desire that built in him. Sawyer was a colleague, more like a boss in many ways, and the brother and son of his actual bosses. Even if Luke hadn't sworn years ago to extinguish any feelings he had towards other males, feeling what he was feeling for Sawyer would still be a very bad idea.

Unbidden, his father and brothers' words infiltrated his mind; the thick, black ooze threatened to overtake him and devour the sense of peace he'd worked so hard to achieve over several years.

"Little gay sunshine boy..."

"Only faggots like the arts..."

"Such a queer little momma's boy..."

As he'd gotten older, the comments had morphed to take on a more sexually sinister tone.

"You like it up the ass, faggot?"

"Damn girly body and blonde hair, no wonder guys want to fuck your queer ass."

"Want us to find a big 'ol gay cock to pound that hole, fag? Would you like that?"

Breath shuddered from his lungs as he stamped down the nausea the memories always brought him. His father had always despised him because of his looks. Luke had a fair complexion, silky blonde hair, and blue eyes. That and his lean, athletic body was a stark contrast to his father and brothers' meaty builds, dark hair, dark eyes, and naturally olive complexions. Not once in his life had he heard a kind word come from his father's mouth in reference to him, his youngest son.

His brothers had taken their father's hatred for him to new and excruciatingly painful heights. The words hurt and still crept into his mind to taunt him, but the physical torture and humiliation they brought down on him was a haunting memory he would battle for the rest of his life. Even if he was ever able to admit he was attracted to men, the physical and emotional scars his brothers had left on him were the shackles and chains which would forever prevent him from experiencing what his body and heart longed for.

A memory of his beloved mother, his friend, his confidant, his protector floated into his mind like a feather on the wind. It had always been her and him against his father and brothers. His mother, Lilly, had never wavered in her constant support and protection of him. When the cancer devouring her body could no longer be held off, she gathered him in her arms and murmured her love to him. In halting gasps and wheezing whispers, she shared her last moments with him. "Luke, my dear baby boy, you've not been shown love from a father, but you were born from the love of both a father and a mother. I'm sorry you will never know the man your father could have been. Please forgive me for allowing you to suffer at their hands. Don't give in, don't let them win..." She stopped briefly to take a breath, but she never finished what she was saying.

At age 15 Luke didn't know what to make of her broken whispers about the love of a father. But, 'don't let them win' were words which would bombard his mind like a spray of bullets each day of his life. He would never let *them* win. His brothers' and father's words would never be true about him. He loved the male form, the hard outlines, the muscles, the hair-roughened skin, but he would never give in to those feelings. Ever. If he allowed himself to find physical pleasure at the hands of another man, his brothers' and father's words would be truth. He'd be exactly what they always accused him of being. *No.* He would cling to his mother's request. He would never let them win.

That promise had never been difficult to keep. He had the constant memory of their hate-filled words to keep his desires in check. If those memories didn't dull the longing, he would allow himself to briefly recall the physical and emotional torture his brothers forced upon him from the moment his mother passed on. The recollection of that humiliation and pain was enough to remind him daily why he could never acquiesce to the inclinations of his body and soul.

Until he walked into the gym and saw Sawyer Morgan.

Driving a hand through his messy blonde tresses, Luke contemplated leaving.

But his movement caught Sawyer's attention. "Who's there? What are you doing here at this time of night?" Sawyer, in contrast to his naturally calm politeness, barked out at the shadows. *What the hell? I just need some alone time and now I've got to deal with this?*

Sawyer's breath caught in his chest and his entire body tightened in response when the man exited the shadows. Only a few lights were on in the gym, and this man stood directly underneath one. The light reflected from his blonde hair and gave him an ethereal look. At 6'2" himself, Sawyer didn't often find men taller, but he judged the athletically lean man standing outside the ring to be about 6'3". His blue eyes were cautious, apologetic, and interested all at once.

"Sorry, man. I didn't know anyone else would be here." Sawyer instantly recognized the new martial arts instructor, Luke Hamilton, and walked the edge of the ring to shake the man's hand.

When a lightning-hot heat traveled between their joined hands, Sawyer took notice, but he also noticed how quickly Luke's jaw clenched and his hand pulled away.

"I apologize for being here this late. I didn't think I'd be interrupting anybody. I can leave..." Sawyer noticed that Luke trailed those last words as if hoping Sawyer would ask him to stay.

"No worries, man, you're welcome to stay. We can go at it

alone or team up and fight out whatever it is we're both trying to rid from our minds." Sawyer stepped away from the ropes slightly and swung his arms open wide in invitation for Luke to join him.

Wondering at Luke's behavior, Sawyer watched as the man shuffled his feet and appeared to have an inner dialogue with himself. Running a hand through his hair again making Sawyer realize it was a nervous gesture, Luke blushed a bit. "I really should leave you to it, but I was hoping to get some issues pounded out tonight so if you don't mind, I think I'll stay. Want to go a few rounds?"

Sawyer's groin constricted and threatened to make itself known with the words *pounded* and *go a few rounds*. Turning his back on Luke, he quickly adjusted himself and mentally scolded himself at the same time. *Damn, man, the guy was just making conversation. Don't turn everything sexual. Besides, you'd be a complete whore to go from one man to another in the same night.*

"It's all good, man. Let's go." Sawyer tossed Luke some spare gloves and headgear. Aside from his brother and cousins, Sawyer had seldom felt an instant kinship with someone he knew next to nothing about. Yes, he had known Hayden would be a friend even if he wasn't a lover, but that was because Katie had already assured him that Hayden was a kindred spirit, another gay man just seeking love and acceptance.

This man, Luke, was a complete unknown. Would he

balk at Sawyer's sexuality when he found out? Was he the type who would have made fun of Sawyer in school? His father had hired Luke, and Sawyer trusted his dad's judgment. Maybe that was why he felt an instant connection with Luke, like he'd known him for years.

They met in the middle of the ring and bumped fists. Their sparring was light and easy in the beginning. They circled each other, swung, and dipped. While they shuffled around the ring, they spoke.

"So, what brought you here tonight? Most people don't come to kick ass on the bag at this time of night unless something is wrong." Sawyer wasn't sure why he was being so nosey. Would he be okay answering the same if it was asked of him?

"Phone call from my father. Those never go well. I hung up pissed off and hurt as usual, so I came here to calm down with some yoga and then get some kicks in on the bag." Luke narrowly missed a right hook from Sawyer. "What about you? Do you come here at this time every night or was tonight a special occasion?"

Your whole family knows now. It didn't go great, but you survived. You have to get used to telling others, might as well start with him. "Well, to be honest, it was a pretty shitty night. I came out to the rest of my family and it didn't go well at all." The hurt threatened him with a jab to his heart, he fought against it by lashing out toward Luke. Sawyer immediately felt bad when he saw the blood ooze from Luke's nose and lip.

"Shit, man, I'm sorry. I forgot where I was for a second. We were taking it easy, and I let my emotions get the best of me. Truly, I'm sorry." Sawyer tossed his equipment into his gym bag and then removed the headgear and gloves from Luke, throwing them in his bag as he led his injured friend to the first aid kit.

"It's all good, man. I've had a lot worse done to me, I can take it. It's just a busted nose and split lip. Nice one you landed there, though I can't say I want to be on the receiving end of your punches again any time soon." He winced against the pain as he tried to smile and walked with his head tipped up in hopes of keeping his nose from dripping on anything.

Grabbing the first aid kit from the wall, Sawyer opened the door to the locker room and had Luke lean against the counter by the sinks. "Grab some paper towel and clean yourself off."

Luke leaned across the sink in front of Sawyer to reach the paper towel. The hitch in both men's breathing added to the palpable tension in the room. Heated sparks jumped from skin to skin when Sawyer's arm brushed against Luke's. Breathing deeply, Sawyer fought the wave of desire that rolled through his body when his brain registered the scent of soap and man.

Almost roughly, Sawyer grabbed the paper towel and ran it under the water. Dabbing gently at Luke's lip, trying to calm his feelings, Sawyer worked until the blood was cleaned away. Using the damp towel, Sawyer managed to clean Luke's nose. Finding a piece of clean gauze, he handed it to Luke. "Keep this until you're sure your nose is done bleeding."

With a last dab of the towel on his lip, Sawyer dug through the kit in search of ointment for the wound. "Here. This should stop the bleeding and maybe numb it a little." Sawyer let his thumb brush lightly over the crack in Luke's lip, wishing he could dip his head and let his lips follow this thumb.

Sawyer watched for several seconds as Luke's chest heaved and his blue eyes darkened. He backed up a bit as Luke abruptly stood up, but he didn't move quickly enough to miss the other man's obvious physical reaction to the situation as it rubbed against his own barely-concealed erection. Glancing upward to make contact with Luke's heated gaze, Sawyer fought the need to wrap his arms around the man and pull his mouth down to his own.

"So, thanks for fixing me up, Doc. I think the sparring is done for tonight, but I'll take a raincheck for another time. And we definitely need to get you through some yoga and meditation sessions; sounds like you could use the benefits of both practices." Sawyer saw right through Luke's attempt to change the subject and avoid the tension between them, but he took the bait.

"Yeah, my therapist has been telling me I should look into some relaxation techniques. Yoga and meditation would probably be just the right combination. I'll definitely take you up on the lessons. Thanks man."

"So, um, I don't know about you, but I'm not tired at all. Must be from the adrenaline of the fight." Luke smiled as brightly as his busted lip allowed him to. "I'm not ready to go to bed yet. You want to grab some coffee at that 24 hour place?"

Sawyer's brain flitted from excitement to confusion. He was thrilled to be asked out for coffee by Luke. However, he got the distinct feeling that, even though there was a definite physical attraction, Luke would fight tooth and nail against anything more than friendship. The thought disappointed and puzzled him. Shaking his head to clear the jumbled thoughts he convinced himself he could delve into the why's with Luke once they knew each other better. And going out for coffee was the perfect way to get to know someone better.

"That sounds good. I'm not sleepy either. Luckily I don't have to work tomorrow. I'm sure I'll end up here at some point, but I can stay up until the wee hours of the morning drinking coffee and be none the worse for the wear tomorrow because I can sleep in." Grabbing his bag and locking the door behind them Sawyer headed toward his car. Halting briefly he scanned the parking lot. His gaze landed on a motorcycle. "Is that yours? Do you want to just ride with me? I can bring you back by here after coffee."

He watched the hesitation flash over Luke's face. Sawyer

read right through him, he wanted to climb into the car, but he wouldn't allow himself to do so.

"Nah, I'll take my bike and just meet you there."

Sawyer swallowed his ridiculous disappointment. *Don't be an idiot. He invited you for coffee. He's meeting you there. It's not a date, you don't have to drive him there.* As he chastised himself he watched with heated eyes as Luke's ass sauntered away.

Climbing into his car Sawyer noticed a message from Hayden.

Hayden: *Hey there.*

Hayden: *So, tonight was really great. Better than I had hoped for.*

Hayden: *Just wanted to check on you and see if you are okay. You seemed distracted when you left. If I know you you're probably feeling guilty about tonight. I'm not expecting a ring on my finger now. Maybe we can make plans for a date soon?*

Hayden: *So, now I'm feeling desperate...I'll stop messaging you. But, call me please.*

Memories of their night together filled his mind. It had been the perfect physical connection and release, and he'd needed it badly after the issue with his family. But even the physical completeness he'd felt when Hayden took him didn't make him feel anything different for Hayden. Later when he'd pushed himself into Hayden's body as he forced away the betrayal he felt from his family, he'd not felt anything but a means to an end. Their time together brought him a phys-ical release, nothing more. He owed it to his friend to be honest and let him know there was nothing romantic going to take place between them.

That's great, Morgan. You've got one guy who would marry you tomorrow and one guy who seems dead set against anything but friendship. And which are you the most physi-cally attracted to? Of course it's the gorgeous man on the motorcycle. You're going to give the 'just friends' speech to one man and the other one is probably preparing to give you the same speech.

Rolling his eyes and scrubbing a hand over his face, he pulled from the parking lot. *It's just coffee with a friend.*

Yeah, keep telling yourself that.

9

*I*t's just coffee with a friend. Yeah, keep telling yourself that. Luke Hamilton was in deep and he knew it, but he was helpless to avoid it.

You could have totally avoided it by not asking the man for coffee. You could have gone home to a cold shower and seen him sporadically at work. Instead, you offer to teach him meditation and yoga and invite him to coffee. Yep, that was real smooth. You promised to avoid your attraction to men at all costs. How's that working out for you right now?

Luke growled in frustration as he leaned into the final corner before arriving at the all-night coffee shop. His head was a jumbled mess of emotions and conflicting thoughts.

On one hand, he'd never been so instantly and completely physically attracted to another man. Yes, he'd found several men attractive over the years, but none so much as to make his promise to his mother hard to keep.

On the other hand, he was supposed to work with Sawyer, he shouldn't be muddying the waters by thinking anything about him other than friendly thoughts. And, he *did* need a friend. He hadn't been in Torey Hope all that long and he'd never really been the social type. He was more of a loner, whether by choice or forced to be because of the shit he put up with from his dad and brothers. But was it wise to befriend the one man who made him rethink his vow to never act upon his attraction to men?

God man, it's just a cup of coffee. Get over it.

Deciding he could be friends with someone without entertaining sexual thoughts about them, Luke climbed from his bike and watched in absolute awe at the beauty of the man walking towards him. Luke was used to being taller than most people, but Sawyer was close to his own height; close enough that he could almost stare straight into the deep brown depths of the man's eyes. His dark brown hair was cut short and styled into a spikey messy look. Everything about Sawyer was hot, but Luke also saw more than that. He saw a man who was hurt, a man struggling, a man in need of a friend just as much as Luke was.

I can be that friend. As long as he doesn't want more from me, I can be there for him.

A small voice in his head taunted, but what if he wants more? What then?

I'll just have to explain that I can't be more. End of story.

The voice was not to be deterred. So you'd give up a friendship? You'd deny yourself happiness? Wouldn't that be like letting your dad and brothers win anyway?

Shut up, just shut up. For now it's coffee and friendship. I can't deal with more than that right now. This will have to be enough.

Shoving the voice and his thoughts down, he fell into step beside Sawyer. Opening the door to the coffee shop for Sawyer, Luke used everything inside himself to avoid looking at the other man's ass as he strode past.

He failed.

Miserably.

"So, what made you decide to come out to your family tonight?" Luke asked Sawyer as they both waited on their piping hot coffee to cool.

"Well, I had already told my brother and cousins a while back, but I just knew it was time to stop hiding it from everyone else. Honestly, I should have admitted it to them years ago, but I've been too afraid of rocking the boat and causing trouble." Sawyer stirred a packet of sugar into his coffee and stared thoughtfully at the brown liquid as it swirled in the cup.

"And from the way you were beating the shit out of that bag, I'm guessing it didn't go well?" Luke asked quietly.

"Nah, it didn't go well. The majority of my family is supportive, but there are three or four who made their disgust and displeasure clear. I think my grandpa calling me hurtful names was the hardest part to take. I've idolized that man since I took my first step, maybe even before, so to hear those words spill from his mouth in reference to me...I guess I just felt betrayed." As he spoke he wondered at how easy it was to talk to Luke.

Luke was quiet for a short time as he let the cruel words from his brothers and father steam roll through his head. Sawyer's question shook him from his thoughts.

"How were your family and friends when you came out to them?"

"I'm not gay." Luke's vehement denial had Sawyer sitting back in shocked silence. He stared at the man sitting across the table from him. Just stared. Because that was all he could do. A million thoughts ran through his head. *No way he's straight. I felt his reaction to me in the gym. My gay-dar can't be THAT rusty. Shit, he seriously thinks he's not gay? Just my luck.*

As Sawyer continued to stare at him, Luke shifted uncomfortably. "Okay, maybe that's not entirely true. I *am* attracted to men. I always have been, ever since my earliest memories. But I can't ever act on those feelings. Ever. End of story." Luke's words and the set of his jaw told Sawyer that he was very serious.

But a flicker of hope burned in Sawyer's chest and a cheesy quote from an old comedy movie played on repeat through his head, *"So you're telling me there's a chance..."* A chance, that's all Sawyer wanted. He wanted Luke in his life, and for now he'd take him in whatever capacity he could get him.

Over the next hour, with coffee drained and long since forgotten, Sawyer and Luke talked and laughed as they got to know each other.

"Favorite food?" Sawyer cocked his head to the side and waited on Luke's answer.

"Pizza. Cliché I know, but the truth. Honestly, pepperoni pizza is my favorite, and I love cold pizza for breakfast." Luke blushed. "You?"

"Cold pizza? Sure, I'm a guy, aren't I?" Sawyer's grin brought a soft glow to his warm brown eyes. "But as far as favorite foods go, I'd have to say my grandma's baked potato bar. We load up these huge potatoes with every topping you can imagine; sometimes it's hard to even find the potato. You'll have to come over some night and let me show you how we eat potatoes here in Torey Hope." As Sawyer made the statement, he felt a flutter in his heart thinking of Luke coming to dinner at his grandparents' house. He wanted to bring him to meet his family, but he knew that scenario was light years away both because of his recent announcement and because of Luke's staunch denial of his sexuality.

"I'll take your word on it for now," Luke replied after he let the words soak in. He appeared touched at the quasi-invitation, and panicked at the same time. Quickly switching to another topic, Luke cleared his throat, "Favorite childhood memory?" As the words were spoken, Sawyer noticed that Luke seemed to regret them.

"I have almost all happy memories growing up. Decker and I had Zach and Kendrick to play with. We've got the best families in Torey Hope, and we had The Center+ from before we could even walk. Granted, it wasn't as elaborate back then, but it still offered us awesome activities. But hands down, I think my favorite memory is when the captain would take us fishing. He's always been strict, but he was fair and patient too. He'd take the four of us boys out to the lake, and we'd spend hours with our lines in the water. He used to pretend like he was asleep under that darn fishing hat he wore, but he'd always pipe up with advice or questions or a joke at just the right time as the day wore on." Sawyer paused, jaw clenched against tears threatening to fall. "I don't know if I'll ever get that back with him, that easy closeness. I miss it already."

Blinking rapidly to clear his eyes, he glanced at the clock. Not wanting his time with Luke to end, but feeling the need to get out of the coffee shop, he made a suggestion that was purely spur of the moment. "Ever gone night fishing?"

An hour later, as a breeze rippled the water, they sat near the lake's edge and watched their lines in the shadowy darkness. The full moon and kerosene lanterns provided just enough light, but the darkness surrounding them offered solitude and the feeling of closeness that allowed for conversations that maybe would have never taken place in the bright light of day.

"So, since we're actually participating in one of my favorite childhood memories, want to share one of yours?" Sawyer's voice was low so as not to spook the fish or his new friend who seemed as jittery as a long-tailed cat in a room full of rocking chairs.

As silence filled the air, Sawyer turned his head slightly. Gazing at the strong profile, Sawyer took note of Luke's closed eyes and gritted teeth.

"Hey, man, it's okay, you don't have to talk about it." It hurt Sawyer to know that memories of his childhood brought Luke pain.

"No, I want to talk about it, it's just that I don't have a lot of happy childhood memories, and the ones I have make me miss my mom. She died of cancer when I was 15." Luke spoke softly, and haltingly, as if he'd not shared much about his life with other people. "I've never really talked about her to anyone else. I didn't have a lot of friends growing up."

His heart hurt to hear Luke say the words. Sawyer knew

nothing of a childhood without friends, and thinking of Luke as a lonely little boy made him sad. And then he felt anger; why would no one want to be friends with Luke?

"Why didn't you have friends?"

"I kept to myself a lot. I didn't want people to be around my dad and brothers; they aren't very nice people, and I didn't want them to spread their ugly words to any of the kids in town." Luke's words were almost whispered as he recalled the memories.

"What about friends at school?" Sawyer was still trying to picture a childhood with no friends.

"My mom homeschooled me. It was easier to be home with her than to be at school and try to avoid my brothers. By the time she died, I was doing school on the computer, so I finished in a self-study program and graduated early. Her will came as a surprise to my father; he had no clue that she had a separate life insurance policy and that the entire amount would come to me. That money allowed me to travel and learn the various martial arts I wanted to study. I also took several yoga, Pilates, and meditation classes over the years. I've always had the same free-spirit as my mother, so traveling brought me peace. The years I had to endure at home after she died almost brought me to my end, so being allowed to take that money and leave as soon as I graduated was a blessing that my mother left me." Luke's story spilled out. Sawyer felt he was getting more information than Luke had ever shared with anyone else, but he sensed there was much more to the story that Luke wasn't sharing.

"So, your mom was your best friend?" Sawyer was very close to his mother, but he didn't know what it would be like to have only her as his friend. And to lose her, leaving him truly alone in the world, would be devastating.

"Yeah. She was the one who understood me. I was her little look alike. We shared the same smile, eyes, hair, likes, dislikes, sense of humor, everything. She was my biggest fan, my confidant, my protector. When she was gone, the hell I'd been living became more painful than I'd ever thought possible." Luke stopped speaking as if steeling himself against the pain of the memories.

Sawyer's hand instinctively reached out to clutch Luke's shoulder and offer support. The shuddery breath Luke took in trembled through Sawyer's hand. The heat of the other man's hand seared his as Luke reached up to grasp his hand. Heartbeat pounding in his ears, Sawyer held his breath as Luke tilted his head so the skin of his cheek caressed the back of Sawyer's hand.

They sat there for what seemed like hours. Sawyer wanting more, but sensing that Luke would balk. So he let his friend soak in the small bit of intimacy he was affording himself. Before long, Luke ground his teeth together and let go of Sawyer's hand. Lifting his head, he cleared his throat and went on.

"My happiest childhood memories include my mom

taking me to the library. She would plan our entire week of study around the programs the library had going on. We were there two or three times a week usually. Most days we would walk there. I remember holding her hand, skipping down the sidewalk. We would stop for ice cream on the way there sometimes. She always brought a large shopping bag to tote all of our books back home." Luke sat with eyes closed and savored the memory. "Even when she got sick, she'd take me to the library. She fought the cancer for several years; the last two she was too sick to take me for books, but by that time I was old enough to go by myself. I'd bring books and ice cream home for her. In the end, ice cream was one of the only things she could eat." Luke's voice caught, "I haven't been to a library since she died. I know it sounds silly, but I miss it. I miss the smell of the books, the quietness, the worlds waiting to be discovered between the pages."

Sawyer had so many things he wanted to say. He wanted to take the hurt away; he wanted to thank Luke for sharing his memory; he wanted to ask about the monsters who were Luke's dad and brothers. But he lost his chance when they were both pulled from their reverie by a pull on Luke's line.

Sawyer hopped up and grabbed the fishing pole. Handing it to Luke, he instructed, "Okay, reel it in, nice and slow." When he saw that Luke was unaccustomed to reeling in the line, he stood behind him. Wrapping his arms around Luke's, Sawyer gripped the reel handle over Luke's hand and began reeling the line in.

Several moments later, Sawyer realized that the fish had long since broken the line. He had lost himself in the feel of Luke's body pressed against his. Becoming aware that he was now firmly plastered to Luke's back for absolutely no reason other than the fact that it felt wonderful, Sawyer slowly released Luke's arms. Before he could force himself to back away completely, Sawyer pressed his luck. Fighting the urge to wrap his arms around Luke's waist, Sawyer satisfied himself with lightly running his nose along the sensitive skin of Luke's neck. Breathing deeply, the scent of soap and man again battered his senses.

Fighting against his heavy breathing and rapid heartbeat, Luke turned his head slightly so that Sawyer's lips were right at his earlobe. Knowing he was about to cross a line he wasn't sure Luke was ready to cross, Sawyer flicked his tongue out and pulled the flesh of Luke's ear between his lips. Bringing his hand up to guide Sawyer's head, Luke tilted his head farther to the side to allow access to his neck.

Sawyer let his lips travel slowly over the warm skin, savoring the musky, salty flavor. Forgetting his earlier battle to keep his hands to himself, Sawyer let his hands grip Luke's hips. Pulling the other man's body flush with his own, Sawyer pressed the evidence of his desire against Luke's ass.

And just like that, Luke shot away from him. Breathing heavily, hands on knees, gathering himself, Luke spoke, "Man, I can't. I just can't. I'm sorry. It's not about you. It's about not letting my dad and brothers win." Dropping to his knees, Luke let his head fall into his hands. Scrubbing his face, he laughed bitterly. "Not letting them win means I lose, but I have to keep my promise. I have to. It's the only thing I have left of her."

Sawyer didn't understand the riddles Luke was speaking, but he instinctively wanted to comfort his friend. Walking to him, Sawyer reached down for Luke's hand. Pulling him to his feet, Sawyer held Luke's head in his hands and forced blue eyes to meet brown.

"I don't know what they did to you or what you promised your mom, but I do know there is something here. There is something between us that I've never felt for anyone. I won't let it just disappear. I will be whatever you need me to be, for now. But I want more. I want you." Knowing he shouldn't press his friend in the emotional state he was in, Sawyer fought the urge to slam his mouth down on Luke's. Instead, he feathered a kiss against the other man's lips. "One day, you'll tell me your story. One day, you'll let me in. Until then..." With one last feathery kiss, he let go of Luke.

After packing up their gear in a tense, yet somehow comfortable silence, both men went home to their separate beds. Neither slept. The emotions of their day had finally caught up to them. Confusion, hurt, and guilt rumbled through their minds. But in that mix of emotions there was also happiness and hope silently making themselves known. After several hours of letting the emotions stew in their heads, a fitful sleep overtook them. Luke and Sawyer both gave in to the sleep as their hearts fed on that happiness and hope.

_____

10

*I*f the old wives' tale was to be believed, Sawyer's ear should have been on fire over the next few days. Several of his most supportive family members went to bat for him with those members of the family who were the least on board with his recent announcement.

Nate sat in his parents' living room and took the sweet tea his mother offered. When Cindy had taken her seat next to John, Nate started to speak. Before he could get a word out, his mother began. "Now, Nathaniel, I'm sure you're here to talk about Sawyer, and I'm glad about that. I think we should talk and form a plan. We can't have this phase of his causing problems for those of us closest to him. So far, I've been able to keep the women at church from learning of his little announcement, but I'm not sure how long I can keep the rumor mill quiet. It's common knowledge that his friend,

Hayden Marsten, is gay and they've been seen together far too often to keep the rumors from starting soon. Now, my thoughts are..." Cindy gasped as John lovingly placed a hand over her mouth.

"Cindy, dear, let's allow our boy to speak." Turning to his son, John nodded. "Nate, the floor is all yours."

Clearing his throat and realizing that he had more of a job ahead of him than he had originally thought, Nate began.

"Mom, Dad, I don't think this is a phase for Sawyer." At his mother's attempt to argue, Nate held up a hand pleadingly, "Mom, just let me speak, okay?"

"Honestly, Libby and I have wondered about Sawyer's sexuality for several years. We were never 100% sure, but we always had it in the back of our minds. At first, when Libby told me she thought Sawyer was gay, I balked. But we talked into the wee hours one night, and we both came to the conclusion that he was our son and we loved him. No questions asked. We want all three of our children to be happy and healthy. End of story. If being with another man is what Sawyer needs to be happy, then so be it. It would be no different than Abby bringing home anyone who didn't match our original picture of who she would end up with. Different race, different religion, I would hope it wouldn't matter. If she fell in love with that person, we would be open minded and support her in that happiness. I don't want Sawyer to get hurt; I think that's one of the main reasons I didn't want to accept his attraction to men. And selfishly, I think I worried about what it would mean for *me*. My son has been and will be made fun of, judged, and disgraced because of something he can't control, yet I was worried about what it would mean for *me*."

Nate took a deep breath as his admission settled in the room. "Sawyer needs us, he needs his whole family. We've always been the strong, upstanding, caring family who lets love shine through all we do. If you turn your back on him or refuse to accept him for who he is then we aren't showing that love."

Nate turned pointed eyes toward his mother. "Mom, you're so concerned about what the ladies at church may say. Of that group of church ladies and their husbands there are at least two affairs, three alcoholics, one with a prison record, one charged with embezzlement, and two with gay children."

When his mother's mouth dropped open in shock, Nate continued. "I have to say that I'm really disappointed. You of all people, the mother of a disabled child, should be the last person to pass judgement. And to worry about what people at church will say? Well, I think the lesson you've always taught us is to love each other and let the judgement come from God at the end of time. Judging is not our job, we are here to love each other. I think about the prayer you used to say with us as children, *'Dear God, be with us as we go through our day. Let your love shine on others through our words and actions.'*"

When his mother's eyes welled with tears, Nate reached out a hand. "I don't mean to hurt you, Mom. But I have to love and support my son in the same way that you always loved and supported Nicky and me. Libby and I really need you and Dad by our sides as we do that. Sawyer needs you." Nate let his plea float through the air and watched as his mother filtered his words through her mind.

Bringing a hand to her mouth, Cindy caught a sob. "Oh my God, Nathan, I'm no better than the ones who used to make fun of Nicky. I let my concern over my reputation outweigh my never-ending love for Sawyer."

Turning ashamed eyes to her husband, she let the tears fall. "John, what have I done? Do you think Sawyer can ever forgive me?"

"Shhh, sweetie, I'm sure Sawyer will just be thrilled to have you in his corner. We will go talk to him soon and clear the air. Saying you're sorry and offering a sincere hug will go a long way." John put an arm around his wife and hugged her to his side.

Several moments later, Nate left his childhood home feeling buoyed with hope. If he could change the mind of his mother, maybe the others could be brought around as well.

"Jeremiah Jordan, you will listen to me and listen good." Audrey stood with arms crossed and hip jutted out in a way that Jeremiah knew meant business.

"Dad, really, this isn't something we should even be

discussing." Kendrick laid his hands gently on his mother's shoulders and guided her to sit down on the couch.

"Listen you two, I'm not going to call him names or be mean to him, I just don't think I can accept my nephew being with a man. I don't want him to be hurt; I saw enough ridicule over sexuality during my time in the military. I don't want that for him." Jeremiah tried to explain his position.

"Dad, if I had come to you and told you I was gay, would you have told me you couldn't be around me anymore?" Kendrick cocked his head to the side and hoped the answer was what he thought it would be.

"Of course not, you're my son, I would never choose to *not* be around you," Jeremiah spoke emphatically.

"Back when you and Mom got together, would you have stood for anyone to judge Beckett based on his disabilities?" Kendrick spoke softly about his older brother, knowing in his heart that his father would have never let anyone hurt his son.

"Beckett was my life, just like you and Megan are, I would have fought tooth and nail against anyone who made him feel bad about himself." Jeremiah's love and resolve for his children was clear.

"If the captain had said he couldn't be around Beckett anymore because Kenja is Asian, would you have stood for that?" Audrey spoke softly.

"Again, of course not. Kenja's race is not something she can control. She's a beautiful girl and she and Beckett deserve to be happy." Jeremiah fought the urge to roll his eyes.

"Does Decker deserve to be happy?" Kendrick asked.

"What? Yes, Decker deserves to be happy. I'm glad he found Katie, they seem good together." Jeremiah huffed.

"But his identical twin, the same little boy who has spent as much time at this house as his own, the man who is one of my very best friends, the boy you used to bounce on your knee and chase around the house...does he not deserve happiness?" Kendrick went on before his dad could speak. "Stop thinking about the rough road Sawyer has ahead of him. Stop thinking of the hurt you've watched others go through. *Start* thinking about the fact that you love Sawyer. He's the same person he's always been. You gave Mom a second chance way back then. You knew some bad shit about her, but you looked beyond that and let love win. Doesn't Sawyer deserve the same? Acceptance and support were what Mom needed and what you offered. Can't you do the same for Sawyer?" Kendrick implored of his father.

With tears in her eyes, Audrey spoke to Jeremiah. "JJ, you saved me all those years ago. If we don't stand together and support Sawyer, who's going to save him? He needs us; he needs the love and strength of his family to ride out the rough road ahead of him. Please say you'll be by our sides as we support him." Audrey watched Jeremiah with hopeful eyes and prayed that they had reached him.

"Daddy, you said some terrible things to Sawyer. Years ago I wouldn't have known how to stand up against you, but now I know. The words you used were ugly and hurtful and you broke Sawyer's heart. If you cut him out of your life, you'll lose more than just Sawyer. You'll lose me and Audrey along with many other members of this family." Libby's eyes shone with tears as she spoke.

"Nate and I have suspected Sawyer was gay since he was a young boy. It's never changed our love for him, and I hope you can take a step back and realize that your love for him hasn't changed either. He's still the same little boy you used to take fishing. He's the same boy you taught to drive a stick shift. He's the same boy you used to play checkers with. None of that has changed. He was gay then, he's gay now. Don't turn your back on him when he needs his family most."

Libby could tell from the glint in his eyes and the set of his jaw that her father was not relenting his position.

"Okay, Daddy, I'll go now. But please know that if you don't come around to accepting Sawyer, you will tear this family apart. No, that's not true. The rest of us will continue living and loving while you sit alone with your hatred and mean words and closed mind."

The weekly family get together was at Jack and Judy Jordan's house. Sawyer knew he was technically not their grandchild, but in a family as large as the one he grew up in, family ties and blood lines got blurred like a chalk painting in the rain. He'd grown up with them being Grandpa Jack and Grandma Judy, and he was grateful that their love for him hadn't changed when he told them he was gay.

Standing in their kitchen, waiting on Decker and Katie to arrive with the pizza, Sawyer noticed the absence of certain family members.

"Why so serious, Sawyer?" Judy patted him on the cheek.

"I guess I was hoping nothing would change, but seeing so many members of the family not show up tonight means that me being gay has changed a lot of things." Sawyer fought against hanging his head in shame. He had vowed to his Uncle Kyle he'd hold his head high, and he wanted to keep that vow. Just like Luke wanted to keep a promise made to his mother. Sawyer also wanted to keep his head high to show Luke that being gay was okay, and they could get through it together.

"Oh, I must have forgotten to tell you, I told the others to be here later. I thought maybe you needed some time to talk to certain people. In fact, I think your Grandma Cindy is in the living room waiting to talk to you." Judy kissed his cheek. "We love you, sweet Sawyer. Don't ever forget that."

Sawyer smiled as he walked into the living room to find Grandma Cindy. What would this conversation bring? Surely Grandma Judy hadn't just thrown him to the wolves.

"Grandma?" Sawyer took a seat across from her.

"Oh, Sawyer, I'm so very sorry for the way I acted. I was selfish and more concerned about my image than I was about your feelings. Please forgive me." Cindy grasped his hands over the coffee table as she pleaded his forgiveness.

"No worries, Grandma. I know what I told you was a shock and a lot to take in. Of course I forgive you." Sawyer squeezed her hands. "Do you have any questions or things you'd like to talk about?"

"Well, there is one thing I've been worried about. Now, don't worry, if any of those judgmental church ladies start throwing stones, I'll just remind them of their own glass houses. But what I'm concerned about is Asher. I mean, he's young and impressionable; he looks up to the four of you and I'd just hate to see him swayed to your side." A genuine frown of concern played over Cindy's face.

Swallowing his laughter, Sawyer smiled patiently. He'd heard many gay friends' stories in college of people fearing sexuality could be caught or spread. "No worries, Grandma. I'm not out to recruit children. If Asher is gay, he's gay. I can't 'rub off' on him or anything like that. His sexuality is safe with me." Sawyer winked and Cindy blushed as if realizing her fear was unfounded and unreasonable.

"Well, I guess when you put it that way I just sound like a silly old woman, huh?" Cindy stood and pulled Sawyer into a hug. "There will probably be times when I put my foot in my mouth, please forgive me. And talk to me if I say anything offensive. Now, before I start musing about how you're going to give me great grandbabies, you better go to the garage. I think there's someone there waiting to drink a beer with you." With a final pat to his cheek, Cindy let him go.

WALKING down the steps and toward the garage, Sawyer wondered who he'd find. His Uncle Jeremiah or the captain? He wanted both of them to accept him, but he knew getting the captain on his side was going to be more of a challenge than his uncle. Knowing he'd take whatever ally he could get, he opened the side door to the garage and stepped in.

The familiar scent of oil and gasoline flooded his senses with memories of his childhood. The four boys had played for hours in and out of the garage while growing up. As his eyes adjusted to the dim light, he found his Uncle Jeremiah and Kendrick leaning against the cabinets of Grandpa Jack's work area.

"Ah, the S of BDSM arrives. Have a cold one, man." Kendrick tossed him a beer and Sawyer accepted it gratefully.

"So, before we have this somewhat awkward conversation about Sawyer being gay, can someone please explain to me what BDSM has to do with Decker and Sawyer?" Jeremiah seemed to be stalling yet genuinely curious.

"Just an old joke. Not a very funny one." Sawyer shook his head and tried to move on, but Kendrick wasn't having it.

"No, let's ease into this discussion." He winked at Sawyer

and then turned to his dad. "You see, I had been dating a girl who wanted me to do all this BDSM shit. You know, the whips and chains and collars. I wasn't into it, so we broke up. But one day I was doodling *BDSM* on my notebook waiting for class to start and realized that the initials were perfect for *Brothers Decker & Sawyer Morgan*. There you have it, the birth of a very clever nickname." Kendrick nodded his head, proud of his creativity.

"Thank God. I know what BDSM is, and I'm not sure I could take it if Sawyer shared he's gay *and* he and Decker are into BDSM." Jeremiah shuddered, and Sawyer threw his head back in laughter.

"No worries, Uncle J, no whips and chains for me. Although, I have a funny story about a blind date sometime when you're up for it." Taking a long sip of his beer, Sawyer waited while he wondered where this conversation was going to go.

Clearing his throat, Kendrick nodded at his dad in a *go on* gesture. Jeremiah shuffled nervously before downing the rest of his beer.

"So, first I want to say I'm sorry for the way I acted when you told the family you're gay. That was wrong of me. I've had some time to think," Jeremiah began, but Kendrick interrupted.

"Yeah, and some time for Mom to lay into him." He smirked as Jeremiah rolled his eyes.

"Yes, there was that too. Anyway, I had some time to

think about what you told us. I think the reason I acted the way I did was out of fear for you. I watched a couple guys get treated terribly during my years in the military all because of their sexuality. One of the men got beat up so badly he was no longer able to be a soldier. Thinking of that happening to you scared me."

Jeremiah stopped for a moment.

"And, while we're being honest, I think I'm also scared of things I don't understand. I don't understand the attraction to men, so I balked at it when one of my favorite nephews told me he likes men. But I've had time to think, and I know that who you like or love doesn't change the fact that I love you and always will." Jeremiah walked to Sawyer and pulled him into a strong hug. "I hate that you've had to face this alone for so long, and I hate that there will be more rough times, but you've got me on your side through it all."

While all three men fought back tears, Jeremiah headed inside and Sawyer and Kendrick stayed in the garage to finish their beers.

"Well, two of three have come around. That conversation went fairly well, huh?" Sawyer was grateful to Kendrick for being there and standing beside him.

"Yeah, it's amazing what having your ass handed to you by my mom can do to change your outlook on things." Kendrick stated matter-of-factly and Sawyer couldn't help but laugh.

"Well, I guess I'll have to thank Aunt Audrey for her ass

handing skills." The cousins laughed and headed inside for pizza.

THE PIZZA WAS delicious as usual, laughter filled the house, and things felt right. Almost. The only thing missing was the captain and Grandma Janie. Their absence hung heavily in the air.

Sawyer's mom, Libby, stated, "Janie said she's giving him until the weekend and then she's going to lay into him. She feels it will be better if he has some time to think about it before she starts in on him."

Sawyer felt the absence of the captain as painfully as he would have felt the absence of a limb. He hated that his secret had broken the family up, even though he prayed it would only be temporarily. He also hated the thought of never having his grandpa back in his life.

Doing his best to ignore the pain in his heart, he looked around at the family members who *were* there and felt his heart swell with hope. He'd shared his secret, and 99% of his family still loved him and supported him. It didn't mean that he'd never have problems, but it meant the world to him to have them by his side. He knew he was lucky, very few of his friends had found the same love, acceptance, and support.

"Thank you all. Thanks for being here for me, for loving me, accepting me, supporting me. My biggest fear was losing you, or causing problems for The Center+. I know the captain may be a harder sell, but I really am grateful to have all of you on my side."

Running his hand through his short brown hair, he continued, "One thing I think we need to agree upon is open communication. If you have a question, ask. If you're worried about something, talk to me. I'm not openly dating anyone right now, but if and when I do, there will probably be talk around town. And I'm worried what will happen when clients and parents at The Center+ get wind of it. Maybe we should have a meeting at work, include all the employees, and set up a planned response if the time for that comes."

Everyone nodded their agreement, and Katie accepted the responsibility for adding it to the agenda for the next meeting.

"Um, you said to ask questions if we had them," Nicky spoke up.

Everyone in the kitchen tensed up. Nicky struggled with a developmental disability from birth. He was smart, but it took him longer to learn things. His speech and gait were affected by the lack of oxygen at birth. He had a beautiful wife who had been through some horrific things when she was younger, she and Nicky had an open, honest, and beautiful love, and they were blessed with gorgeous, perfect children.

Nicky was known for speaking his mind; if it came to his head, he said it. He was never purposely rude or hurtful, but he was blunt to say the least. So, if Nicky had a question for Sawyer, there was no telling what he was going to ask.

Nate jumped in. "Nick, why don't you tell me your question first?" Nate leaned in to let his brother whisper into his ear, and his face took on a pink hue.

"So, how about those of you who want to be a part of this fairly detailed question head to the garage for some beers, and the rest of us will clean up the mess from supper. How's that? Good? Okay then." Nate pushed Nicky and Sawyer out the door.

A grinning Kendrick followed. Zach and Zoey, Decker and Katie, and Aly all trouped out the door as well. The kitchen was left with the older generation.

"Trust me, it's best if the younger ones field Nicky's questions." Nate blushed again, and everyone nodded their understanding.

"I DON'T WANT to drink beer. Beer is alcohol and it can impair your judgment. I have to drive Carly home tonight, so I won't be drinking." Nicky always had statistics to spout. Alcohol, cigarettes, condoms, he knew stats on all of them.

"No worries, Uncle Nicky, you don't have to drink beer. In fact, maybe we should all stick with water for now." Sawyer knew drinking made Nicky uncomfortable so he passed waters around to the group.

"Okay, what's your question?" Sawyer was mentally trying to prepare himself for anything that could possibly come from his uncle's mouth.

"I didn't know what gay means, but I looked it up in the dictionary and it said *happy*. That didn't make sense because I don't know why the captain would be angry that Sawyer is happy. So I asked Carly, and she said gay means when a girl likes a girl or a boy likes a boy. At first, I was still confused because I like lots of boys and I know Carly likes lots of girls, but no one gets angry about that. So I kept asking Carly about it, but she just turned red and said I should ask someone else. So, I called Beckett because he's my friend and he's very smart, even though he's much younger than me. Did you know we used to go get ice cream when he was a little boy? Anyway, I called Beckett and I asked him. He said it's when a boy or girl wants to be with another boy or another girl the way I want to be with Carly." Nicky stopped to take a breath.

Sawyer relaxed a bit, so far there was nothing awkward, but one could never tell what Nicky might blurt out next.

"When Carly and I wanted to make babies, Nate taught me how to kiss, but he wouldn't tell me what to do to get a baby. He said we'd just know what to do when the time was right." Nicky kept on talking as if this was a discussion he had every day.

"Okay, with that, I'm out! Can't handle the parents having sex discussion. Sorry all, you can give me the summary of this conversation at a later date. Preferably when I've had many beers." Zach hugged a laughing Zoey to his chest and then backed out of the garage, nodding gratefully when his sister, Aly joined him.

Nicky, nonplussed by his children's exit, continued. "So, after we kissed a lot, we figured out what to do to get a baby. And making babies is a lot of fun. We even make babies now even though we don't want any more babies. Carly says she's too old to have babies, but we aren't too old to have fun making babies. It's also called *sex*, but that word makes me feel funny when I say it." Again, Nicky stopped to breathe.

The conversation was starting to feel dangerous, like any second Nicky was going to throw a curve ball. Sawyer remembered the red tint on his dad's cheeks, and realized Nicky's question was going to get very personal very quickly. Taking a deep breath, he looked around at the remaining members of his crew. Kendrick was biting his lip to keep from laughing. Decker's jaw was clenched tightly, but he had a smirk as he realized just where his uncle was headed. Katie was openly smiling and watching Nicky lovingly.

"So, I know where I have to put my penis to make a baby with Carly. But what I don't understand is where you put your penis if you want to make a baby with a boy." Nicky looked at Sawyer expectantly.

Using what he'd learned in a public speaking course he took years ago, Sawyer waited a bit to gather his thoughts before he spoke. Knowing he probably couldn't get so lucky to get out of this question easily, he decided to attempt it anyway.

"Well, a boy can't make a baby with another boy. If I want to have kids, I'll have to adopt them." Sawyer hoped beyond all hope that this answer would satisfy his uncle.

"That would be nice, there are many children out there just waiting for the love of a family." Nicky had obviously seen an adoption commercial recently. "But if you can't make babies with a boy, what do you like about being with a boy? Can you kiss him?"

"Yes, kissing is nice. I think a lot of people like kissing."

"Do you like to get naked with a boy?"

Hard swallow. "Yes, that part is nice too."

"I like when Carly puts her mouth on my penis. Do you like that? Do you put your mouth on a boy's penis?"

Yep, he went there. Nodding in a way that showed his disbelief at this conversation, Sawyer confirmed, "Yes, I like that and yes, I do that."

"So, you just put your penis in his mouth?"

Knowing he could have left it at that, but feeling like it would be wrong to mislead his uncle when Nicky already struggled grasping so many things in life, Sawyer knew he had to be honest.

"Well, no. There is another place a man can put his penis." *I seriously can't believe I'm talking about this with my uncle.* One look at his brother and cousin told him they were having the exact same thought. Katie was just smiling sympathetically.

"Girls have two holes, but Carly said I can't put my penis in her other hole because it hurts. Boys only have one hole. Is that where you put it? Do you put it in the hole that hurts? Do you let boys put their penis in your butt?" Nicky had just pieced the information together and now spoke to Sawyer incredulously.

"Yes, that's what many gay men do." Sawyer thought it was good to keep the answer short and sweet.

Nicky finished his water while he seemed to be thinking about the information he'd just been given. Before heading back to the kitchen to find Carly, he hugged Sawyer to him.

"I hope you can find a boy you like. And when you do, I hope you can put your penis wherever you want to."

Once he was clearly out of ear shot, the four busted out laughing. They laughed until tears streamed down their cheeks. Leave it to Nicky to lighten the mood.

11
———

"*R*obert Decker, as I live and breathe, I won't watch you do this to your family any longer. You are entitled to your opinions, but you are not entitled to crush your grandson's heart with your words and judgments." Janie, having given her husband some time to come around, had finally reached the end of her rope.

"I married you because you were a kind, fair, loving man. I watched you with your grandkids, especially those four boys, and I knew you had so much love in your heart for them. The basketball, the trips to the park, the fishing...it was so evident that they were your world." Robert looked at her with fire in his eyes when she paused.

"My family *is* my world, you know that." The words escaped defensively between gritted teeth.

"Then just be there for him, support him. Apologize for

the derogatory words you used against him. He just needs to know he hasn't lost you." Janie's words came out soft and pleading.

"But how can you ask me to support something I think is wrong? Am I supposed to let my morals fly out the window and just cheer on the fact that my grandson is having physical relations with other men?" The stress of the past few days had caught up with him, and Robert lashed out.

A soft hand reached out for his. "No, Captain, you don't have to like it. You don't have to agree with it or understand it. But for the sake of this family, please don't pass judgment. Don't withhold your love from Sawyer. Of all times, he needs your love the most right now. Remember that towheaded little boy who used to come to you with a scraped knee? The same kid who used to beg for 'just one more' piggyback ride? The child who cried on your shoulder when they were rough-housing and broke my flower vase? He's the same man who now needs your love and support more than ever. Don't let him down, Robert."

Whispered words spilled out through tears, "I just don't want him hurt. I don't want others to judge him or make fun of him. I love that kid more than anything; the thought of him hurting kills me."

"*You* are hurting him. You broke his heart when you spewed those words at him the other night. He's going to hurt; he's going to be judged. That's real life. But with his family on his side, he will get through it. You survived the death of

Lois, alcoholism, and the brutal things those men did to your daughter. There's no doubt in my mind that you will survive this. Whether Sawyer loves a man or a woman, it's not our place to pass judgment. In the end, all that matters is that we show love and that our family is strong, healthy, and happy." Walking into his embrace, Janie tensed waiting for her husband's response.

"I just don't know, love. Those other things just about killed me; I'm not sure I'm strong enough to watch Sawyer go through the hurt he's facing."

The words he spoke were not the ones she'd been hoping for, but they buoyed her hope that the captain would eventually come around. She sighed, and smiled against his chest.

A WEEK HAD PASSED since Sawyer and Luke had gone night fishing. Sawyer felt like he was in high school again. He planned his trips out of his office in hopes they would coincide with Luke's trips out of the gym. When they would *happen* to run into each other, his heart always found its way into his throat and his palms inexplicably needed wiped on his pants.

He had taken to eating his lunch at the same time as Luke, and only felt slightly embarrassed that his brother and cousins had caught on to that change in habit quickly.

"You okay, bro? You used to eat in your office, but now

you're eating in the break room. I could always set my clock by you eating at 1:00 p.m., but this week you're eating at 11:45 a.m. on the dot. Anything you want to talk about?" Decker fought against the smile that threatened to break through his attempt at looking serious as he spoke to his brother.

"Yeah, man. We're all worried. You've changed your eating location and schedule; you leave your office more than I've ever seen you do before, and your workouts have changed too. You've gone from the treadmill and weights five days a week to Pilates, yoga, and tae-kwon-do three days a week. In my experience, all of these changes can only mean one thing." Zach grinned broadly, not attempting at all to hide his smile as he spoke to his cousin.

When Sawyer rolled his eyes and ignored his brother and cousin's barbs, Kendrick took the bait to keep the fun rolling.

"What, Zach, *what* do changes like this usually mean? Please, dear cousin, tell me that our Sawyer isn't in dire straits. Is it something that can be cured?" Kendrick's overly dramatic play acting brought a smile to Sawyer's face against his wishes.

"Well, Kendrick, it's pretty serious, but there *is* a cure for what ails him." Zach's tone took on a faux seriousness.

Grabbing Zach's shirt by the chest, Decker joined in the fun. "Zach, tell me and tell me *now!* What is this ailment Sawyer is suffering from and *how* can we cure him!?"

"Well, it's a very common ailment and it affects millions

around the world. It's called..." Zach paused for dramatic effect.

"Spit it out, man!"

"It's called, being in *love!*" Zach's cheesy grin and the slap he landed on Sawyer's back reminded him that they were just having fun.

"What?! *Love?* I've heard of this before. Hold on, I think the internet has common cures listed." Kendrick made a show of pulling out his phone and pretending to type in *cures for love.* "Ah, yes, here it is. *To cure a case of love, the patient should grow some balls, ask the martial arts instructor out, and spend a night getting down and dirty in his bed.*"

The four men busted out laughing. When they settled themselves down, Sawyer spoke.

"I wish it was that easy, guys. Luke is great. I like him. Like *really* like him."

"So, go for it. It's obvious he's into you. Anyone with two eyes and a brain can see it every time you two are within 5 feet of each other. He can't keep his eyes off you, and he gets all squirmy and weird. Plus, he doesn't even glance at the girls we have working here. No question, he's got it bad for you." Kendrick nodded his head sagely as he spoke.

"That's all fine and dandy, guys, but Luke is dead set against accepting or acting on his feelings towards any man, especially me it seems." Sawyer shrugged his shoulders as if it was a done deal. "For now, I have to accept that we are friends. I really don't know if it could ever move past just friends. It's something about his dad and brothers and a promise he made to his mom before she died."

"Man, when have you ever backed down from a challenge? The laser tag wars, fishing competitions, grade comparisons throughout school...you never backed down from anything. Growing up it was almost like you had a battle inside to prove yourself to everyone. You gonna let Luke's initial freak out over his reaction to you keep you down? Nah, man, you need to step up and get your man." Kendrick clapped him on the back, and Sawyer felt a glimmer of hope.

"You know, you're right. Luke knows he's gay. I just need to turn on the charm and wedge my way into his heart the way I used to wedge my way into Abby's room when she'd put up the *Keep Out* sign. All I've got to do is get a foot in the door, then I can muscle my way in. I'd never force him into anything, but I think if he starts thinking with his heart more than his head, I have a better chance." Sawyer checked the clock and realized he was due in the break room for lunch shortly. "Thanks guys, I better go, I have a challenge to meet."

SAWYER KNEW Luke took his lunch at 11:50 because Zoey was teaching a class until 12:30, and Luke could be finished in time for his class at 12:45. They had fallen into a comfortable routine during the week. The break room could hold around twenty people if needed, but 11:50 wasn't a popular time for the rest of the staff to eat lunch. Sawyer's immediate family either went home, went out, or ate in their offices.

As they were eating, Sawyer noticed Luke seemed upset. He let him talk for a bit about something funny which had happened in his last class. But then, Sawyer could wait no longer. When Luke got up to throw his trash away, Sawyer followed and cornered the other man between the trashcan and the refrigerator.

"What the fuck, Sawyer? We're at work, and I've told you I can't do this." Luke's words were heated, but more by desire than actual anger.

"Tell me what's wrong. I can tell you're upset; I want to know what's bothering you." Sawyer pressed in close until the heat of their bodies met. He felt like he was about to go up in flames.

"Nothing is wrong. I was just thinking about how normal things are between us and how I wish I could do this with you for real, not just as friends. I guess I was just feeling sad that it can't go past this." Luke let his gaze meet Sawyer's as he spoke.

"It *can* go past this, and it *will* if I have anything to do with it. I was reminded earlier that I don't back down from a challenge. Ever. So, consider yourself warned, you are my challenge, and I intend to win. Enjoy this *friendship* for now, because I have plans for it to become much more. Maybe not today, maybe not tomorrow, but someday you and I will be what our bodies and hearts want us to be."

Sawyer, feeling energized from the adrenaline pumping through his veins, leaned in and grazed his lips against Luke's cheek and whispered, "This *will* happen. Count on it."

Both men jerked back and separated when they heard Kendrick's voice booming down the hallway outside the break room.

"He's probably eating lunch, *Captain*! Let me see if I can find him for you."

Sawyer was grateful for Kendrick's loud warning. He walked to the sink to rinse his lunch dishes. Luke was gathering up his lunch belongings just as the captain walked into the room.

"Damn, boy, I'm not deaf. Stop that yelling. And I'm pretty sure I can find my own grandson in a lunch room." Robert spoke in a disgruntled tone towards Kendrick's retreating back as he opened the door to the break room.

His eyes immediately found Sawyer. Then he scanned the room and realized they weren't alone. His gaze flitted back and forth between Luke and Sawyer for several seconds before piecing things together in his head. He closed his eyes, rubbed a hand over his face, and breathed deeply.

"Captain, good to see you, sir. This is Luke Hamilton, our new martial arts instructor. Luke, this is my grandfather, Robert Decker." Sawyer easily made the introduction, without tripping over the nerves jangling about in his head and heart.

"Captain Decker, it's good to meet you. Sawyer speaks highly of you, sir." Luke held out a hand to shake.

"Well, I'm sure my name's been mud as of late." The captain looked a bit chagrined as he shook Luke's hand. He appreciated the other man's strong grip. This guy didn't fit all of the stereotypical gay images Robert had floating around in his head.

"Sawyer, son, could we talk? Maybe in your office?" He spoke to his grandson through a mixture of nerves and hope.

Sawyer had never once seen his grandfather seem anything but sure of himself, so to see him nervous and doubting was a bit unsettling.

Trying to put the man at ease, Sawyer spoke, "I've got one better than that. How about I take the rest of the day off and we go talk over some fishing poles and bait?" Sawyer raised his eyebrows in question as he offered an impromptu invitation to his grandfather.

Sawyer turned to Luke. "Could you take care of anything that comes up while I'm gone? You've got my cell; call if you need me. I'll let Decker know I'm leaving."

"No problem. Enjoy the fishing." Luke smiled at Sawyer and then turned and nodded at the captain before leaving the room.

"Alright, let's get the fishing supplies and hit the lake. Let's see who can catch the most. Winner gets to choose where we eat dinner." Sawyer felt nervous anticipation about their upcoming discussion, excitement over doing something so familiar with his grandpa, and a giddy sense of hopefulness that maybe things between them could eventually turn out right.

SAWYER LEANED back in his folding lawn chair on the bank of the lake, letting his legs stretch out before him, and sliding his cap down over his eyes to shield what sun the shade tree couldn't catch. Their lines stretched before them, and their bobbers floated silently in the calm water. The captain took the same position, and Sawyer sensed that he would need to wait for the man to start talking.

Thirty minutes later, Sawyer was roused from a sound sleep when his line jerked. Sitting up quickly and standing to get a better footing, he expertly reeled in the large fish on the end of his line. They got the fish off the hook, quickly weighed it, and threw it back in. Captain Decker made it a point to only keep the fish if they were planning a large fish fry.

As Sawyer settled back into his seat, he slyly pushed his luck with the captain as he mouthed silently, "That's one," while holding up one finger and winking at his grandpa's disgruntled face.

Mostly to himself, but loud enough under his cap that he knew the older man could hear, Sawyer taunted, "Mmmm, I'm thinking dinner at that steak place sounds good." Sawyer wasn't sure what his grandfather wanted to talk about, but he knew that it felt fantastic to be spending this time with him, even if it only lasted for a small amount of time before shit hit the proverbial fan.

About ten minutes later, Sawyer heard the captain rustle about in his chair, but he kept his eyes closed and the cap over his face. He figured that it may make it easier for the older man to speak if he wasn't looking directly at him.

"Sawyer, my boy, I need to say some things. I hope you'll let me speak without interruption, or I may not get this all out." When Sawyer remained silent, Robert continued. "I owe you an apology for the words I spoke to you the other night. I'm sorry. I should have never said those things, and I realize they were hurtful. I never meant to hurt you."

Sawyer swallowed thickly and squeezed tears from his eyes. *Thank you, Captain. You have no idea how much that means.*

"I don't know that I'll ever be completely on board with you being gay. I think it will take me some time to accept the idea that this isn't something you've chosen for yourself but the way you've always been. In the grand scheme of things, I don't want to see you get hurt. I don't think two men together is right, so it may take me a while to come around to seeing you with another man. But none of my other grandkids blatantly make out with their significant others in front of me, so I doubt I'll be seeing that from you either."

Sawyer wasn't sure if the captain was finished, so he waited it out just a bit.

"In the end, I just want you to know that I love you, and nothing will ever change that. We've had a difference of opinion on things before, and I'm sure we will many more times over the years, so this difference of opinion doesn't have to come between us. I hope you can forgive me. I just want you to be happy boy."

Sensing that was his chance to speak, Sawyer sat up and removed his cap.

"Thank you, Captain. Your words mean the world to me. When I thought I had lost you, lost this, I was crushed. Thank you for talking to me. I promise no making out in front of you. Now, Kendrick you may have to watch out for." Sawyer smiled at his grandpa, and they both laughed, knowing Kendrick was the wild card of the bunch.

"So, that young man you introduced me to at The Center+, Luke? He as sweet on you as you are on him?" The captain blushed a bit as he spoke, his voice gruff.

"How do you know I'm...how do you know I like him?" Sawyer couldn't bring himself to use his grandpa's old-fashioned term.

"Boy, I may be old, but I wasn't born yesterday. I've seen sparks from fireworks burn with less heat than the looks passing between the two of you. Always thought I'd see you look at a girl that way, but nevertheless, it's clear the two of you have something for each other. That who you're dating?" Now that the man had started talking, it seemed he didn't want to stop.

"Nah, we're just friends for now. There are some issues that have to be worked through, especially for Luke. Until then, I'll just be his friend." Sawyer spoke softly and his grandfather noted the disappointment.

"Well, starting off as friends is a good thing. That's how it was for my Lois and me. And then your Grandma Janie was my friend long before I asked her out for the first time." The man's eyes lost their focus as his heart and mind traveled back in time. Clearing his throat, he regained his focus. "My advice to you, my boy, is don't wait too long. You never know what the future holds, don't wait to be happy until it's too late."

Sawyer nodded at him as the older man returned to his lounging position and pulled his fishing cap down over his eyes.

Understanding that their talk was over for the time being, Sawyer stretched out again and pulled his cap down. Beneath the hat, his eyes streamed tears and his face glowed under his smile. He had his grandpa back in his life.

At the end of the day, Sawyer had caught four fish to the captain's three. They decided on beers and greasy burgers and fries at the local pub. They laughed about the ass kicking Robert was sure to get when Janie found out about the cholesterol-laden meal.

Sawyer hugged his grandpa good-bye. "Thanks for the talk, Captain. I really appreciate it. I'm not going to say that everything will be easy from here on out, but it will be a whole lot easier knowing you're all standing behind me." With a final hug and *I love you* shared between the men, Robert headed home.

Sawyer climbed into his car. He pounded his fists against the steering wheel and shouted *Yes!* with a fist pump into the air. He had known the captain's reaction was weighing on him, but he hadn't realized just how heavily. Having the man on his side made him feel damn near invincible. His heart raced, and his smile could have lit the entire town of Torey Hope. Feeling on top of the world, he knew there was only one person he wanted to share this with.

LUKE STEPPED from the shower and wiped the mirror with his towel. Pulling on a pair of mesh basketball shorts, he ran the towel through his hair before heading to the kitchen. He had eaten supper at The Center+ before his last class, but the nervous energy reverberating inside of him had him wanting a snack. Grabbing a yogurt, he padded to the living room and pulled out his laptop. He had every intention of watching a movie until he couldn't keep his eyes open.

His plans were interrupted by a knock on the door.

The sound gave him pause. He didn't have many friends

in Torey Hope, and he'd never told any of them where he lived. He had no idea who could be at his door. His heart beat wildly at the thought of who he *hoped* was on the other side of the door. *Stop. Why in the world would he come here? And how would he even know where you live?* The chastisement he gave himself did nothing to calm the heated reaction his body was having at the thought of Sawyer coming to see him. *You better hope it's not him. Sawyer coming here would be a very bad thing. Very bad.*

Reaching down to adjust himself in hopes of hiding his excitement, Luke laughed self-deprecatingly.

You idiot. Your luck it's the old lady down the hall coming for a cup of sugar or to give you some cookies again. You're going to look like a total perv opening the door with a hard-on.

As he swung the door open, his heart and mind battled over who they hoped it would be. His overjoyed heart won, and his disgruntled mind left the scene shaking its head in disbelief.

SAWYER STOOD outside of Luke's door, hands on the frame, head down as he contemplated showing up on the man's doorstep unannounced and uninvited. If he didn't answer in the next ten seconds, Sawyer would just leave, and no one would be the wiser.

His head knew it would be best to turn around and go

home, but his heart? His heart longed for Luke to open the door. He wanted to talk to him, spend time with him, be close to him.

Five, four, three, two, one...he should just go.

"Sawyer, is everything all right?"

Sawyer dragged his eyes from the tops of Luke's bare feet up to his equally bare chest before forcing himself to focus on the sparkling blue eyes in front of him.

Luke took in the beautiful sight of Sawyer, leaning on his door frame, warm golden eyes watching him, and knew he was in trouble. When Sawyer pushed off the doorway, Luke sensed he was planning to leave. Knowing that was probably for the best, but not wanting it to happen, Luke stepped back in a silent invitation.

"Hey, man. Sorry, I know it's getting late, and I shouldn't have just popped up uninvited..." Sawyer spoke as if he was waiting on Luke to tell him to leave.

You really should just tell him to go home. Nothing good could come from this.

Your heart is beating faster, you want him here. You want to see just what could come from this. No matter what, wouldn't it be nice to just have a friend to spend time with?

"No problem, man. You're always welcome here." Luke grabbed two waters and tossed one towards Sawyer. As both men took long swallows of their water they studied the other. Discarding their unfinished bottles on the counter, Luke walked to the living room.

Sawyer followed.

"Hey, man, like I said, you're always welcome to come by, but I've got two questions." Luke smirked a bit as he spoke.

"Yeah? Ask away." Sawyer couldn't help the cockeyed grin he shot back.

"One, how did you know where I live? And two, why are you here?" Luke wasn't sure how to ask the questions without sounding blunt and to the point.

Continuing to smile, Sawyer chuckled and ran a hand through his caramel brown hair. Blushing slightly, eyes twinkling, he admitted, "Well, I *may* have looked at your application at work. And I *might* have done a drive-by to see the place for myself." Letting his hand drop to the back of his neck, Sawyer huffed out, "Yeah, that sounds so much worse when I say it out loud."

"Nah, it's all good, man. I mean, who wouldn't want their own private stalker?" Luke laughed as Sawyer's cheeks pinked. "And you decided to pay me a visit..." He let the question hang on the air.

"Well, I had an awesome day with the captain, and when it was over the first person I thought to tell about it was you. I just wanted to share it. With you," Sawyer finished lamely. "And again, that sounds really pathetic when it's spoken out loud. I'm sorry man; I was riding a high from getting my grandpa back, and I acted without thinking. I'll leave you to your evening and just talk to you at work." Sawyer started to turn toward the door.

The hand that snaked out to grab his wrist was an electri-
fied lifeline; his heart stuttered and soared as the hand tugged
him back around.

"Sawyer, wait." Luke's voiced was strained. "Stay."

Sparks jumped between their bodies as they stood facing
each other. Close enough to feel the heat from the other's
skin, but not touching.

"I've never had anyone want to spend time with me; no
one has ever thought of me when they had something they
wanted to share." Reaching out and grasping Sawyer's hand,
Luke continued, "Thank you. It means a lot that you thought
of me. Now, tell me all about your fishing trip with the
captain."

Pulling just hard enough on his hand to make Luke step
forward a tiny bit, Sawyer leaned his forehead against Luke's.
"If I promise to tell you about it, and I promise not to take
anything too far, can I do something first?" Sawyer's gruff
whisper was full of longing and hope.

Luke knew he should say no. But his heart and body
wanted....wanted more, wanted Sawyer, wanted to feel what
he'd never felt before. Breathing heavily, body trembling,
Luke nodded his head and closed his eyes. He wanted to
savor every moment of what Sawyer was going to do.

Hands skimmed up his torso, cupped his shoulders to pull
him closer, and tangled in the curls at the nape of his neck. "I
promise to go slow. I'll stop when you need me to. I just need

to taste you." Sawyer's lips hovered lightly over Luke's as their heated breaths mingled.

For the rest of his life Luke would remember the unique scent of this man. His body craved, his mind fought, and his heart wept. Wept for what he knew could never be.

"Kiss me, Sawyer, but please don't be mad when it can't go anywhere from here." Luke's eyes glittered with tears. Tears over hurting Sawyer, tears for what he knew he was missing out on, and tears for what had been done to him. If it hadn't been for his past, maybe he'd have some sort of future.

Warm lips touched his, and his entire world seemed to shift on its axis. As Sawyer's tongue danced across his lips, Luke's body molded to every hard plane of the man in front of him. He allowed his hands to roam across the rock hard chest. He had longed for this, for this man, for this touch for as long as he could remember. And in moments it would end. It had to end.

But you can enjoy it before it does. His heart teased him as his body reacted.

"Sawyer, I can't let this happen. It's not fair to you. It would be wrong for me to let it go on. You should find someone who can openly be with you, someone who doesn't have a fucked up past." His breath was heavy as he tried to get his body under control.

"How can you say this is wrong? Your mouth on mine doesn't seem to think it's wrong. Your hands all over my body don't seem to think it's wrong. That impressive heat between your legs doesn't feel wrong." With a fist gripping loosely in blond curly hair, Sawyer forced Luke's sexy-as-sin mouth to tip up and crystal blue eyes to look at him. Flicking his tongue out to lick a perfect, soft bottom lip, he whispered, "How is this wrong?"

Hard hands pushed at Sawyer's chest as he felt the thrust and retreat of hips against his own. Luke tried to fight him, but he was fighting his feelings and inner demons even harder. Sawyer's strong hands cupped Luke's face, foreheads pressed together, chests heaved with desire. With a deep groan Sawyer's tongue swept Luke's top lip and his teeth pulled at the bottom one.

Moving his hand from Luke's neck, Sawyer let his palm run down the hard abs until it flattened against the heat under mesh shorts. "You say you don't want me, but this says differently. I won't force you; I know this is a lot to take in. But don't lie to me; don't lie to yourself; you want me just as much as I want you."

When the hands on his chest applied harder pressure, Sawyer let himself be pushed away. Adjusting his hard length behind his zipper, he smirked as he watched the movement mirrored in front of him.

"Sawyer. I'm not lying. I know I want you just as much as you want me. But it can't happen. Ever. Maybe someday I'll tell you more, but for now I need you to just believe me."

Luke let a shaky hand rub over his face while he tried to squelch the longing and heartache.

Sawyer heard the man speaking; he heard the words. But he'd also felt how that body responded to his hands, to his kiss; he knew Luke had something horrible in his past, but he also knew there was something between them. Something real. Something worth fighting for. And Sawyer had every intention of fighting.

Placing a soft kiss on Luke's lips, Sawyer gathered him in his arms. "One day you will tell me about your past. No matter what happens between us, I'll always be here to listen to you." Trailing his nose softly along Luke's ear, Sawyer whispered gruffly, "But know this, there is something between us, and I won't go down without a fight." After a final hug and drawing in a deep breath, Sawyer backed away. "Can we sit? I'd still like to tell you about my day."

Luke's eyes shone with tears, but he smiled and gestured towards the couch. "Yeah, sure, I'd love to hear how everything went with the captain."

After an hour of talking and laughing about the fishing trip, Sawyer glanced at the clock. "Man, it's getting late, I better go. Thanks for, well, you know, for....just thanks." As the men stood, Sawyer drew Luke into a full-body hug. Luke stiffened and tried to pull away, but Sawyer held tight. "Don't fight it, just let me hold you." Luke relaxed and let his body soak in Sawyer's warmth and strength.

"Sawyer, I want you as a friend. Honestly, I want so

much more, but I can't have that, so I'll settle for friends. Are you going to be able to just be friends?" Luke's eyes pleaded with him.

Just friends? Hell, no. But until he's ready to admit there's more here, yeah, I'll have to be content with just friends. "Sure. For now." Sawyer smirked.

"Sawyer, I'm serious. What happened tonight can't keep happening." Luke was getting angry that Sawyer wasn't taking no for an answer. "If you can't accept being just friends, then maybe we should agree to disagree and keep our distance."

The thought of not having Luke in his life made Sawyer's chest hurt. "No, I need you."

When Luke's eyebrows raised in question, Sawyer smiled and went on. "Not like that. Well, *yes,* like that, but I mean I need you as a friend. So, I promise no repeats of tonight unless you want it to happen."

Leaning in, he gave Luke a soft kiss. "No more after this last kiss I mean." Deepening the kiss, Sawyer sighed when Luke moaned into his mouth.

With a long, lingering kiss, Sawyer whispered, "And believe me, you *will* want more of this to happen. Someday." With a wink, Sawyer headed out the door.

Luke padded through the living room and kitchen in a daze. He tossed his half-eaten yogurt and water bottles in the trash. When he crawled into bed, he prayed for a restful night. Instead, he got glimpses of what could be with Sawyer swirled with nightmares of his father and brothers. He woke several times during the night, in a cold sweat, trembling. The dreams were so real, he could hear the venomous voices spewing hate, feel the pain burning through his body. No, no matter how badly he wanted something more with Sawyer, he could never let his father's and brothers' words and actions define him.

12

"Sawyer, there's someone here to see you. I tried to get him to make an appointment, but he was insistent you would want to see him." Katie looked over her shoulder and then scampered into the office, closing the door quickly behind her.

"Seriously, Sawyer, I happened to see this guy at the front desk. He was giving the new assistant a hard time so I stepped in. I think he's harmless, but I'm not sure you'll want to deal with him. However, he says he's your friend." A knock on the door made Katie's eyes go wide. "Do you want me to have Decker get rid of him?"

"Katie-girl, I don't even know who it is. I'm sure I can handle whoever is on the other side of that door. Feel free to call..." Before he could mention his brother's name, Sawyer heard a ruckus on the other side of the wooden divider.

"Decker Morgan, you sexy beast! Come over here this instant and give your Adam a hug. And any other type of physical contact you want to give would be perfectly acceptable." The man all but purred, and Katie swung the door open in shock.

"Decker? You know this guy?!" Katie tried to smile politely, but seeing the petite, dark skinned man clinging to Decker was enough to have her laughing out loud. "Well, it appears you *do* know who this is. Want to introduce us?"

Adam climbed down from his perch around Decker's waist. "Is this little hellcat yours, Decker? You might want to tell her to put her claws away. Down girl." Adam made a scratching motion toward Katie.

"Whoa, *ladies*, let's all put the claws away." Turning to Katie, Sawyer smiled and put his hands on her shoulders. "Katie-girl, this is my friend from college. His name is Adam, and he's obviously forgotten his manners."

Turning to Adam he pulled him into a hug. After releasing him, he spoke, "And Adam, this beautiful, strong, talented, smart girl is Katie. My old girlfriend from high school and Decker's better half nowadays."

Looking between the two, Sawyer shook his head. "I take it you two got off on the wrong foot. Let's start over."

"Adam, this is Katie. She means the world to Decker and me. Katie, this is Adam. Decker tolerates him, and I survived college in part thanks to him. So, let's all get along, shall we?" Sawyer motioned the other three into his office.

"Adam, it's very nice to meet you. I'm sorry I gave you any trouble out front; I didn't realize you were a friend of Sawyer's. I shouldn't have insisted that you make an appointment." Katie held her hand out. Sawyer knew it was killing her, but she was ever the professional.

Holding his hand out as if he expected her to kiss it, Adam rolled his eyes when Sawyer cleared his throat and shook his head. Moving his hand so that he could shake Katie's hand instead, Adam sniffed. "Well, you could have just believed me when I said Sawyer would be happy to see me. But apology accepted." Pulling her into a hug, Adam squealed, "*Now*, you've got to tell me where you got that nail polish. It is to *die* for."

With Adam and Katie getting along, Decker headed back to his office with a promise they would all meet up for drinks later.

"Adam, it was so nice meeting you, but I really do need to head back to my office to get some work done. I'll see you for drinks tonight." Kissing his cheek, then pulling Sawyer into a hug, Katie winked. "Have fun you two."

Leaning in to whisper to Sawyer, she giggled. "Torey Hope isn't going to know what hit them."

Sawyer threw his head back and laughed. But he knew she was right. Torey Hope hadn't ever seen the likes of Adam.

"Well, sugar, Adam is here. Take me out on the town, show me around, let's spill some T."

"Spill some T? Seriously, Ad? Can't you just say 'talk'?"

Sawyer shook his head. "Did you purposely wear your loudest outfit so you could make a grand entrance?" He took in the vibrant hues of his friend's clothing.

"Well, I couldn't come to town looking like everyone else. You *know* how I like to stand out. Speaking of *out*, are you? Out?" Hooking his arm through Sawyer's, Adam began leading him toward the door. As they walked past the gym, Adam slowed to a crawl and barely contained his drool.

Sawyer glanced past Kendrick and Zach, but his own heart sped up and he worked to control his breathing when he saw Luke was there with them.

"Day-um, Adam likes. Remind me to say hello to Kendrick, Zach, and friend when we return. Please tell me they'll be joining us for drinks." Adam turned large eyes toward Sawyer and batted his lashes.

"I'll ask them. Kendrick and Zach probably will. I don't know about Luke." Sawyer tried not to show any emotion when he spoke the other man's name. It had been a week since he'd shown up unexpectedly at Luke's door, and things had definitely been tense between them as of late.

"Oh, *Luke* is it? And just what does Adam need to know about this *Luke*? Is he your baby, your lover, your butt-buddy? Do you want to marry him with rainbows and unicorn decorations? Mmmm, Sawyer is blushing, Adam must have hit the nail on the head. Tell me, Sawyer, do you want to *nail* Luke or do naughty things to his *head*?"

When Sawyer shifted uncomfortably and rolled his eyes,

Adam clapped and bounced up and down. "Ohhhh, you *so* want him. This visit just got totally delish. Let's go grab lattes and dish, sugar."

Following Adam to his car, Sawyer could only shake his head.

SAWYER AND ADAM settled into their seats with steaming hot lattes. Sawyer had chosen the little coffee shop in town knowing it would be less crowded than the larger one a few miles away.

"So, you big, sexy man. Tell Adam all about what's been going on." Adam munched daintily on his shortbread cookie.

"Well, one thing that hasn't changed is you talking about yourself in 3rd person." Sawyer took a sip of his latte and smirked at his friend. "So, I came out to Decker and my cousins fairly soon after coming home from school. I just recently told the rest of my family. It's been a bit rough with some of them, but overall, I totally lucked out and have their support."

"Really? How did you do it? A big dramatic announcement? Text or email?" Adam, always ready for juicy stories, barely contained himself in his seat.

"Well, I didn't come in on a pride parade float wearing a mankini and dancing to Lady Gaga..." Sawyer deadpanned.

"Hey! I only did that *once*. It was hilarious and you know

it." Clapping his hands again, Adam laughed at the memory Sawyer had brought up.

"Yeah, well, I did it with less show. Took Decker camping and told him. Invited the other guys up and told them too. We had a good evening. They were very supportive and curious." Sawyer smiled as he recalled the camping trip and conversation. "I told my parents pretty much right after. They were upset, but supportive. They weren't shocked like I expected them to be; they said they'd had suspicions for several years."

Sawyer still felt like he'd dodged the proverbial bullet when it came to his parents' support. So many friends had been less than lucky when it came to telling their parents.

"One of my grandmas, an uncle, and my grandpa took a bit to come around. My grandpa was the worst. Some really hurtful things were said, but we recently took a day to go fishing and talk, and things seem much better. The beauty of it all is that I can see myself overcoming it eventually. Friends and family are accepting me. I think everything is going to be all right." Sawyer offered a genuine smile.

"Okay, that's great. I'm happy for you. Yay!" Adam nodded his head enthusiastically. "Now, skip to the good stuff. Who are you kissing, blowing, fucking, and loving?" He smiled coyly and raised his eyebrows in anticipation.

Sawyer's cheeks pinked and he immediately took to studying his latte.

"Oh. My. God. You are totally doing all of those things,

aren't you!? Tell Adam who the lucky guy is." His eyes were wide with anticipation.

"Well, I guess it would depend on which guy you want to hear about..."

Sawyer ducked his head and grimaced at Adam's shrill "*Whaaat?!?*"

"Shhh, keep it down. Finish your latte and we'll leave. I'm not talking about this with you in the coffee shop. We need an open place where you can squeal and bounce around until your little heart is content." Downing his drink, Sawyer stood and walked to the trashcan.

Turning around he almost knocked over an elderly lady. She stood her ground, hands on her hips, giving him an evil glare.

Shaking her finger in his face, she spoke lowly, "I told her. I told her this would happen. Well, not *this* exactly, I surely wasn't expecting *this*, but I told her." The old woman gave him the stink eye once more then turned around to the counter. "I'd like a hot tea. To go, please. I've got somewhere to be." She cast a final threatening glance over her shoulder in Sawyer's direction.

"Sugar, I don't know what you did to make that granny angry, but we better leave. If she had a cane, I think she'd be beating you with it by now." Adam hooked his arm with Sawyer's and snuggled against him. "Let's go, you've got some explainin' to do."

With a confused look back at the lady, racking his brain as

to why the she seemed so angry with him, Sawyer let Adam lead him out of the coffee shop.

Arriving at the park, they walked to the duck pond. Sawyer laughed as his friend paid a quarter for duck feed and spent the next fifteen minutes calling, "Here ducky, ducky, ducky. Come see Adam you little quackers, I've got food for you."

"You don't get out much, do you?" Sawyer rolled his eyes as Adam threw the last of the feed to the ducks.

"I get out plenty, I just don't visit many towns this small. Let me enjoy being quaint for a bit." Rubbing his hands together, Adam settled cross-legged onto a rock and indicated Sawyer should sit on the adjacent bench. "Now, let's start at the beginning. Who are you kissing?"

"Um, I've recently been kissing Hayden and Luke," Sawyer admitted.

Adam raised his eyebrows in question, but continued.

"And blowing?"

"Hayden."

"Fucking?"

"Hayden."

"Loving?"

Sawyer turned away. "I don't know that I love him. But I know he doesn't love me."

"Who? Hayden? He must be an idiot." Adam pursed his lips together.

"No, I don't love Hayden. He probably believes he loves

me." Running his hands through his hair, Sawyer sighed. "Uhhhh, I'm not being fair to him, I know it."

"Okay, now you've got to give Adam a bit of time to figure this out." Taking a deep breath and blowing it out slowly, he continued. "You kiss Hayden and Luke, right?"

Sawyer nodded.

"Hayden may love you? He blows you and vice versa? And you've fucked him? And him you?" Adam lists the points on his fingers.

Sawyer again nodded.

"So, what's the problem? Is he mean? Ugly? Bad in bed?" Adam questioned as if Sawyer had lost his mind.

"It's just not there, that spark. We are friends, and we've enjoyed each other's company, but I just don't feel it." Sawyer gazed out across the pond. "He's not..."

"Ahhhh, Adam gets it now, it's all becoming clearer. Hayden isn't *Luke*. Your eyes don't go all dreamy when you talk about Hayden, but you start breathing funny when you mention Luke. Does Hayden know he's competing against Luke?" Adam was smug.

"There's no competition, Ad. There was nothing between Hayden and me even before I met Luke. Believe me, I wanted there to be something. Hayden is perfect, attractive, established, steady, ready for commitment. But I feel like I'd be settling if I took things further with him."

Closing his eyes, Sawyer thought back to the night before when Hayden had stopped by. Sawyer should have just been honest with him, right then and there, but he'd let Hayden stay. He'd allowed a kiss. He hadn't stopped Hayden's roaming hands. Why? Because he was thinking of Luke the entire time.

When Hayden had inquired if Sawyer was feeling okay, he'd quickly grasped onto the excuse and run with it. "Just tired is all. Probably just need a good night's sleep. How about we catch up later?"

Sawyer had seen the shadow of doubt flicker across Hayden's face when he showed him to the door. Closing the door behind him, Sawyer leaned against it. *Cut him loose, Morgan. He's got a lot to offer. Don't keep him hanging. It's not fair to keep him around until you're sure this thing with Luke is or isn't going to work out. Hayden deserves better than that.*

"So, when are you going to give Hayden the 'it's not you, it's me' speech? Sugar, you can't just keep him in your back pocket as a backup. First, because he'll find out, and how do you think that will make him feel? Second, Sawyer Morgan doesn't string guys along. Cut the man loose." Adam imparted his sage advice with a knowing nod of his head.

"Now, what about Luke? There's been kissing?" Adam was hopeful.

"Yes, there's been kissing." Sawyer touched his lips absentmindedly as he recalled their sensual kisses.

"There's been more than kissing?" Adam's hopeful anticipation made Sawyer smile ruefully.

"No, there's been nothing more than a few kisses. And I don't think there ever will be. Luke had a really rough past, lost his mother to cancer, mistreated terribly by his father and brothers. He admits to being attracted to men, but swears he can never act upon that attraction due to a promise to his mother. Something about not letting his dad and brothers win."

Sawyer's forehead crinkled in concern. "I'm pretty sure he's been hurt, badly. He likes me; he wants me, but he's scared and not willing to break a promise he made. I haven't been able to get him to tell me all about it, yet, but I'm working on it."

"Mmmm, well, I saw the man, so I understand the desire to have him around, but if he's not giving it up do you really want to put a lot of effort into a relationship that has a very low chance of yielding any results?" Sawyer got the feeling Adam was purposely goading him.

"It's not just about 'yielding results,' Ad. I like the guy; he's my friend, and I enjoy spending time around him. I'm not just going to give that up because he doesn't want to sleep with me." Sawyer was irritated, both at Adam and the situation with Luke.

"Good answer, sugar. Let me tell you what Adam thinks you should do. First, be his friend. Sounds like he's got a lot of baggage that he needs to sort through before anything else can happen. But with you by his side, maybe he'll be able to sort quicker. Second, say good-bye to kissing, blowing, and fucking Hayden; it's just not right and you know it. You may have to endure a dry spell for a while, but you seem to think this Luke is worth it, so suck it up and get used to spending late nights with your right hand. Third, invite *everyone* out for drinks tonight. I want to spend time with the guys before I leave, and I bet Katie is a great dancer. Hayden and Luke should come too, since they are your *friends*. Invite them." When he started to protest, Adam held a finger to Sawyer's lips. "Shhhh, just let Adam plan everything and it will all work out just fine."

After Sawyer popped into the restroom and Adam fed the ducks one last time, they headed out of the park.

Sawyer's phone vibrated in his pocket. Smiling at Katie's picture on the screen, he slid the button and answered, "Hey, girl, what's up?"

"Sawyer, where are you right now?" Katie sounded flustered.

"Adam and I are at the park, why?"

"Stay there. Decker and I need to see you."

"Katie, is everything okay?"

"It will be, just give us a minute to get there."

Sawyer and Adam walked to the front of the park to meet Decker and Katie. Instead of Decker's sleek black car, they pulled up in a retro station wagon. Sawyer and Adam exchanged questioning looks.

Before Sawyer could understand what was going on, the back door opened and Adam gasped. "Look out, sugar! It's the angry granny!" He jumped behind Sawyer and used him as a shield.

"Gee, Ad, why don't you just throw me right to her?" Shaking his head at his friend's antics, Sawyer watched the trio approach. He simultaneously recognized the older woman as Katie's grandmother and realized what had made her so angry in the coffee shop.

"Hello, Grandma, I'm sorry I didn't recognize you in the coffee shop. How are you today?" Sawyer spoke politely, but everyone could hear the smile in his voice.

The elderly woman jutted her chin out and just glanced back and forth between Decker and Sawyer. Katie raised her eyebrows at her grandmother and jerked her head toward Sawyer in a *speak to him* manner.

The older woman crossed her arms and huffed.

Uncomfortable with the silence, Adam piped up, "She doesn't look nearly as scary when she's not yelling and pointing fingers."

"Grandma! You *yelled?* In the coffee shop?" Taking a deep breath and trying to calm herself, Katie spoke evenly. "You owe Sawyer an apology."

Understanding dawned on Adam and he snickered. "Let me guess, she didn't know you had a twin?" He smiled at Decker and looked sympathetically toward Grandma.

"Pishaw! I knew he had a twin, I just didn't realize how exactly alike they look when they aren't in the same room together. When I see them standing next to each other, I can see the difference, but I *may* have mistaken Sawyer for Decker earlier." Trying to keep her dignity while still admitting her mistake wasn't working out very well for the older woman.

"Grandma..." Katie began.

"Hush, girl." Turning to Sawyer she lifted her chin proudly. "I'm sorry I yelled at you. I jumped to conclusions and thought you were Decker cheating on my Katie with a man. I hope you can accept my apology."

Adam continued to giggle. Sawyer shot him a *be quiet* look.

"Apology accepted, Grandma. Decker and I have fooled some of the best, our parents included, so don't feel too bad." He leaned down and whispered dramatically in her ear for all to hear. "Plus, I may be gay, but does he really look like my type?"

Everyone laughed, and Adam propped a hand on his hip. "Sugar, you just *wish* Adam was your type."

"Well, I'll let you take me home now. Again, so sorry for the display and confusion." As Grandma turned toward the car, they heard her mumble, "That other boy should be in the dictionary under the word *flamboyant*. Darn bright colors, makes me want to wear sunglasses."

Katie rolled her eyes, and the men laughed.

"And I'd put you in the dictionary under '*spitfire* see also *character, spunky*,'" Adam called out to Grandma good-naturedly.

Waving him off with a blush and a wink, Grandma settled into the backseat of her old car.

Katie and Decker waved, calling out, "See you at 7:00."

Katie added, "Oh, Adam, I took care of that thing you wanted me to do. It's all set."

As they drove off, Sawyer looked at Adam suspiciously. "What did you do? And when did you have time to do it?"

"Ahh, sugar, these fingers are magic in more ways than one. It only took that one restroom break by the pond for me to fire a message off to Katie from your phone. She's a good girl, she understands that Adam knows best." Patting Sawyer's cheek, he said, "Now, let's get you home and fancied up before our date."

Heading to the car, Sawyer protested, "I don't need to be fancied up, and it's not a date."

His words fell on deaf ears.

13

———

"*T*urner, table for 8? We've got you all set up, follow me." The hostess snaked through the crowded restaurant.

"One day, you'll be putting our reservations under *Morgan*." Growling in her ear, Decker wrapped his arms around Katie and pulled her body close to his as they reached the table.

As she giggled, Kendrick patted him on the back. "Dude, keep it in your pants. This is a family establishment."

Sawyer eyed the eight chairs. "Who else is coming?"

Zach and Zoey sauntered in filling the table with six people.

When no one answered him, Sawyer eyed both Katie and Adam. Before he could ask again, they both busied themselves with their menus, and Sawyer felt a presence behind him.

"Luke, Hayden, glad you guys could make it. Have a seat." Katie smiled at the two men and skillfully avoided Sawyer's glare.

"Here Hayden, I saved you a seat." Adam patted the chair next to him and winked at Hayden. Not one to ruffle easily, Hayden smiled with a nod and thanked Adam as he took his seat.

The one chair left was next to Sawyer. Luke settled himself and instantly took an interest in his menu. It was clear he was attempting to avoid looking at Sawyer.

"Hey. Good to see you. I'm glad you could come." Sawyer spoke softly to Luke while he longed to wrap his hand around his neck and pull him in for a kiss.

"Yeah, Katie said it was going to be a big group thing and I should come." Luke seemed apprehensive about being around so many of Sawyer's family and friends.

Hayden, clearly charming and at ease with a large group, spoke to Katie, but made it feel as if he was speaking to all present. "Thank you very much for inviting me. Being new in town means I haven't made a lot of friends. It can get lonely sitting at home."

Turning to Sawyer, Hayden spoke, "Feeling better today? Hope you got some rest after last night."

Adam's eyes went round, Katie's mouth dropped into an

O, and Luke choked a bit on his water. Sawyer thanked his lucky stars when the waitress arrived to take drink orders.

For three hours, through drinks and appetizers and shared desserts, Adam kept them all entertained with stories from college. He was a total nut, but deep down inside he had a good, albeit fragile, heart. Sawyer had figured out long ago that Adam dressed and acted and spoke the way he did because it helped to hide his hurt and his fears. Watching him spin stories and keep his family and friends laughing, Sawyer felt his heart warm. It was so nice to no longer have to hide his friend, dating history, sexuality.

Everything felt right.

Everything except the thick tension between himself, Luke, and Hayden.

He excused himself to head to the restroom, partly because he'd had too many drinks, partly because he needed to escape the heated looks from Hayden and the electricity sparking between him and Luke.

Flushing the urinal, he walked around the partition to the sink.

Finding Hayden leaning against the sink almost stopped his heart.

"Damn, man, you scared the shit out of me. I didn't hear you come in." Sawyer tried to avoid the look in Hayden's eyes as he maneuvered around him to wash his hands.

He felt the man's heat against his side, his breath in his ear, before the words washed over him. "We don't have anything exclusive, Sawyer. But I want that, I want to have you all to myself. He's never going to come out, accept himself, accept you. With him it would be more hiding and pretending. With me, you could be yourself, have a future." Hayden reached down and palmed the front of Sawyer's jeans. "We are good together; we could be great together if you'd just let it happen." Hayden turned to leave, but was met with Luke hesitantly coming in the door.

Luke's eyes traveled from a sultry Hayden to a flustered Sawyer.

Hayden's eyes flitted over Luke and glanced meaning-fully at Sawyer.

Sawyer ran his hands through his hair and squeezed his eyes shut.

As Hayden left, Luke approached Sawyer slowly.

"He likes you." A statement.

"Yeah. He does." An admission.

"And you like him?"

Grabbing him around the waist, Sawyer quickly spun Luke around against the sink. "No. Damn, I wish I did like him the way he likes me. But, no. He's my friend. I feel nothing for him romantically. Nothing like I feel for you." Sawyer let his lips brush against Luke's, lighter than a feather.

Allowing the kiss to deepen momentarily, Luke clung to Sawyer's shirt.

"No, you promised, no more of this." He shoved Sawyer backwards a bit. "He would be good for you. He's very into you; he seems smart and stable; you guys could have a nice future."

"I promised no more kissing unless you wanted it to happen. The way your lips moved under mine tells me you definitely wanted that kiss." Reaching up to cup his cheek, Sawyer whispered painfully, "And I don't just want a nice future, I want *you*."

With heavy hearts and desire laden bodies, Luke and Sawyer separated reluctantly before their restroom rendezvous was interrupted.

When they arrived back at the table, Hayden had said his goodbyes and headed out. Knowing looks filled the faces of most present, but no one mentioned the obvious.

Luke did his best to avoid Sawyer's eyes as he mumbled his quick goodbyes.

Katie and Zoey headed out for dancing, and Adam begged to accompany them.

The four remaining men paid their bills and headed out into the evening.

"You guys want to play some Madden?" Zach asked.

"Hell yeah, we haven't played that forever. It's about time I beat your asses." Kendrick clapped them on the back.

THEY SPREAD out over the living room, controllers in hand, and let the games begin.

After about five minutes, Zach spoke over the volume of the game. "So, was it just me or did our sweet Sawyer have two men panting over him tonight?"

Decker cracked a smile and winked at his brother. "Yeah, man. I thought Luke was going to spontaneously combust when he sat next to you. And the heat from Hayden's eyes could have set the place on fire."

Sawyer just smirked, preparing for the razzing he knew was coming.

"Yeah, I'm surprised the three of you could even walk with all the fiery steel between your legs after that restroom break." Kendrick made a crude gesture at his crotch.

The men laughed and fell silent to play the game for several more moments.

"Oh yeah! Take that fuckers!" Kendrick stood and did a victory dance which consisted mostly of the middle finger, hip thrusts, and tongue wagging.

Decker took a minute to text Katie. Zach, too, pulled out his phone.

"Checkin' on your girl, bro?" Kendrick asked.

"Yeah..." both Decker and Zach answered.

When three sets of eyes zeroed in on him, Zach flushed. "I mean, I was just making sure Zoey and Katie were okay. I didn't want them to drink too much and try to drive." He stumbled around on words, "I didn't mean it like she's *my* girl..." He trailed off and excused himself quickly for the restroom.

"There's a story there, I can feel it." Sawyer had a thoughtful look on his face.

The men sat quietly for a moment as they chewed things over in their heads.

"You mean to tell me you think Zach is doin' our cousin?" Kendrick spoke loudly on purpose, knowing his cousin could hear him in the restroom.

"She's not really our cousin, fucker!" Zach yelled from the restroom.

Kendrick laughed silently, rolling on the couch. "I love giving him a hard time."

Decker and Sawyer glanced at each other and then at Kendrick.

"You seriously think there's something between Zach and Zoey?" Decker seemed shocked.

"Well, if you two would pull your heads out of your asses, or your dick from some guy's ass as the case may be, you'd notice that those two are practically inseparable." Kendrick sobered a bit.

"They've always been close, so what's different now?" Sawyer asked.

"They've always been close, but now they share secret looks and heated stares. I don't know what, if anything, has happened between them, but I think something is going down." Kendrick spoke softly to the twins.

As Zach returned from the restroom, Kendrick piped up, "Well, man, at least you let Sawyer drop his gay bomb before you told the family you want to fuck your cousin. Maybe your announcement won't seem so bad after Sawyer's." Sticking his tongue out crudely, Kendrick laughed and dodged the fist Zach halfheartedly pounded on his arm.

"She's not my fucking cousin, man. Let it go." Zach gritted his teeth.

"No, but she could be your *fucking* cousin. Get it? Because you want to..." Kendrick ran out of the room toward the kitchen laughing hysterically as Zach threw a pillow at him.

As the four met up in the kitchen, Decker spoke with a glint of humor in his eyes. "Well, looks like I'm the only one with a good thing going in my love life right now."

When the other three sobered and scowled at him, he continued, "Sawyer is in his own little love triangle, fighting Hayden's advances and Luke's non-interest. Zach wants to hook up with the girl we've known as a cousin our entire life. And Kendrick needs to be checked weekly for STDs based on the number of girls he's sleeping with." Nodding his head, trying not to laugh at the looks on their faces, Decker was smug as he purposely pushed buttons.

All three spoke at once.

"It's more complicated than that..."

"She's not actually related to us, and no one said anything about hooking up..."

"Hey, I always wrap it before I tap it. Gotta protect the goods..."

Decker couldn't help but laugh as his brother and cousins defended themselves. He sat at the kitchen table and gestured that the others should do the same.

"Okay, where should we start? I'm not sure there's any fixing Kendrick." Decker rolled his eyes in his cousin's direction. "Zach? Want to talk about anything?"

"Nothin' to talk about. Zoey's my friend. End of story." Zach sulked defensively.

"Let us recall not long ago that I walked in on you and Zoey in a fairly intimate embrace. I wasn't thinking clearly at the time, and I'd forgotten about it until just now, but that hug looked more than just friendly." Decker stopped talking and looked at Zach pointedly.

As if he'd forgotten Decker had seen him with Zoey in the gym, Zach chewed the inside of his cheek. "Now's not the time to talk about it. Maybe I can and will sometime soon, just not now. Can we let it go?"

"For now, we can let it go because I think we've got a much more pressing matter at hand." Decker turned his eyes toward Sawyer.

"Yeah, but just who's hand is pressing and where? I believe that is the real question." Kendrick winked and chuckled at his own joke.

Running his hands through his hair, Sawyer sighed. "Do you guys want the whole story or the shortened one?"

"Start with the short one, then we'll decide if we need the long one." Kendrick waited for Sawyer to begin.

"Hayden likes me, I don't feel it. I want Luke, he wants me, but swears it can never happen." Sawyer looked at the other men expectantly.

"Elaborate." Decker issued the command softly.

"Hayden is perfect, attractive, nice, successful, stable, ready to commit, in it for the long haul." Sawyer listed the man's attributes.

"Damn, I almost want to date him." Kendrick laughed. "What's the problem then?"

"There's no spark, no heat, no desire." Sawyer held his hand up before anyone could speak. "And before you go there, I knew this long before Luke was in the picture."

"Correct me if I'm wrong, bro, but hasn't Hayden spent some time here with you and you with him at his place? How serious is it?" Decker questioned.

"If by serious you mean physical, it's pretty much as serious as two guys can get. If by serious you mean emotional, that's a one-sided relationship, at least in my mind." Sawyer spoke bluntly, but saw the unspoken question on their faces. "I know, I know, I have to tell Hayden. It's not fair that I've used him or strung him along. I just don't want to hurt him."

"If Luke packed up and moved to Timbuktu, would you want something with Hayden?" Zach asked.

"No, like I said, even before Luke, I felt nothing but platonic feelings toward Hayden." Sawyer shook his head as he spoke.

"Yeah, man, you really need to be fair to him. I know

you've had a lot going on, and I'm sure having Hayden to turn to was comforting, but you can't let it go on any longer," Decker reasoned with him.

"I know. I'll talk to him. Soon."

"So, what's up with Luke?" Kendrick asked.

"Everything. It's all up in the air, unlabeled, disorganized, and messy." Sawyer rubbed a hand over his face. "We've kissed a few times. He is totally into me, except that I'm a guy and he can't be with men. Or so he says. I've still not gotten him to talk about his past very much. I don't even think he's afraid of coming out or being seen in public with me, I think it has more to do with something his dad and brothers said or did, but mostly it's about the promise to his mom."

"Well, if you're in this for real, you've got to be patient. Be his friend, take him on dates without him realizing they're dates, don't let him get away without worming your way into his heart. But Sawyer, I think you may have to realize that sometimes people never overcome their pasts." Kendrick spoke softly and sincerely.

"A date without knowing it's a date? How do I do...Wait! I think I have an idea. Thanks guys, I need to make some plans." Sawyer popped up from his chair and headed to his room.

14

*A*fter a fitful night's sleep and an uneventful day at work, Sawyer stood apprehensively on Hayden's front step. He knew what he had to do, but he feared losing a friend.

"Sawyer, what a nice surprise, come in." Hayden was still in his business shirt and dress pants, his tie loosened around his neck.

"Sorry to just show up like this. I didn't even give you time to relax after work." Sawyer stood nervously at the doorway, not sure if he should stay standing or sit down.

"Nonsense, I'm always happy to see you. Go have a seat, I'll get us drinks. I actually wanted to talk to you about something." Hayden's face flashed a hint of regret before he disappeared into the kitchen.

Taking a seat on the chair closest to the couch, Sawyer wiped his palms on his jeans.

Hayden appeared with iced teas and sat on the couch, close enough so their knees bumped.

"Hayden, I need to talk to you..." Sawyer began, but he was interrupted by his friend.

"No, wait, Sawyer, let me talk first." Hayden took a deep swallow of his tea as if to calm his nerves and build his strength.

"I need to apologize for the scene I made in the restroom." Hayden reached for Sawyer's hand and held it as he continued. "I found myself in the awkward position of being extremely jealous of Luke and not knowing exactly how to handle it. I acted rude, possessive, and condescending towards your relationship with him, and for that I'm truly sorry. I'm not that type of person. I think I saw my hopes of something deeper happening with you being dashed as soon as I saw the way you and Luke looked at each other, and I was desperately grasping at straws to salvage what may have been left of us."

"Hayden..." Sawyer started, but he was stopped.

"Wait, let me finish. I've known from the first day we met that there wasn't really a chemistry between us. You're extremely attractive and a great guy, but we don't have that spark. I'm willing to forgo the spark for a comfortable friendship and solid future." Hayden paused and Sawyer tried quickly to think of a response to let him down gently.

"But then I saw the fire in your eyes when Luke walked into the room and took his seat beside you. I could never compete with that fire, and I'd never want to hold you back from experiencing a relationship like that." Hayden took a deep breath. "So, basically what I'm saying is I think we should just be friends. And as your friend, I think you should not let go of whatever you have with Luke."

Sawyer's eyes stung with unshed tears. He dropped his head. Looking back up at Hayden, Sawyer took their joined hands and brought them to his lips. Kissing Hayden's skin lightly, he spoke, "Hayden, that's possibly the sweetest, most selfless thing anyone has ever done for me. Thank you."

Leaning in to kiss Hayden's cheek, Sawyer sat back and smiled. "You deserve that fire in a relationship too. I hope someday, when you're least expecting it, you'll find it."

Finishing their tea over random small talk, the men smiled warmly at one another.

"I better be heading out. I have a secret date I'm attempting to sneak in on a certain martial arts instructor tomorrow." Sawyer smiled.

Hayden's broad smile lit up his face. "Well, I have to say he's a pretty lucky guy, even if he doesn't realize it just yet. Have fun, you deserve it."

Hayden reached out a hand to shake, but Sawyer pulled him into a hug. "Thanks again, man. You are a total class-act."

SAWYER MADE himself wait as long as possible the next morning before bounding out of bed and heading to Luke's. It was a Saturday and the place he wanted to take him wasn't open until 10:00 a.m.

Forcing himself to walk at a normal pace, Sawyer checked his clothes again. He'd purposely dressed casually, both because the location they were headed called for it and he didn't want to appear too date-like. The faded jeans, soft t-shirt, and simple tennis shoes made him feel relaxed and comfortable, but inside, his heart was beating a mile a minute.

What if he's not home? What if you can't get him to leave the house with you? What if he balks when we get there? The thoughts hummed around Sawyer's head like race cars around a track.

Taking a deep breath to calm his nerves, Sawyer knocked on the door.

A still-sleepy Luke, dressed only in low-slung sweatpants greeted him several moments later with a confused look on his gorgeous face.

"Sawyer? Um, good morning?"

The two men stood stock-still, their eyes voraciously traveling from head to toe, breathing and heart beats ramping up several notches.

Shaking himself from his trance, Sawyer silently chastised himself. *You're here to show him a nice day, not to show him you're barely more than a hormonal teen.*

"Mornin'. Hope I didn't wake you..." Sawyer hedged at an apology if one was needed.

"Nah, man, I was up, just hadn't gotten out of bed yet."

The image of Luke tangled in sheets, quickly pulling on sweats and nothing more when he heard the knock at the door, made Sawyer's mouth go dry.

"So, listen, I have some errands to run today and wanted to know if you wanted to tag along. Thought it might be a good way to see the town and get out of the house." Sawyer put the invitation out there and silently begged Luke to accept.

He watched as Luke's head and heart battled for several seconds. Seeming satisfied with whatever the outcome of their feud had been, Luke nodded. "Sure, just let me grab a quick shower."

He stepped back so Sawyer could enter. "Just make yourself at home. There's OJ in the fridge or I can make coffee." Luke hesitated as he waffled between heading to the kitchen or the bathroom.

"No, one of the things I wanted to do was stop at my Grandma Janie's bakery for breakfast and caffeine. Go ahead and get ready." Sawyer nodded his head toward the hall he knew Luke would soon disappear down.

Running through his plans for the day while Luke showered, Sawyer glanced around furtively. Once he heard the water running and was sure Luke was in the shower, Sawyer stood and roamed the living room and kitchen looking for what he needed.

He found exactly what he was searching for on the small table in the kitchen. Running a hand through his hair, he argued with himself whether or not he should do what he was contemplating. Reaching out a hesitant finger, he slowly moved the items around, glancing at each one to see if it would do. When he heard the shower stop, he grabbed the first item he could get his hands on and quickly shoved it in his pocket as he returned to the couch. Two minutes later, a freshly showered Luke appeared with still-damp hair. Sawyer allowed his greedy gaze to travel down Luke's bare chest before a shirt was pulled over his head and covered the perfection.

"Ready?" At Luke's nod, Sawyer headed toward the door. "Oh, hey, make sure you have your wallet and ID."

When Luke looked at him strangely, Sawyer shrugged, "Just never know when you might need it, ya know?" Trying to appear nonchalant, Sawyer let himself out the door and headed toward his car.

Once they were settled, Sawyer pulled the Honda out onto the street. "Okay, breakfast first. Grandma Janie makes the best scones, but her cinnamon rolls are to die for."

Making their way to The Cakery, Sawyer waved at his grandmother as they walked inside. The scent of baking pastries and fresh-brewed coffee assaulted their senses.

"My sweet Sawyer, it's so good to see you." She came

around the counter and gave him a hug. Turning to Luke she stuck out a hand, "Good morning to you. I'm Grandma Janie."

Luke smiled and returned the hand shake. "Nice meeting you, I'm Luke Hamilton. I'm the new martial arts instructor at The Center+."

"Of course you are! I've heard the name, but we've not been formally introduced." She gathered him into a hug before turning to Sawyer.

"What can I get you boys?"

"Let's have a cinnamon roll and a buttermilk scone with lingonberry preserves. And two lattes please." He glanced at Luke, raising his eyebrows in silent question of the order. When Luke nodded and smiled, they headed to a small table in the corner.

While they waited for Janie to bring their breakfast, Sawyer spoke quietly. "Janie is the captain's second wife. My biological maternal grandmother died when my mom was very young. The captain was a lonely alcoholic for several years, trying to raise my mom and Aunt Audrey. Many mistakes were made over the years. Audrey probably suffered the most. I haven't been told the entire story, and honestly, I don't think I'd want to know all the sordid details, but Audrey went through some bad stuff. She and my mom had a rough relationship for several years. It culminated with Audrey doing something to my dad that was actually punishable by law, and he and my mom and the captain setting up an intervention to get Audrey straightened out. My understanding is it was really bad for a while. But not long after, everyone involved started healing and moving on and that's when Grandpa met Janie. They dated for a while and married soon after. She's treated all of us kids like precious treasures ever since." Sawyer stopped talking and winked at Luke as Janie came out of the kitchen with a tray full of goodies.

"Here you go, boys." She sat the food and drinks down along with napkins and forks.

"This looks delicious Mrs. Decker, thank you." Luke's eyes widened as he took in the size of the cinnamon roll and scone.

"None of that Mrs. Decker nonsense. You can call me Grandma or Janie or Grandma Janie. Mrs. Decker is what the doctor's office calls me." Janie smiled and reached her arms out to both men so she could pat them on the shoulders. "Now you boys enjoy your breakfast and don't even think about paying, it's on the house. Not every day I get to start my morning with two attractive young men prettying up my place." She winked and walked away.

"I'll be sure to tell the captain that," Sawyer called out as she left.

"The captain is still on my list for eating enough to send himself into cardiac arrest the other night, so he can just get over it." She stuck her tongue out playfully at Sawyer before disappearing into the kitchen.

"I like her, she's sweet." Luke looked at the food in front of him. "Wow, I had no idea these would be so big."

"Yeah, that's why I just got the two, I figured we could split them."

When they had finished their meal and gotten refills on their lattes to go, Sawyer waited until Janie's back was turned and stuffed a $20 bill into the tip jar on her display counter. "She never lets me pay, but I always make sure she gets a big tip." Sawyer winked as he whispered to Luke.

Upon leaving The Cakery, Sawyer nodded toward a building to their left. "I need to get a new library card, I lost mine sometime while I was away at school. You up for a trip to the library?"

Sawyer knew that Luke hadn't been in a library since before his mother died, and he knew his plans for today could backfire terribly. But he also knew that Luke missed the library, he'd said so himself, so Sawyer took a chance.

Luke's head nodded almost imperceptibly and they began walking toward the old stone building. When they reached the steps, Luke stopped and stared up at the sign announcing Torey Hope Public Library, Corey Hope, Illinois. "Wow, it's been such a long time. I didn't realize just how much I missed it until right now."

Entering the library, Luke slowed and breathed deeply. "It's not the same library, but it's the same smell. The leather and paper and dust. Mmmm, smell that." He smiled crookedly at Sawyer.

They walked to the main desk. "Good morning, gentle-men, may I help you?" The lady who greeted them was one of Torey Hope's biggest gossips, and Sawyer suddenly felt a twinge of worry.

"Well, I need to get a replacement library card." Turning to Luke, he whispered, "You want to get a card while we're here?"

Luke left the shelf of books he was studying and walked to the desk. "What would I need to get a card today?"

"Just your ID and proof of address." The clerk spoke as she pulled out the information sheets.

"I'll come back another day, I've got my ID, but no proof of address."

"Um, as long as you won't turn me in for mail tampering, I *may* have borrowed a piece of mail from your kitchen table while you were in the shower," Sawyer whispered sheepishly.

Luke stared at him for several beats before taking the envelope from his hand and digging his ID out of his wallet.

Five minutes later, Luke was the proud carrier of a Torey Hope Public Library card. A disgruntled Sawyer was out $25 because his replacement card didn't come for free.

They headed towards the shelves with Sawyer grumbling, "Geesh, you'd think they'd give a guy a break. I was gone for four years."

Luke shook his head at him and began to eagerly fill his complimentary book bag with titles both old and new. Sawyer wandered through the shelves pretending to look at books while, in reality, he was too busy watching Luke to have a single clue as to what books he was stuffing in his bag.

LUKE SAT at the little table with his head in his hands. As he thought about his day, he couldn't help but smile. But that smile quickly turned into a frown because he could never have this for real with Sawyer. It wasn't fair to make him miss out on a true relationship just because Luke had so many demons to deal with.

"Hi, Luke. You look forlorn. That means sad. It's the Word of the Day on the calendar Carly bought me. Why are you so sad?" Nicky Morgan, Sawyer's uncle sat down across from him.

Luke lifted his head and smiled at the man. Nicky was limited in some things, but possibly more observant and wise than most people in other aspects of life. Luke glanced toward the ice cream shop and saw Sawyer standing in line. When Sawyer waved and smiled, Luke couldn't help but return the gestures.

"You're the boy he likes," Nicky spoke bluntly.

When Luke had no reply, Nicky continued. "I know Sawyer is gay and that means he wants to kiss boys and do other things. You're the boy he likes. He smiles at you and his eyes twinkle the same way Nate looks at Libby or Jeremiah looks at Audrey."

Again, Luke sat mutely, not knowing how to respond.

"And you like Sawyer. Your face brightens just like Kyle and Josie when they look at each other across the room." Nicky glanced back and forth between Sawyer and Luke. "Do you kiss him and want to marry him?"

At that point, Luke knew he had to speak. "It's not that easy, Nicky. I do like Sawyer very much, but I can't ever be with him like that."

"But you like him, and he likes you. Why would you not want to spend your life with someone you love?" Nicky's forehead crinkled.

"When I was growing up, some people were really mean to me. I promised my mom when she died that I would never let those mean people win. If I love Sawyer, those mean guys win and I can't let that happen. I don't get to love, but that means they won't win." Luke spoke in defeat.

"But by not loving Sawyer you're making yourself sad, which means those mean people win anyway, right?" Nicky questioned.

"It's not quite that simple, but yeah, I guess they win either way."

"Well, I don't like mean people, and I don't like when my friends are sad." Nicky stood up to leave when he noticed Sawyer was heading their direction. "Just remember, Luke, you can't help who you love. You should just worry about keeping yourself happy and forget about those mean people. They aren't here now, but you have friends in Torey Hope and we all want to see you and Sawyer happy." Nicky waited until Sawyer handed one of the ice creams over to Luke then pulled his nephew into a warm hug.

"He likes you. Be nice to him and love him. Maybe he'll let you..."

"Whoa, Uncle Nicky, let's not forget that some things aren't for talking about in public." Sawyer quickly halted where he thought the man was going.

"I was just going to say maybe he'll let you marry him. I know it's not appropriate to talk about holes and penises in public." Nicky spoke solemnly before walking away.

Sawyer closed his eyes at his uncle's words and slowly turned back to face Luke.

"Yeah, so that was Nicky and he says anything and every-thing that's on his mind, no matter who is around. He's a wonderful guy, great father, and honest to a fault. But truly, you just never know what might come out of his mouth." Sawyer babbled nervously, hoping Luke wasn't offended by what Nicky had unknowingly insinuated.

"He's a good guy, it's obvious he loves you very much." Luke smiled as he licked ice cream to keep it from dripping.

They ate their ice cream in silence for several moments, the only communication being between their flirty smiles and glances across the table.

"Are you ever going to tell me more about your past? Help me understand why you fight this so much?" Sawyer asked as he finished his ice cream.

"I want to, and I will. It's just hard to think about it, let alone talk about it. I'm afraid you'll think differently of me after I tell you." Luke knew in his heart that Sawyer would never judge him for what he'd lived through. But it was an easy excuse to use.

They stood to walk, Luke grabbing the bag of books by his feet.

Arriving at his apartment, he invited Sawyer in. Dropping the bag at his feet, Luke hesitantly reached his hands for Sawyer. "I know what today was. Thank you. You knew I hadn't been to a library in years, so taking me there was really special. The books and the ice cream brought back memories of my mom, happy memories."

Sawyer ran a strong hand down the side of Luke's face. "I enjoyed my day with you, I loved seeing you relax and just smile."

"This is so wrong, but I can't seem to help myself." Luke curled his fists into Sawyer's shirt.

"What? What is wrong?" Sawyer questioned.

Without speaking, Luke captured Sawyer's lips with his and kissed him fervently.

Sawyer quickly spun Luke around and pinned him against the door. The kiss deepened.

In a movement which clearly portrayed his desperation and desire, Luke muscled Sawyer across the living room bringing them to a stop against the hallway wall.

Luke's hands traveled under Sawyer's shirt. As his hands

roamed the muscles, Sawyer watched him lean his head against the wall breathing heavily, as if trying to get a grip on himself.

Sawyer took advantage of Luke's neck being on display and leaned in to drop heavy kisses against the man's salty skin. Running his tongue from neck to jaw to ear, Sawyer let his lips pull at the ear lobe before traveling back down to focus on the hollow of Luke's collarbone.

Knowing he was pushing his luck, but not wanting to stop, Sawyer slowly worked his hands under Luke's shirt. He'd seen the man without the shirt, but seeing did nothing compared to feeling the tight muscles and fiery skin under his fingers.

"I'm going to regret this, and I need you to know it can't keep happening, but I need to touch you." Luke spoke gruffly even as his hands moved down to cup the front of Sawyer's jeans.

Wasting no time, not wanting Luke to change his mind, Sawyer made quick work of both his buttons and Luke's. He knew he'd stop as soon as Luke said the word, but he couldn't think about that at the moment.

Both men eased tentative hands under elastic and groaned when skin met skin. They reveled in the solid heat. Luke's head fell back against the wall when Sawyer's hand maneuvered them so their erections rubbed together.

Sensing Luke was almost at his breaking point, Sawyer allowed the connection to continue, but moved his hands to the other man's shoulders. Chest heaving, Sawyer rested his forehead on Luke's and pressed his groin gently against his. With soft, short rocking motions, Sawyer continued his assault on Luke, knowing he needed to tread lightly. Gripping the back of Luke's head, Sawyer whispered gruffly in his ear, "You can't keep fighting this. It's too good, too right. I'm stopping for now, because I know you're not ready, but rest assured we will continue this one day." Brushing a kiss softly against Luke's lips, Sawyer backed away.

For several seconds, he watched as Luke leaned against the wall with his eyes closed. Sawyer longed to reach down and stroke him until he fell apart, but he knew the man was fighting his inner demons. Buttoning his own pants first, then finishing up the buttons on Luke's jeans, Sawyer walked them both to the kitchen.

Leaning against opposite counters, the men stood silently for a few moments.

"Listen, I'm sorry about that..." Luke began.

"Stop, Luke. Don't ever be sorry about that. There's something between us, something stronger than either of us can deny. I am trying really hard not to push you too far, but having you react to me like you did tonight is definitely nothing you need to apologize for," Sawyer spoke sincerely, his eyes locked with Luke's.

"Um, do you want to stay for dinner or something? I mean, as long as it's not too awkward. We could order pizza or Chinese?" Luke's face held a mixture of hope and fear.

"Man, it kills me to have to turn you down, but tonight is Adam's last night in town and I promised dinner before he leaves." Sawyer stepped the short distance across the kitchen and slid an arm around Luke's waist, pulling him flush to his body.

Luke groaned and rested his forehead lightly on Sawyer's.

"But, how about this? Tomorrow you come to my grand-parents' house for lunch and then we can spend the day playing video games at my house with the other guys." Sawyer cocked an eyebrow hopefully.

Taking a deep breath, Luke blew it out. "Gonna have to pass on the lunch invite, but I could probably do video games at your place." When Sawyer's face fell, Luke cupped his cheeks in his hands and spoke softly, "Baby steps, Sawyer, I need baby steps."

Sawyer left Luke's a bit later feeling buoyed with hope. He was strung like a tight rope and saw no end in sight other than a cold shower, but Luke had said he needed baby steps. Someone who was completely against moving forward wouldn't have asked for baby steps. He had made progress with Luke throughout the day. He could only hope that Luke wouldn't start regretting what had gone on between them.

SAWYER AND ADAM enjoyed a nice evening, and Adam left with promises to check in and visit again soon.

Lunch at John and Cindy Morgan's was the usual upbeat, fun atmosphere Sawyer had grown up in. He only wished Luke could have been there. Not just because he wanted him by his side, but because he sensed that Luke needed the love of a family.

"Hey, guys, I told Luke he could come over and play video games today. Hope you don't mind," Sawyer spoke casually to his brother and cousins.

"Nah, man, that's cool. I'll actually probably be at Kate's until late, so don't count on me for games." Decker winked at his girl as he spoke to his brother.

"No gaming for me tonight, man. I told Asher I'd help him on some project he's working on. I'll probably just stay at Kyle and Josie's on the couch tonight." Zach shrugged and gave Asher a fist bump. Asher was a teenager and tried his best to be cool, but his gangly awkwardness was evident every time he was around his older cousins.

"No can do, bro. I've got a hot date and even hotter plans for after that date. I won't be home until the wee hours. Enjoy your games. Be sure to use your joystick safely." Kendrick threw his head back and laughed.

Sawyer looked around at the group of men. "Are these all legit plans or are you just making them up so Luke and I will be alone? I mean, I really did invite him over for video games, so you all don't have to leave on our account." He wasn't sure whether to be upset the guys weren't going to be there to keep things light, or excited that he'd have Luke all to himself.

After the other three convinced him they truly had previous plans, he walked the short distance across town to his house, his mind churning the whole time. By the time he'd reached the house, he had a plan. Pulling out his phone, he called Decker and Zoey to be sure all of Luke's classes would be covered and to let Decker know he and Luke were each taking the next day off.

"Really, bro? You've never taken a day off this sponta-neously. Everything okay?" Decker asked sincerely, but Sawyer could hear the smile in his voice.

"Yeah, man. I just hope I can get Luke to agree to it." Sawyer smiled as his plan grew in his head.

He ran through his plan once more as he straightened the place up, and then sat down to wait on Luke. He'd get Luke to agree to the plans for the next day, make him promise to go with him, and then see where the night took them.

A slight knock on the door pulled him from his thoughts. Swinging the door open, he stepped back so Luke could enter.

Trying to gauge Luke's mood, he leaned in and placed a gentle kiss on his cheek.

"Hi." He smiled at Luke.

Luke grinned and shook his head as if laughing at himself for being nervous.

"Hi to you, too."

"So, I guess I didn't plan this very well. My brother and cousins all had something else going on this evening and

won't be back until late or at all. So, we've got video games on our own all night."

When Luke glanced at the game choices, Sawyer continued, "So, what's it going to be?"

They decided on a racing game and spent the next hour shouting and smack talking and laughing as they competed against each other. When they tired of the racing, Sawyer grinned mischievously and popped in a dancing game. Between the two of them, they had quite a few dancing skills and battled it out for over an hour before collapsing on the couch sweaty and tired.

"Man, I need a shower. You're pretty much my size, you can shower and borrow some clothes. Then we'll order some pizza for dinner and figure out what else we want to do." Sawyer spoke the words before he realized they could be taken in a suggestive way. "I mean, like a movie or something."

Luke smiled. "I knew what you meant."

"Hey, before we get cleaned up, I wanted to ask you something."

Luke turned around and faced Sawyer. "Sure, what's up?"

"So, there's a new aquarium in the next town over. It opened this weekend. I was wondering if you'd like to take the day off work and go with me tomorrow." Sawyer saw the look of hesitation pass over Luke's face.

"I've already cleared it with Decker. Zoey's got your

classes covered, and I'm sure Zach will be there to help her out." Sawyer closed the space between them, whispering softly in Luke's ear, "Come on, you know you want to."

Chuckling, Luke just shook his head. "How can I argue with that? Okay, sure, I'll go with you tomorrow. Sounds fun."

They headed up the stairs. Sawyer showed Luke to the bathroom and let him take a shower first. Tossing a change of clothes on the bathroom counter, Sawyer willed himself not to let his eyes wander to the frosted glass shower door.

When Luke exited, Sawyer quickly jumped in the shower and spent about five minutes letting the cool water take his breath away as he attempted to calm himself down.

When the pizza arrived, he gathered up plates, napkins, and drinks and carried them to his room. "All my movies are up here. Settle in." He motioned to the bed.

If Luke was hesitant, it didn't show. He plopped down on the bed and grabbed two slices of pizza. They laughed and chatted and watched the local news while they ate. The connection and comfortableness between them felt as if it had been there forever rather than just the short amount of time they'd known each other.

"So, I really wish you'd come to lunch today. Not as my boyfriend or anything, *yet*, but just because it's fun, and my family would love you," Sawyer spoke as he cleared up their dinner mess.

When Sawyer began thumbing through his movies, he

heard Luke take a deep breath and mumble something to himself. Turning around, he questioned, "What?"

Shaking his head, closing his eyes, and breathing for what appeared to be a count of ten, Luke finally spoke. "Hear me out, okay? If I don't get to say everything, I may never say it."

The two men sat on the edge of the bed facing each other.

"So, I'm not completely ready to tell you about my past. Let's sum it up to say that my dad and brothers said and did some horrible things to me and made me ashamed of who I am. I swore to myself I'd never let their words be true. I promised my mom I'd never let them win. But talking to your uncle the other day, he made me seriously stop and think." Luke paused for a moment.

"Yeah, Uncle Nicky can do that to you." Sawyer smiled encouragingly.

"So, he made me stop and think about the fact that if I'm miserable and lonely, they still win." Luke shook his head, like his was trying to solve a puzzle in his mind. "That's a thought which has always been in the back of my head, but hearing someone else say it made it more believable."

Sawyer nodded understandingly. He knew Luke needed to talk, and he was just there to listen for the time being.

"I'm not ready to do certain things with you, physically, but I think I'm ready for other things. I want to be with you. Tonight." Luke turned hopeful eyes toward Sawyer. "If you'll let things move at my pace and only what I can handle."

Sawyer reached a hand up and cupped Luke's cheek.

"We can do as little or as much as you want. Anything you want to try, I'm yours." Leaning in, he kissed him softly.

The kiss deepened until Sawyer found himself on his knees in front of a still seated Luke. Fingers in the waist band of the sweats he'd loaned him, Sawyer's eyes questioned Luke. At the nod of his head, Sawyer pulled the pants down and swore when he saw Luke wasn't wearing anything underneath.

"You didn't give me any underwear, and I didn't want to put the other pair back on." Luke smirked.

"No worries, it would have just been another layer to get through." Leaning down, without giving Luke a chance to think about things, Sawyer drew him into his mouth.

Luke leaned back on his arms and hissed as Sawyer's heat engulfed him.

While Sawyer would have continued until the end, Luke pushed at him and then pulled on his shoulders to get Sawyer up on the bed. "Can I...I mean, if you're okay with it, I'd like to..." Luke flushed and stuttered over his words.

Sawyer smiled sympathetically.

"Sorry, I'm totally new to all of this. I've had sex with a couple girls, but I've never been with a guy, even though it was always guys I was thinking about when I was with girls. I want to have sex with you, but I need to be the top." A look of panic and pain crossed Luke's face. "I just can't do bottom, and I'm not sure I'll ever be able to."

"Baby, you can top me every single time." Sawyer drew

him in for a rough kiss. "But I need to know you are really ready for this. You just let me give you a blow job, and now you're wanting to have sex with me. Last week, even just yesterday, you were vehement about never being able to act on your attraction to me." Sawyer paused to give Luke a chance to answer.

"I don't know how to explain it, and I can't promise I'll not freak out during or after, but I just know I am so drawn to you I can't keep fighting it any longer. I have to at least give it a shot."

Sawyer hesitated. "Luke, I want to help you work through things, but I also want to be more than an experiment." His eyes begged Luke to correct him.

"I don't mean it like that. I've always pushed aside my feelings towards men. I've never allowed kissing or touching let alone the things we've done. Sex with women wasn't satisfying, but it was expected, so I let it happen occasionally to keep up appearances." Luke leaned in and kissed him. "I've tried pushing my feelings aside this time, but they're too strong. I think there are things we can do together that will allow me to feel, but keep the painful memories at bay."

"Okay, I'll let this happen for now because it would probably kill me to tell you no. But I need you to know that I'm going to keep at you to tell me about your past. I need to know what I'm up against, so I can figure out ways to help you fight through it." Kissing Luke gently, he continued, "But for now, let's save the talking for later." He smiled and laid back on the bed.

Luke joined him on the bed, propped on his elbow.

"Now that we've decided what to do, I feel like I want to savor the moment." Luke smiled.

"How 'bout we savor the moment and each other? Take off your clothes," Sawyer commanded as he stripped his own shirt and pants quickly, and watched as Luke followed.

Aligning their bodies, they both breathed deeply and let the heat and desire overtake them.

Reaching down between them, Sawyer grasped Luke's length and his own, rubbing them together and letting the friction increase the heat.

When Luke pulled back abruptly, Sawyer looked at him with concern.

"Sorry, there's a very good chance this isn't going to last very long to begin with, and it was going to be over before it even started if I let you keep doing that." Luke smiled sheepishly.

"Condoms and lube are in the drawer." Sawyer nodded his head in the direction of the bedside table.

"Wow, always prepared huh?" Luke appeared to be slightly hurt.

"They've only been in there since I met you. Until then, I kept one in my pocket for 'just in case,' but that's all." Sawyer kissed Luke's nose.

"Do you think, for now or at least until I'm more comfortable with it, we can skip any finger or tongue foreplay?" Luke asked.

"Yeah, that's fine." Sawyer leaned in and whispered in Luke's ear, "But it can be all sorts of fun. Maybe someday."

Sawyer stroked his hand up and down Luke's length a couple times before rolling on the condom. Handing the bottle to Luke, he watched as the man coated himself and then dribbled the liquid on Sawyer.

"Are you going to stay on your back like this?" Luke looked uncertain.

"Yeah, I want to be able to see your face." Sawyer planted his feet on the mattress, his knees bent.

As Luke aligned himself with Sawyer's body he closed his eyes and inched in slowly.

Sawyer pushed against him, and ordered, "Open your eyes, look at me."

Luke panted as he fought against the heat threatening to end things too soon. Opening his eyes, Sawyer saw Luke glance down at their joining. He also saw the tears pooling in his eyes.

"You okay? We can stop." Sawyer laid his hands gently on Luke's shoulders.

"No, I'm good. It's just a little overwhelming to see and feel something I've been longing for my whole life," Luke spoke through gritted teeth.

With that admission, Sawyer choked out in desperation, "Then move, Luke. I need to feel you move."

Stroke after long, slow stroke, Luke could take no more. Just as Sawyer encouraged his body to unleash, Luke shuddered and pushed deep inside one last time.

Sawyer gathered Luke in his arms when the other man collapsed on top of him.

"Sorry that was over so quickly. I guess I should have been working on some stamina." Luke hid his face in Sawyer's neck.

"I told you to never be sorry for what we do together." Sawyer gripped Luke's chin and forced their eyes to connect. "It was perfect and beautiful, and I feel so lucky that I got to share it with you."

Several moments later, Sawyer stirred to take his second shower of the night.

Exiting the bathroom, he spoke to Luke, "Shower's all yours. It's not too late, we can go ahead and start that movie now if you want."

He stopped short as he entered his empty room. Walking to the bed, staring at the piece of notebook paper as if it were a viper ready to strike him dead, his knees buckled, and he dropped to the floor.

Dear Sawyer,

I'm not running away. I just need some time to sort some things out. I thought if I only let you put your mouth on me, and I was always the top, I could make this work. But after tonight, I know in my heart it won't be enough. I need to work through my past. When I come back, I'll tell you all about it, and we can hopefully see where this thing is heading.

Please don't be mad that I left. I wanted nothing more than to spend the night with you, but the next time we share a bed, I don't want my past to be sharing it too.

Can I get a raincheck on the aquarium?

Love,

Luke

Sawyer panted heavily as he read the letter through three more times. He's not leaving you; he wants to work this out, just give him some time.

Rubbing a hand over his face roughly he blew out a deep breath. "Damn it, Luke, I just wish you would let me help you work it out." His words echoed in the empty room.

WALKING into work the next day, the look on Sawyer's face made it evident to everyone he met that they should steer clear of him. Everyone but his twin and cousins.

When he grabbed his lunch and stalked into his office, planning to eat alone, he rolled his eyes and groaned as the three of them followed in behind him and shut the door.

"Please, please. Come on in. Have a seat. I was really hoping you'd come butt into my personal life today," Sawyer spoke sarcastically.

"Dude, you slept alone last night. Luke's not here; you're

here when you asked for the day off, and your face spells *Fuck Off*. What happened?" Kendrick asked.

Rubbing a hand over his face, Sawyer sighed. "I don't know. Things went from zero to sixty last night. One minute we're playing games, dancing, eating pizza, the next minute I'm flat on my back having sex with him. By his choice I might add." When he stopped, he had to laugh at the look of shock on their faces.

"But after I took a shower, I found this letter." He waved it in front of them enticingly.

Decker grabbed at it and they all read it.

"Man, I don't think this is a bad thing." Zach pointed to the letter, "It sounds like he wants to make something work with you."

"Yeah, man, I agree. So why such a pissy attitude?" Kendrick pressed.

"I don't know. I guess having him sneak out hurt. And knowing he's probably going to have to go through some bad memories to work out his past, it just worries me. I want to be there to help him through it all." Sawyer closed his eyes and laid his head on the back of the chair.

"Luke's used to doing things on his own. Let him do what he needs to do. When he comes back, maybe you can help him get used to having someone around to turn to." Decker and the other two stood to leave. "Enjoy your lunch, bro. Let us know if we can help in any way."

Sawyer was left to his solitary lunch, but he didn't feel much like eating.

15

*L*uke had been gone for almost a week. The annual community meeting was scheduled for that evening. Sawyer brooded for over an hour trying to come up with a legitimate excuse not to attend. The Center+ had been having community meetings for several years as a way to pull the citizens of Torey Hope in and let them see the variety of programs being offered. But The Center+ also held these meetings so they could hear what the town wanted or needed. Sawyer had never minded the meetings before, although he'd not attended one in four years, but his bad mood over Luke taking off didn't bode well for the evening.

"No way, fucker, I see what's going through that head of yours. You're trying to weasel out of the meeting tonight. You're not going to use the heartache card, or the too busy card. Hell, you got laid, you should be bouncing off the walls.

He'll come back. Now, get your ass off the couch, you're going to the meeting." Kendrick spoke most of this diatribe while fixing a sandwich in the kitchen which meant both Decker and Zach also heard it.

"He's right, man. You can't skip the meeting. We need to present a united front now that we're back in town and running things more at The Center+." Decker tossed his brother's shoes on the floor beside the couch. "Get up."

"Yeah, at least you're having sex. If anyone should be grumpy, it should be me." Zach grumbled as he inhaled the cold pizza he'd grabbed from the fridge.

Loading up in Zach's truck, the four men headed to The Center+.

"Looks like a good-sized crowd tonight." Decker mused as they pulled into the parking lot. "I do wish Luke was here so we could introduce him to the town."

When they walked inside they were greeted with hugs and smiles from many of Torey Hope's townsfolk. Most of the people were milling about munching on cookies and sipping punch while they waited for the meeting to start.

Nate and Jeremiah started the meeting several moments later. A slideshow presenting both new and old programs being offered was shown. New staff members were personally introduced or their picture at least shown on the screen. Sawyer's heart squeezed when he saw Luke's picture appear.

Zach and Zoey talked about the new fitness classes and took questions. Kyle smiled broadly at Josie as she and

Sawyer presented the new painting techniques they planned to teach. Sawyer and Katie, along with Zach and Zoey, showed some of the new dance moves which would be taught during the dance classes. Libby and Audrey laid out the curriculum planned for the year along with what community parties were already scheduled onto the calendar.

The captain leaned over to Sawyer and chuckled as Nate took the podium again. "This is where he opens it up for questions or concerns. Last year we almost had a knock-down-drag-out over the weekly bingo games; one little old lady accused her neighbor man of cheating every week, and she wanted him arrested. It was a sight to see."

Sawyer smiled at his grandpa and attempted to focus on what his dad was saying.

"Okay, we've shared with all of you what the next year holds for your families and friends here at The Center+. It's now the time in our annual meeting where we let you share your questions and concerns." Nate paused to let hands be raised.

A diminutive elderly lady in the front row stood with the help of her cane. The captain nudged Sawyer and smiled.

"I want Old Man Barker banned from the weekly Bingo game. He's a cheat and a liar!" The old woman turned to face a man who Sawyer could only assume was Old Man Barker and pointed her finger in his direction.

"Tilly Mae, you sit yourself down. You're making a fool of yourself *again*. Just because Mr. Barker wins and you lose money every week doesn't make him a liar *or* a cheat. I've played Bingo with you, you jabber on so much about the town gossip there's no way you can pay attention to those ten cards you insist on playing every week." Katie's grandmother had stood and walked toward Tilly and finished quietly, "Maybe you should ask the man out on a date like we all know you want to rather than embarrassing yourself and him every year at this meeting."

When Tilly's face turned red and she sat down, Nate quickly scanned the room for other people with questions. When he didn't see any other hands, he smiled and spoke to the crowded room, "Thank you all for coming, and thank you for continuing to make The Center+ an integral part of your families and this town."

As people began to stir and gather their belongings, Sawyer noticed the doors to the meeting room swing wide and three men entered the area. He recognized them as three of the kids in his older cousin Beckett's class who had always tried to give Beck a rough time. He smiled slightly as he recalled how Beckett had always just replied with a funny little quip and walked away, never letting the wannabe bullies bother him. Sawyer had always looked up to Beckett and appreciated his ability to let things roll off his back. He felt that he'd learned a lot of his own outlook on mean-spirited people by watching both Nicky and Beckett over the years.

Looking at the men at that moment, he noticed they hadn't changed much in their attitude and swagger, but physically they'd each lost some hair and filled out their bellies. He was lost in thought as he watched them, so he barely caught the beginning of what the man in the middle, Matt, said.

"Whoa, hold on there good people of Torey Hope. Ben, Joe, and I actually *do* have some concerns about how things are being run here at The Center *plus*. We think there may be a little too much *plus* being added without our knowledge."

As soon as the man started speaking and nastily emphasized the word plus in the business title, Sawyer instinctively knew what was coming. His heart began to pound and he broke out in a cold sweat, but he was cemented to his seat with no hope of escape.

Several people sat back down, while others paused momentarily against the outer walls of the room.

Nate, who had never put up with bullies and hadn't appreciated these men picking on his nephew Beckett as kids, took a deep breath and blew it out, but responded diplomatically. "What can we help you with, gentlemen?"

The three men puffed their chests and smirked a bit while they walked to the middle of the room. "What we'd like to know, and I'm sure every citizen in this room would be interested in knowing, is if you're ever going to make it public knowledge you've got a couple *faggots* working here."

Before Nate could speak, Katie stepped to the podium. "Ben, Joe, Matt, while The Center+ appreciates your concern and would be happy to discuss our hiring and employment policies, we are not in a position to allow the use of discriminatory actions and words against our employees." She spoke smoothly, not even a hitch in her voice, but Sawyer saw the anger flaring underneath the surface.

"That's all well and good, Ms. Turner. I see you learned well in your human resources and management classes. But we still feel it's in the best interest of Torey Hope for this type of information to be shared and not hidden." Matt, obviously the spokesperson of the three, continued while Joe and Ben stood idly by nodding their heads in agreement.

Nicky stepped to the podium. "Do you tell all of Torey Hope that you're bullies and you enjoy hurting others? Because if we're making things known, you should probably share that as well."

Many of the townspeople laughed out loud at Nicky's comment.

"The point here is that you've got young impressionable children and attractive men in and out of this place all day. The least you could do is warn your clients that they need to keep an eye on the two queers. That's all I'm saying." Matt cast a hate-filled look toward Sawyer, but shrank back a bit when the captain stood and crossed his arms across his chest.

Decker, Zach, and Kendrick all walked toward the three men as Katie spoke strong and sure once more. "Again, we will happily discuss the hiring and employment policies we have in place here at The Center+, but your language and actions here tonight will not be tolerated. This meeting will be adjourned for now. If we feel a more detailed meeting about our hiring and employment practices needs to be held, we will let the town know. Until that point in time, the citizens of Torey Hope can rest assured that The Center+ always has been and always will be run with the utmost care and safety of our clients in mind."

As she finished, Sawyer's brother and cousins ushered the three men out the door and the rest of the attendees began milling about. He noticed the furtive glances and whispers that started among some groups of people. His head was spinning; this was straight out of his worst nightmare. One of the biggest reasons he'd kept his sexuality hidden for so long was for fear of causing trouble for the family business, and now it looked like that trouble was starting. He glanced at the faces of his family and the other employees, seeing pity and worry etched across most of them, he turned to leave the room.

Walking to the break room, he took a deep breath. He longed for Luke to be there with him, but he was also glad he wasn't there to witness or experience it. Luke's openness about his sexuality was new and fragile, an incident like this could send him backwards several steps.

The door swung open and the entire family poured inside.

Once everyone settled in to chairs or against counters, Sawyer took a deep breath and spoke.

"I'm so sorry..." He tried to speak without his voice catching, but he failed.

The screech of chair legs across the floor brought the attention of everyone in the room to the captain. Sawyer felt the remnants of what little he'd eaten earlier threaten at the back of his throat. Closing his eyes and bracing for the worst, Sawyer prayed that whatever his grandfather had to say wouldn't be too painful.

"Boy, you don't have a damn thing to apologize for. Open your eyes and look at me, don't you hang your head in shame." The captain walked over to where Sawyer was seated and motioned for him to stand. Placing his hands on Sawyer's shoulders, the captain spoke through threatening tears, "Sawyer, this is what some of us feared the most. Not because it hurts *us*, but because it hurts *you*. Those men are the worst type of people, meddling, stirring the shit pot, just begging for a reaction. I'm sure Katie and Decker have already thought of what's next, but I don't want you to hang your head over this. I'll fight them tooth and nail, hell, I'll run them out of town if I have to. This family, this business, we won't fall because of the likes of them." Pulling his grandson into a hearty hug, the captain spoke once more, "I may never be thrilled with your lifestyle, but that will never change the fact that I love you and will stand up for you every single time."

Drying a tear, Sawyer whispered, "Thank you, Captain, that means more than you'll ever know."

Stepping to the middle of the room, Katie began laying

out the plan. "Okay, first things first, we put out feelers, talk to people around town, get an idea of how much those assholes have stirred up. If it appears we have an actual issue, then we call another meeting and focus on our hiring and employment procedures. We keep to the fact that we hire only employees with a proven work history and no past issues with the law. We mention that The Center+ has to follow good hiring and employment practices or we could be the subject of several law suits and forced to close." Katie glanced around the room. "This isn't a great situation, but it's also not doomsday. I know we're all upset about the incident tonight, and we want to protect Sawyer from it, but let's just stay calm and see if anything comes from it."

Decker joined Katie. "And that right there is why we are lucky to have Kate on our team. Until we hear differently, it's business as usual. Got it?"

The families nodded.

And then they sat around avoiding the large elephant in the room. Sawyer felt the weight of the beast crushing his chest. Silently giving every member of his family a hug, he accepted their words of encouragement with a false smile, and then bid his farewells.

"I need a little time by myself; I'm just going to head home." Sawyer gave a small wave and headed out the door.

Upon reaching the parking lot, Sawyer remembered he'd ridden with Zach. Shrugging it off and realizing a bit of a walk would help him clear his head, he started toward home.

Knowing there was a quicker way, but wanting to enjoy the evening, he cut through the park. Stopping at the duck pond, he smiled as he recalled the day Adam fed the 'little quackers.'

Sawyer took a seat on the large rock and breathed deeply. His head and heart couldn't wrap around all of what had happened. The whole town of Torey Hope now knew he was gay. He wasn't upset about that; he was no longer hiding. But he was angry that his secret had come out the way it did. With a bitter laugh, he thought back to the look of disdain on the library clerk's face the day he and Luke went to the library. She was Matt's sister-in-law. There was no doubt in his mind that she was the one who told Matt about Luke and him. But what did she say? Two men came in and got library cards? It wasn't like they made out between the book shelves.

He was used to working past the anger over the unfairness of situations out of his control, but he couldn't help it as he felt the fear inch its way in. He had always feared of causing problems for The Center+, and no matter how Katie tried to sugarcoat it, he knew this was going to turn into an issue. Before the fear had a chance to completely settle in his heart, he was overcome by the feelings of love and acceptance he'd gotten from his family, especially the captain. The fact that his grandfather wasn't completely on board with his sexuality, but was still willing to stand up for him purely because he loved him, meant more than Sawyer could even begin to describe.

Rubbing hands over his face and glancing around to see how dark it had gotten, Sawyer stood and headed toward his house. He knew Decker and the other guys were probably wondering where he was.

Taking the trail he knew would come out just down the street from home, Sawyer continued to think over what could possibly come from the night's events. Being lost in thought, he had no warning when Joe and Ben stepped in front of him, blocking his path. He was instantly alert, his stomach free-falling to his knees.

"Well, lookie here, Joe. We've found ourselves a real life homo walking in the woods. What do you think we should do with him?" Ben laughed and rubbed his hands together.

"I didn't know they let queers and faggots walk these trails, Ben. I think we should teach this fag a lesson." Joe sneered.

"Whatcha say, fairy, want us to teach you a lesson?" Ben punched a fist into his palm.

"I'm not looking for any trouble, gentlemen." Sawyer knew they heard the quiver in his voice. Two against one wasn't fair, but he also knew if Ben and Joe were in the park, Matt couldn't be far behind. As if on cue, he heard Matt's cruel voice from behind him.

"Not looking for trouble, huh? Maybe just looking for a cock to suck or a dick in your ass?" Matt pushed him forcefully. Sawyer caught himself before hitting the dirt path. Knowing he couldn't take on all three at once, Sawyer figured his best chance was to let them talk and try to get to the other side of them so he could sprint home.

His hopes of doing that were dashed when Ben, the biggest of the three men, grabbed him from behind in a full-nelson type hold. With his arms pinned and his midsection wide open, Sawyer knew instinctively things had gone from bad to worse.

"No one in this town wants you queers. Faggots like you and your little boyfriend don't belong here." A sickening crunch sounded in his ears as pain spread throughout his face from the punch Matt landed.

"You can't be working at that place and wanting to fuck all the men. Next thing we know, you'll be making all our kids go gay. You can do all the sick, perverted shit you want, but not around me or my children." Sawyer fought to breathe and contain the contents of his stomach as Joe's fist pounded his gut.

His knees buckled, but Ben hoisted him up to take the onslaught of abuse headed his way.

Several more insults hurled while fists pounded, bones crunched, and wicked laughter filled the night. Finding himself suddenly dropped to the ground, Sawyer struggled to breathe. He attempted to open his already swelling eyes, but the blood pouring from his eyebrow made a stinging red curtain through which he could not see.

With no sight, he relied on the sound of the voice to recognize when Matt leaned down and filled his ear with the oily filth pouring from his mouth, "You make me sick, you fucking fag. The world would be a better place if you died right here, cock sucker. But assuming you'll live, you better not run your pansy-ass mouth to anyone. If we find out you tell anyone we did this, we'll shut the family business down and track you and that faggot boyfriend of yours down, and next time we won't go easy on you, queer."

As Matt's words faded away, Sawyer's body exploded in pain. Heavy boots took turns kicking at his back, ribs, stomach, and face. Feeling the fire of pain sear through his body, Sawyer mentally called for Decker before his body succumbed to the excruciation.

His body was on fire, every breath like a razor. From far away he heard voices, but the pounding in his head and fog in his brain were too much to overcome, and he gave in to the precious darkness again.

Minutes, hours, days later? He felt the cool touch of a cloth against his forehead. He winced as the movement brought stinging and throbbing. "I'm sorry, baby, I know it hurts. Just sleep. We're all here, you aren't alone. You're going to be okay, but just sleep if it helps the pain." He wanted so badly to open his eyes and see his mom, but he swore they were superglued shut.

As time went on, his wakefulness became more frequent

and less painful. But memories of what had landed him in this bed, in so much pain, came crashing down on him, and he wanted nothing more than to crawl back into the black hole he was in and stay there forever.

Until the voices invaded his mind and he knew he had to wake up.

"I don't care, I'm going to beat the shit out of each and every one of them," the captain roared.

"Daddy, I know you're upset, but I don't think Sawyer would want you fighting violence with violence. Let's give him time to wake up, let him talk to the police. I know this is so hard on everyone, but we need to let Sawyer have a say in all of this," Libby spoke softly to her father as she held Sawyer's hands in hers.

Forcing his eyes to open, blinking against the scratchiness and working doubly hard to make them focus, Sawyer looked around the room. Squeezing his mom's hands, he tried to speak, but his throat was too dry.

"Here, man, here's some water." He hadn't heard Decker in the room, but he knew without asking that his twin had been beside him the entire time he was out.

"Oh, Sawyer! I'm so glad to see those beautiful brown eyes." Libby gently hugged him through tubes and wires draped across his chest. "Nate, go get the doctor."

Before leaving the room, Nate walked to Sawyer's bed and leaned in close to place a soft kiss on his forehead. "I love you, son. We all love you."

The doctor entered shortly thereafter with a smile, but Sawyer sensed his underlying concern. "Sawyer, it's good to see you awake. We kept you pretty heavily sedated for a few days to help your body heal and to keep you out of pain the best we could." The doctor looked around at the family members present. "I need to do an exam and speak to Sawyer briefly. Could you all give us a moment?"

The captain set his jaw, but Libby touched his elbow gently and led him out of the room. Everyone else followed.

Before he left, Decker grasped Sawyer's hand. "I heard you, man. I'm so sorry we didn't get there in time." A tear rolled down Decker's cheek.

"Stop, it's not your fault. I'm just glad you came for me." Sawyer pulled his brother into a hug the best he could from his prone position.

Once he was alone with the doctor, Sawyer reached for the remote to sit himself up higher in bed. The movement caused screaming pain in his ribs, his breath catching as he tried to find a comfortable position.

Looking at the tag on the man's coat, Sawyer watched as Dr. Hardin reached out and picked up another remote type gadget. "Push this button when the pain is too much. You can only use a certain amount, so no worries on overdosing."

Sawyer instantly pushed the button, praying relief would come soon. As the searing pain in his ribs subsided slightly once he stopped moving, he noticed the dizziness and pounding in his head were worse while sitting up.

Closing his eyes against the dizziness just brought more spinning.

Dr. Hardin took the remote from him and moved the bed so that he was only slightly angled. The room stopped spinning, so Sawyer gratefully just stayed in that position.

"Sawyer, I'm very sorry about what happened to you. I know the police want to speak to you, so whenever you're feeling up to it, I'll allow them to come in. Luckily we were able to get some partial foot print photos from the bruises along with a perfect outline of one of the attacker's rings. We've already turned all of that information over to the police. First, though, I want to speak to you about your injuries and gather some information we weren't able to get from your family."

When Sawyer nodded, the doctor handed him more water. "Your throat is probably dry, drink this."

Dr. Hardin settled in on a rolling stool. "So, your injuries are bad, but could have been much worse. You've got a concussion, which is why your head is pounding and you're dizzy. You received 14 stitches in the gash above your eyebrow. It's a good bet your nose is broken, but it's not crooked, so we left it alone other than just packing it. You've got 2 broken ribs, those are probably the most painful and will take the longest to heal. Your kidneys are bruised from the kicks you sustained, but we've run some tests and they seem to be functioning normally. We checked your spleen, but found no swelling or other issues with it. You're going to have some black eyes and a busted lip for several days. All in all, you're in pretty rough shape." The doctor looked at the stitches, felt around on his abdomen, and handed him more water. "You'll need to keep drinking so that your kidneys can continue to work and heal."

Sawyer sensed there was more the doctor needed to say. "Okay, so what are you not telling me?"

"Well, based on the type of injuries you came in with, and the fact that your family was pretty sure they knew who did it and why, we ran a rape kit as a standard precaution."

Sawyer felt the room shift. "Shit, I think I'm going to be sick." Closing his eyes, he breathed as deeply as his ribs would allow. "What did you find? I don't remember that happening, but I know I passed out at one point."

"Well, the examination did show recent evidence of anal penetration, but when speaking to your brother privately he was able to tell me that you'd recently had sexual relations. Can you confirm that for me?"

Swallowing thickly, Sawyer nodded, "Yes, not long before the attack. So, you don't think I was raped or sexually assaulted?"

"No, the examination didn't show any tearing or bruising that would be associated with a violent penetration, so I'm fairly certain you were not raped." The doctor placed a comforting hand on his knee as Sawyer breathed a deep sigh of relief. "We also did an oral swab to confirm there was nothing forced into your mouth while you were out. That was clear as well."

"Your family reports that you've seen a therapist in the past, is this correct?" The doctor consulted his notes. "A Dr. Parks?"

"Yes, I've been seeing him for a while now. I'm thinking it may be a good idea to up the appointments to a couple times a week for now, huh?" Sawyer tried a sarcastic smirk, but his busted lip prevented it.

"Yes, I will contact Dr. Parks and let him know the basic facts of the incident and have his office contact you about getting some appointments set up." Dr. Hardin checked his notes again. "As long as you're able to go to the restroom on your own and your kidneys continue to look good, I think you should be able to head home tomorrow afternoon. Do you have any questions for me?"

Shaking his head slightly, trying to avoid the dizziness, Sawyer closed his eyes. "No, doc, I think I've got it all. Whoa, when the meds kick in, they kick in hard. Tell my family they can come in, but make sure they know I'm about to pass out." Sawyer's tongue felt thick as he slurred his words to the man.

16

Sawyer spent most of the next day giving a statement to the police officers who came to speak to him, and trying to get his grandpa to stand down. The man was pissed, as was Sawyer, but he was trying to convince the captain that fighting violence with more violence was not the answer.

"They beat you up and threatened you, the business, and Luke, Sawyer! They deserve to be punished!" The captain paced the small hospital room.

"And they will be. The police officers said this appears to be an open and shut hate crime case. My lawyer has already assured me that she will fight for the toughest punishment allowed by law against all three of them. Heck, she even told me that their lawyers don't hold out much hope; their job now consists of getting them the lightest sentences. There are security cameras all around that park, the police already confirmed that Joe, Ben, and Matt were seen entering that trail and then running back out of the woods about 15 minutes later. I've given my statement, I've identified all three of them, and they've already been arrested. The ring imprint on my face matches Matt's ring; he squealed like a pig and turned the other two in. I also heard he slipped during the interrogation and basically outed himself when he found out I spoke to the police."

The captain was not to be pacified, so Sawyer caught his hand. "Grandpa, I appreciate you wanting to fight back for me, but more than anything, I just need you by my side. I need you to help me heal and stand up to the hatred by coming back strong."

When the older man finally relented and nodded his head, Sawyer sighed with relief.

Later, as the nurse took away his lunch tray and promised to get busy on his discharge papers, Decker and his cousins entered the room and shut the door.

Zach spoke first. "Man, I'm so sorry. I didn't even think about you leaving by yourself and not having a way home."

"Those fuckers better never darken our doorway again. I won't lower myself to their level, out of respect for your wishes, but I'll make sure the entire town of Torey Hope knows just what twat wads they are. I wouldn't be surprised if all three of them lose their jobs after someone places a few well-meaning phone calls to their places of employment." Kendrick winked, and Sawyer had to just shake his head.

"I'm so sorry, Sawyer. I know you said it's not my fault, but I just feel like I should have heard you sooner, gotten to you quicker." Decker sat in the chair beside his bed, head in his hands.

"Deck, don't feel guilty. I didn't even think to let your name run through my mind and call out for you until the very end. You probably got there right as they were finishing me off." Sawyer reached out his hand and held Decker's in his. "The twin connection comes through once more." He smiled at his brother.

Sawyer looked at his twin and cousins. "We're going to get through this. I will get through this. As long as I have you all on my side, we can do anything. I think a meeting with the town would be best at this point. If I need to step down, I will." He held up his hand to halt the protests. "If it comes to that, we'll deal with it then. But no guilt or hard feelings between us. I want to go home and start feeling better. I won't let the hatred of a few ruin what I have found with my family and friends."

The four men hugged and stepped apart just as Hayden, Katie, and most of the rest of his family entered the room. The next three hours were spent with laughter and love filling his room to bursting. When the nurses finally kicked them out so Sawyer could change into street clothes Decker had brought him, his brother stalled at the door.

"Hey, Sawyer, I wanted you to know that we thought about calling Luke, but we figured you might want him to see you at home rather in the hospital. I hope that was okay."

"Yeah, man, that's exactly what I would have wanted you to do. Thanks." Sawyer pulled him into a hug. "I'll see you at home. There's no way Mom and Dad are letting me leave here without them giving me a ride and making sure I'm all settled in."

The twins laughed, both knowing it was true.

IT HAD BEEN a couple of long, painful weeks, but Sawyer felt he was back to about 100%. He had insisted on only missing a couple days of work, but agreed to take it easy while he was there. Therapy had been going well. He'd long since grown accustomed to overcoming the anger of unfair situations based on his sexuality. There was hatred in the world and he knew he couldn't control or end it all, but he knew he *could* work to end the fear, lack of understanding, and hatred in his small town.

His therapist had him working more now on overcoming his feelings of guilt. He felt guilty that The Center+ was going through some bumpy waters because of him. Although, his therapist was helping him reframe those feelings into "The Center+ is going through a rough time because of the choices and actions of others. I can't control those people. I can only control myself, my own actions, and my own feelings. I will accept the support of my family and friends and move on in positive and productive ways." He wasn't completely over the guilt, but he was getting there.

Sitting in the weekly staff meeting, Sawyer knew he was next on the agenda. When Katie finished her part, she turned to him smiling. "And now the stage belongs to Sawyer."

The meetings were always fun and relaxed, so Sawyer pretended to bow and blew kisses as the staff clapped for him in jest. He took a position at the head of the long table and cleared his throat.

"So, most of you have probably heard through the grapevine, but I thought I'd keep you updated on the legal stuff. Matt, Joe, and Ben have all been sentenced to a year in jail for the attack. They'll serve their time outside of town since Torey Hope's small jail can't accommodate them. Last I heard, their families were planning to leave town as well, both to be closer to them and to avoid any problems here. I'd like to think Torey Hope wouldn't treat their wives and children poorly just because of what those three did, but I can't control that. Luckily, the evidence against them was fairly damning and they didn't do themselves any favors during their police interviews. So, I just wanted to say I appreciate all of you letting the law take care of things. I am truly grateful that the judge was able to make a quick decision and get their sentences handed down so we can all move on."

Sawyer took a drink and rubbed at the healing scar on his forehead.

"The next thing I wanted to talk about is that I think we should have the follow-up meeting with the town. I've noticed some people being very supportive, but I also think some would feel better if we addressed the situation and put their fears to rest." Sawyer glanced around the room.

"I don't like that we even have to calm fears. Some people are letting their lack of knowledge and predetermined notions about homosexuality play too big a part in their decision making. But if Sawyer wants a meeting to clear the air, I'm for it." Decker spoke to the rest of the room and everyone nodded their agreement.

SAWYER NERVOUSLY WAITED for the room to fill and the hands on the clock to hit 7:00 p.m. When Decker stepped to the podium and began speaking, Sawyer couldn't help the feeling of pride and support he felt listening to his brother.

"Good evening. The Center+ has been around since before I was born. It's made many changes over the years, and our family is proud to be the owners and managers of this integral part of Torey Hope. We hope that you will agree the changes we've implemented over the years have allowed for bigger and better programs and opportunities for you and your families."

Taking a sip of water, Decker continued. "In light of the incident that took place a few weeks ago, we've decided it would be best to address any concerns you all might have in a public forum so that all questions can be answered. I'm going to hand it over to Ms. Turner so that she can explain our hiring and employment procedures and practices. Kate..." Decker stepped back and allowed Katie to take the podium.

"As Assistant Manager here at The Center+, I'm proud to be part of an ethically and legally sound business. When we hire any employee, a full criminal history is obtained. We follow every legal hiring procedure to ensure the safety of your families here at The Center+. In accordance with the Illinois Human Rights Act we are prohibited from discriminating against employees on basis of race, color, religion, sex, sexual orientation, national origin, ancestry, age, marital status, or disability. If we were to deny employment to qualified candidates based on any of these, we could be sued and forced to close down. That doesn't even begin to get into the Non-Discrimination Laws we are also required, and pleased I might add, to follow. The Center+ prides itself on being a family-oriented, inclusive, fun, safe place where learning and enrichment can be found. We also pride ourselves in being open, fair, and equal to all members and staff."

Katie shuffled her notes a bit, and then spoke. "I'm going to hand the stage over to Sawyer here in a moment. Before I do, I'd like to remind you that you're allowed your opinions and your questions will be answered to the best of our abilities, however, hate speech will not be tolerated and we reserve the right to ask individuals to leave if they are in violation of Illinois Non-Discrimination Laws."

She let that statement soak in while gathering her notes and stepping away from the microphone. Walking past Sawyer as he moved to take her place, she leaned in and kissed his cheek, whispering, "If at any moment you feel uncomfortable, just look at me, and I will step in."

"I got this, Katie-girl. But, thanks." Sawyer winked at her and took his place.

"Good evening, Torey Hope. I'm happy to see so many of you came out tonight either as a show of support for The Center+ or to get your questions and concerns addressed. One of the biggest foundations for hatred and discrimination today is the lack of knowledge about a certain subject. We fear that which we don't understand; giving knowledge to that lack of understanding takes away the basis of fear. So, I commend those of you seeking knowledge and clarification this evening."

Sawyer took a long drink of water and almost choked when the back door of the room swung open and Luke stood watching him. There had never been a better or worse time for the man to return to town. Sawyer fought the urge to rush across the room and gather him in his arms. Heart beating double time, Sawyer took a deep breath and opened things up for questions while forcing his eyes not to follow Luke's every move.

Sawyer allowed comments and questions to be shared first in order to gather himself and see if a general theme was present in most of the concerns. He found quickly that the general themes of the fears were worry that he would sway the children who attended The Center+ or that he would basically come on to every man who walked through the doors.

Forcing himself to take the apprehensions seriously, Sawyer swallowed the laughter and smirk which were threatening. Letting his eyes skim over his brother and cousins, he had to fight harder to stamp down the laughter when he saw Kendrick's eye roll. Watching Luke intently for a few seconds, he then returned his attention to the crowd.

"First, I want to offer my sincere promise that I'm not trying to recruit your children. I would never wish for a child to go through the struggles that accompany being gay....just as I would never wish for a child to struggle with diabetes or a learning disability or a physical disability.....being gay is not a choice or a whim. If a child or teen were to come to me and express he or she thought they were gay, I would offer them support just as I would to a child or teen struggling with self-harming or bullying or abuse or suicidal thoughts. I'm not here to press my sexuality upon anyone, but this is who I am. I'm here to teach classes and offer training to our students. I can be a role model in several different ways without my sexuality ever being brought into play or questioned. I love what I do, and I'm good at it. I hope that my sexuality won't deter you from allowing your child to learn all of the various art forms we offer here at The Center+ just as I would hope you wouldn't keep your child from enrolling in classes if the instructor was of a different religion or race. As for me hitting on every male client, I'd like to ask if you hit on every member of the opposite sex."

When laughter erupted and heads shook in the negative, Sawyer smiled and continued, "Just like I don't hit on every member of the same sex. We all have different tastes and what we find attractive. I would never hit on someone unless I knew the feelings were reciprocated, and members of The Center+ are firmly on my Do Not Date list." More laughter erupted, and Sawyer allowed for more questions. When none were presented, he stepped aside for Katie to conclude the meeting.

Feeling satisfied that he'd said all he could on the subject, Sawyer stepped from the podium and slipped through the side door with one goal in mind, finding Luke.

STORMING into the break room and locking the door behind him, Sawyer forced himself to slow down. His chest heaved, and he saw Luke was breathing just as heavily.

He crept toward Luke like a lion stalking his prey. When he reached the other man, he was momentarily thrown off when Luke launched himself at him and slammed a kiss against his mouth. Several hot, rough moments later, they surfaced from one of the most memorable kisses in Sawyer's recollection.

Clinging to each other, foreheads pressed together, they just stood and absorbed each other.

Finally speaking, Luke smiled. "That was quite the speech. Seems as if I may have missed quite a bit while I was gone."

"You have no idea." Sawyer smirked.

Luke gently swept a hand across the fresh scar on Sawyer's head, and let his hands feather down the yellowing bruises on his face.

"Want to take me home and tell me about it? I have some things to tell you as well." Luke presented the invitation casually, but Sawyer knew there was more to it than that.

Bringing his lips down on Luke's again, Sawyer savored the taste he'd missed so much. "I'd be glad to take you home. But I think there's something else I want to do before we talk." He winked at Luke and they both laughed.

Walking out of the break room, they passed Decker, Kendrick and Zach.

"Hey, Sawyer won't be home tonight, and we likely won't be in to work tomorrow. If that's okay with my boss?" Luke smiled at Decker.

Smiling broadly at Luke and his brother, Decker laughed. "I think I can allow it this time."

"Gee, Zach, I'm confused. What could Sawyer possibly need a whole night at Luke's to do?" Kendrick played it up.

"I don't know, Kendrick, maybe they're having a movie marathon or an all-night video game session." Zach smiled as he teased his cousin.

"I bet you're right, I bet they are going to play video games. Probably a lot of new moves, secret buttons, joystick positioning, I bet it's going to be all sorts of fun. Hey, Sawyer, can we come over too?" Kendrick was outright laughing.

"No."

"Please, we want to play video games too."

"Nope."

"You two are awfully selfish with your joysticks." Kendrick pretended to pout as Luke and Sawyer walked away.

17

"As romantic as it would be to have you whisk me home and spend all night in bed, I didn't actually think this through very well." Luke blushed as they walked to the parking lot. "I have a plan for all day tomorrow, but it requires me to go to the store."

"No problem, I'll go with you." Sawyer leaned in and kissed his cheek.

"No can do, man. It's supposed to be a surprise, so I can't have you with me when I'm buying the things I need." Luke laughed at Sawyer's scowl. "Since we both have our vehicles here, why don't you run home and pack for tonight and all day tomorrow. Jeans and t-shirt with comfy shoes will be fine. I'll run to the store. Meet me at my place in about an hour and fifteen minutes?"

They had reached Sawyer's car, and he wanted to press

Luke against the door and kiss him senseless, but he wasn't sure where Luke was with public displays of affection just yet. Instead, he opened the door and gently maneuvered Luke into the angle of the door. "Can I kiss you?" Sawyer's voice was gruff and desperate.

Eyes locked with his, Luke nodded. "You never have to ask."

Sawyer's body warmed, and his heart swelled as their mouths met in a sensual coupling.

Breaking away, a shy smile played on Luke's lips. "I'll see you in a bit." He climbed onto his motorcycle and Sawyer sighed deeply as he watched him drive away.

Pulling in at home, Sawyer noticed his parent's car. He had to smile, they'd been extra protective the last couple weeks. He knew he just needed to let them work out their fears for his safety on their own. And having them drop by and bring food multiple times a week wasn't a terrible thing.

Walking into the kitchen, he found his mom and dad talking to Decker and Katie.

"Hey, baby boy, how are you?" Libby reached up to brush his scar and pulled him into a hug. "That was a fabulous speech you gave tonight. We are so proud of you."

"Thanks, Mom. That means a lot." He hugged her back and walked to hug his dad as well. "Listen I need to pack up a few things, but we'll visit a bit when I come back down, okay?" Sawyer winked at Decker and Katie as he left the kitchen.

Throwing a couple pairs of boxers in a bag, he grabbed jeans, a clean t-shirt, and socks as well. Pulling open the side table drawer, he tossed in lube and condoms too. A toothbrush finished off his packing, and he headed back downstairs.

His parents smirked knowingly at him. "Son, Luke's been gone for a while. Do you think it's wise to rush into something with him? I'm not trying to dissuade you, I just want you to be thinking with the right head, if you know what I mean."

"Nate! I can't believe you just said that!" Libby blushed and smacked her husband playfully on the arm. "I think your dad is just wanting to know if Luke has worked out his issues, and if the two of you have had time to discuss where it all leaves your relationship." She raised he brows at Nate, and he nodded in agreement.

"Yeah, what your mom said." He smiled.

"Well, we haven't had a chance to talk yet, but he promised we'd talk tonight."

Everyone in the kitchen jerked their heads to the doorway when Kendrick breezed in with a fake cough covering his "Bullshit..."

"What? I'm just saying, I don't think there's going to be a lot of talking going on tonight. That's all." Kendrick winked at Sawyer.

"Really? In front of my parents?" Decker rolled his eyes at his cousin.

"Sorry, Aunt Libby, Uncle Nate. Just callin' it like I see

it." He kissed Libby on the cheek and shook Nate's hand before leaving the room.

"Anyway, we are going to talk tonight. I have a feeling his past is really bad. I have to admit I'm a little afraid he's not ready or able to completely move past it." Sawyer leaned heavily on his arms as he starred thoughtfully out the window above the sink.

"Sawyer, sometimes a person's past is just too much and they never overcome it. But if Luke has something worth fighting for, it may be the motivation he needs to work through the demons. Heck, many people thought there wasn't enough therapy in the world to get Audrey and your mom and I past our issues, but we worked through everything and came out better for it in the end. Look at all that Kyle and Josie overcame to be together. Only Luke can know if he's willing to fight through the hard stuff to get to the good stuff." Nate hugged his wife to his side and kissed the top of her head.

"That was beautiful." Katie wiped a tear and snuggled into Decker's arms.

"Okay, well, with that, I'm heading to Luke's. I'll be back at work the day after tomorrow." Sawyer gave hugs all around and headed out the door with a definite skip in his step.

He arrived at Luke's and let himself in quietly just as Luke was putting the last of the groceries away. Sneaking up behind him, Sawyer wrapped his arms around his waist and nuzzled Luke's neck. "Mmmmm, I've missed you so much."

Luke feigned surprise and confusion, and turned in Sawyer's arms. "Oh, hi Sawyer, I wasn't quite sure who you were." Trying to look innocent, Luke batted his lashes playfully.

"Yeah, yeah...tease all you want. You knew damn well who it was." Sawyer pulled him in for a soft kiss, and then spoke in a whisper, "I mean, I don't think you hooked up with a bunch of guys while you were out of town. Did you?" A flash of worry crossed Sawyer's face.

"No, I had a whole lot more going on in my mind than worrying about random hook ups." Luke wet his lips, and continued seductively, "Besides, there was only one hot guy on my mind the entire time I was gone." Letting Luke control the kiss, Sawyer just held on and enjoyed the ride.

Luke walked him backwards, stopping only when they reached the countertop. Rocking his pelvis against Sawyer's, Luke groaned. "I want this so bad."

Breaking away, attempting to catch his breath, Sawyer cupped his hands on Luke's cheeks. "I want this too, but do you think we should talk first?" Unable to control himself, he placed kiss after kiss on Luke's lips, his neck, his forehead.

"How about a compromise?" Luke suggested.

"I'm listening."

"We do this, then we talk, then we do this again. I want to be focused when I'm telling you about my trip, but right now I can't seem to focus on anything but touching you and kissing you." Luke showered kisses along Sawyer's collarbone.

"I think that sounds like a fabulous plan."

Sawyer reached for the bottom of Luke's shirt, pulling it quickly up and over his head. Mimicking the move, Luke made quick work of Sawyer's shirt.

Luke, being only slightly taller than Sawyer, seemed to have found a power and desire within while he was gone because he muscled Sawyer to the bedroom, never breaking their kiss.

"You seem a lot more confident this time around." Sawyer couldn't help but note the observation as Luke pushed him down onto the bed.

"I am very sure." Kiss. "Sure that I want you." Kiss. "Sure I need you." Kiss. "Sure that I want to see where this could go." Kiss.

Sawyer raised his chin so that Luke could trail kisses down his neck to his stomach. Stopping at his waistband, Luke looked up at Sawyer with lust-filled eyes. "I want this, I want you. But before it goes any further, I need you to know it's not just about sex."

Sitting up and rolling up to his knees, Sawyer pulled Luke into his arms. Forcefully turning him and dropping him down to the pillow, Sawyer let Luke's body feel the full weight of his own. "That's good, because this has been about much more than just sex for me since the moment I saw you outside that boxing ring." Crushing a kiss against waiting lips, Sawyer rubbed his rock hard length against Luke's.

With pants and boxers removed in the blink of an eye, Sawyer stretched out on his side, facing Luke. Caressing a hand along Luke's face, down his torso, stopping to brush knuckles gently along his erection, Sawyer savored the salty taste and musky scent of Luke's skin as his lips followed his hand's path. He smiled inwardly as he heard the swift intake of Luke's breath when he took him in his mouth.

Luke allowed the act to continue longer than the first time, but pushed him away long before Sawyer was done. "Sorry, still working on that stamina." Luke smiled.

Sawyer worked his way back up Luke's body. Grasping the man's hands, he stretched them over his head and held them there while he kissed and licked his fill. Sawyer lifted up and turned Luke over, fitting his body underneath his own. Pressing his erection against Luke's ass, Sawyer felt him go still.

"What's wrong? You know I'd never hurt you, I'll never push you for something you're not ready for." Sawyer whispered and kissed along the outer edge of Luke's ear.

Luke pushed up on elbows so that he could roll over. Once again, they laid on their sides, facing each other. "That's part of what I need to talk to you about." Luke pushed Sawyer to his back and crawled on top of him. "But first I need to be inside of you." A desperate kiss, and a desperate plea. "Please."

"It's the only place I want you to be." Sawyer reached for the condom he'd placed on the bedside table earlier. Quickly rolling it onto Luke, Sawyer rolled to his stomach. The sexy look thrown over this shoulder was all it took before Luke took hold of his hips and pulled him into the perfect position. With a slow thrust, Luke gritted his teeth and fought to catch his breath.

Several hot, sweaty moments later, Luke collapsed on top of Sawyer.

Sawyer tried not to laugh, but Luke noticed the tell-tale shaking of the man's shoulders underneath him.

"What's so funny?" Luke questioned.

"We need to wash these sheets, unless you plan to sleep in the wet spot." Sawyer chuckled and Luke joined him.

"We'll wash the sheets, wash ourselves, and then talk. By the time we're done talking, the sheets will be ready." Luke eased off of Sawyer's body.

Pulling him down for one last kiss, Sawyer laughed again. "Just in time to dirty them up again."

They showered, ate huge bowls of cereal, and then settled in on Luke's couch to talk. Luke fidgeted with his hands; Sawyer noticed he was extremely nervous. Moving to the corner of the couch, he leaned back and opened his arms and legs. "Come here, let me hold you while you talk."

Luke's eyes welled with tears. He crawled across the

couch and met Sawyer with a sweet kiss. "Thank you. Thank you for being patient, for listening, for just being you." Luke turned and nestled his back against Sawyer's chest, and sighed as Sawyer's arms wrapped around him.

Kissing the side of his head, Sawyer whispered, "Take your time. It's just me, and nothing you tell me is going to change the way I feel about you."

Closing his eyes, Luke began.

"I don't remember everything I've told you. I know I've shared more with you than with anyone else in my entire life, but I'm sure you'd like to hear it all, so I'm going to tell the entire ugly story."

Luke breathed deeply and Sawyer watched his profile for a few moments before letting Luke's story transport him to a past nightmare.

"My father hated me. I don't know why, but the only memories I have are of him spewing hatred at me or neglecting me. I'm pretty sure the only reason he didn't starve me to death is because of my mother. He was never mean to her. I think he had truly loved her at one point even though I never saw love between them that I can recall. His obvious hatred of me was confusing." Reaching down, Luke grabbed Sawyer's hand.

"I was always blonde with fair skin and blue eyes, I looked a lot like my mom. My dad and older brothers weren't tall, I'd describe them more as stout and beefy. Not overly fat, but definitely not built the same as me. They all three had dark hair, olive skin, and deep brown eyes. I always tried to stay hidden from my father; it was as if the mere sight of me would make him angry. He wasn't a bad father to my brothers, he hung out with them, played sports with them, took them places. Except for the hate-filled words he spat at me when I wasn't quick enough to hide from him, he all but acted as if I didn't exist."

Sawyer squeezed Luke's hand. "That must have been a really confusing and hard way to grow up." He leaned in and kissed the side of Luke's head again. "Go on."

"He never physically abused me, I know my mom would have left him for that. Sometimes I would wonder *why* she stayed, but I knew she loved her older sons too. And even though he didn't do it gladly, my father did provide food and shelter; had she left she wouldn't have been able to provide for me. I think she was just doing the best she could." Luke's voice softened and Sawyer's heart lurched to hear him defend his beloved mother while still trying to make sense of the hatred shown to him by his father.

"My father and brothers all three teased me mercilessly, of course only when my mother wasn't around or couldn't hear. Luckily, I was almost always with her, so I didn't have to endure the teasing much." Luke stopped briefly, as if waiting to see if Sawyer would ask what he knew he was dying to ask.

"What did they tease you about?" Sawyer whispered, although he had a feeling he already knew.

"They'd call me things like *faggot, queer, fag*." Luke's

voice gruffly mimicked the words used against him. "Nothing new or original, but at the time I didn't understand the words, and I just knew they were meant to hurt."

"As I got older, and especially after my mom got sick and wasn't able to be around to protect me as much, their words turned more sexually demeaning. They'd ask if I wanted certain things done to me and then laugh when I didn't know how to answer them. At the time, I knew I was more attracted to males than females, but I didn't really understand the words and phrases they were hurling at me. I just knew they scared me." Luke shuddered and Sawyer wrapped his arms around him.

"You're doing great, thank you so much for allowing me into your story." Sawyer just sat quietly, holding him, until Luke was ready to go on.

"The day my mom died, she brought me to her bedside and began to speak. Her voice was ragged and so very soft, like every word and every breath caused her pain. She pulled me close and whispered words that I will never forget. *'Luke, my dear baby boy, you've not been shown love from a father, but you were born from the love of both a father and a mother. I'm sorry you will never know the man your father could have been. Please forgive me for allowing you to suffer at their hands. Don't give in, don't let them win...'* She stopped to catch her breath, but she never spoke another word. She died a few minutes later, with me holding her in my arms." Luke sniffed.

"Babe, if you want to take a break, we can stop for a while," Sawyer offered.

"No."

Sawyer smiled into Luke's shoulder. "Okay then, keep going."

"I didn't understand most of what she whispered to me, I was a distraught 15-year-old. But *'don't give in, don't let them win'* has stayed with me from the moment she breathed her last breath. I knew that very day that I could keep my mom's memory alive; I'd never give in to my attraction to men. If I never let a man touch me, or me touch him, if my body and heart never got what it longed for, *they* would never win. I was determined to never give in, never let them win."

When Luke paused in his story, Sawyer closed his eyes and breathed deeply. Understanding of Luke's panicked reactions and determined rejections made more sense now, but he knew there was much more of Luke's story still to come. And he feared it was going to get uglier before it got better.

"I thought I'd had it bad when my mom was still alive, but when she died my life became a living hell." Breathing deeply as if to prepare himself for what was coming, Luke continued. "Remember I told you that my mom had taken out a separate life insurance policy and her will stated the money was to go solely to me? Well, I graduated early and the lawyer in charge of her will made sure I got the money. I took off and never looked back. I feel grateful to her every day for leaving me that money; without it, I would have had nowhere to turn,

and I don't think I would have survived them any longer than
I did."

Sawyer knew he really didn't want to hear what Luke had
lived through, but he also knew that it would probably help
him to talk about it, and it would help him personally to know
what demons haunted Luke. "Can you tell me about what
they did to you?"

Shifting slightly to curl into Sawyer's body more fully,
Luke whispered, "It started the day of my mother's funeral.
My father never physically hurt me, but he was just as bad
because he'd let them do it; he'd just watch and smirk while
they hurt me. It was like he was proud of them for giving me
what I deserved." He stopped, and Sawyer wasn't sure if he
was going to give more detail or not.

"In the first few days, it was just fists and kicks along with
the hateful taunts. But then they started dragging me to the
shed outside the house and hitting me with sticks, chains,
belts. I learned quickly not to fight back, or it just lasted
longer." Briefly lost in his memory, Luke paused before
going on.

"They beat me like that two or three times a week. I
started hiding food away and gratefully accepting the breads
and cookies and muffins the neighbor lady would sneak to me
when my father and brothers were at work and school. I
remember her asking about my bruises; I know she didn't
believe my excuses, but she never said anything more about
them. Part of me wishes she would have turned my father and

brothers in, but part of me feels like my past brought me right here where I'm supposed to be, so I can't be too terribly upset with her." He lifted up to kiss Sawyer gently.

"I had about a month left to go in my schooling, and I could see the early graduation date looming ahead of me. It was my carrot, my prize, the only thing that had kept me going during the months of abuse. I knew as soon as I graduated, I could leave there and never look back."

Sawyer sensed the worst was about to be told.

"What they did next almost killed my spirit, my will to live, and I sometimes wished they had just killed me." Swallowing deeply, Luke gripped Sawyer's shirt in his fist. "They started using things on me when they'd beat me. A hair brush handle was first, but they quickly moved to the dirty, dry, rough handle of a rake. The searing pain would take my breath away. I was usually already so exhausted from the beating, I thankfully would pass out from the pain most times. The pain never got better, but waking up in the shed after that first time with the rake, I seriously thought I'd died. The pain radiated throughout my body, and I felt the blood pour down the back of my legs as I attempted to walk. I used to laugh bitterly to myself as I tried to sooth the injuries and block the pain that at least they waited to unleash this horror on me until the very end of my stay there. The last week of school before I graduated, they took me to the shed one last time. They chained me up, assaulted me with the rake handle while laughing and calling me a fag and asking if I liked it that way. My oldest brother laughed wickedly as he made my other brother orally assault my mouth. I fought, but it just egged them on. I ended up gagging so hard I puked and passed out. I woke up on the dirt floor, the taste of puke and filth in my mouth, the pain and shame screaming through my body."

Sawyer had stopped breathing as Luke's story continued to pour out.

"I left that night. I couldn't take it any longer. I lived on goodies the neighbor lady gave me and snuck into the library to use the computers so I could finish school and graduate. The day I was officially awarded my graduation certificate, I went to the lawyer's office and claimed the money. He helped me set up a bank account; we put the money in it, and I never looked back.

"It took several months to heal from their physical and sexual assaults, and even more for my mind to heal from the abuse. The martial arts, yoga, and Pilates all helped me to center myself and work through the physical and mental anguish. And being here with you has helped to calm the demons too." Luke kissed Sawyer again.

They were silent for several moments, each reacting to the story they'd just told or heard.

Sawyer fought anger and sadness like he'd never felt before. He wanted to lash out, to hurt, to cry; he wanted to hold, to protect, to comfort. Taking Luke's hands in his, Sawyer fought back the tears. "Luke, thank you so very much for sharing your story with me. I hate what they did. I hurt for you, but I feel like I understand you so much better now." Kissing him gently, lingering softly, Sawyer feared his next question, but he knew it had to be asked.

"Like I said, I appreciate you sharing with me, but I have to be honest and say that I don't understand what happened to change your mind about accepting your feelings and wanting to be with me." Sawyer's brow crinkled.

"Ah, that's where my trip out of town comes into play. Now we're getting to the good stuff." Luke smiled and stretched slightly before continuing.

"I went to my father's house. I wanted to confront him and my brothers. Turns out my father died of a heart attack not long after I came to Torey Hope. My oldest brother is in jail for domestic battery. The other is dead of a drug overdose. My dad's house was just left abandoned when he died. He was already in foreclosure and it was such a junked out mess by that point, the bank took valuables and personal items out and bulldozed the house. I learned all this from talking to people around town. So, I headed to the bank and asked if I could see any of the personal items. They required the lawyer who had handled my mother's will to identify me, but once that was done they opened a safe deposit box. There wasn't a lot in the box of monetary value or even sentimental value. I had no need for my father's watch or his wedding ring." Luke paused and let his words hang in the air.

"Okay, so what else did you find? You're killing me here." Sawyer smirked at him and Luke laughed at him.

"The anticipation is the greatest part." Luke smiled.

"No, the greatest part is seeing you happy and home in my arms." Sawyer tipped Luke's chin and kissed him firmly. "Right where you belong."

"Nowhere else I'd rather be." Luke kissed him back.

"Now, stop dragging out the anticipation and tell me what you found."

"Okay, okay, so as I was digging through the box I came across this letter. It was addressed to me and dated about a week before my mom died. Inside the envelope was a small note to my mom's lawyer asking that he see to it I got the letter along with the money. I'm not sure what happened, but the letter obviously never got to the lawyer. I have a feeling that my father had something to do with that." Luke's anger and hurt towards his father was still evident.

"So, they allowed me to take the letter out. I walked to the library and sat in one of the areas Mom and I used to sit in. I swear I had to read the darn thing at least ten times and by that time tears were pouring down my face so hard that people kept looking at me and asking if I was all right." Luke gingerly pulled a letter from this back pocket. "Would you like to read it?"

"Hmmm, I don't know, I'm not sure I'm all that interested." Sawyer feigned indifference before rolling his eyes and kissing him. "Of course, I want to read it!"

"Come over by the window, the light is better." Luke walked to the window and held the letter out for Sawyer.

Taking it gently from him, Sawyer leaned against the window sill to read it.

My dearest Luke,

If my lawyer has given you this letter it means I'm no longer with you, but you now have money to escape and live your life freely.

I owe you an apology, baby boy. So many apologies actually.

First, I'm so sorry for keeping you in that home with those mean spirited, hateful men. You did not deserve that, and I should never have stayed.

Second, I'm sorry for keeping the truth from you for so long. I should have run away with you and told you the entire story from the time you were born. I regret so much, but this especially.

The man you grew up calling your father was not your father. The man who was truly your father was a man I fell in love with one summer while working as a waitress at the local café. He was a wanderer, much like my spirit wanted to wander, and much like I assume you will want to wander and live life to its fullest. I regret that I was not faithful to my husband, but sadly, by that point, he'd had so many mistresses I'd lost count. Your real father, Lucas, was the spitting image of you. He was kind, gentle, soft-hearted, and just a good man. He was only to be in town a week, but we struck up a friendship and neither of us could bear to think of him leaving. We gave in to the love between us, and you were the result. I've never once regretted that. You were born from the love of two people, and I know Lucas would have worshipped the ground you walked on.

He came back through town about a year after you were born. My husband had obviously put two and two together and realized you were not his biological son. I wanted so badly to leave town with Lucas, saving myself from a life absent of love, and saving you from a life of blatant hatred. Lucas gave me his address and told me to pack what I could and come to him. He watched you with such abject adoration, it killed him to leave his baby boy for even the short time it would take him to return home. We had such plans. We were to be a family. I packed a small bag and your baby essentials and waited until your father took his 'real sons' to a baseball game. Throwing our bag in the car and strapping you into your car seat, I left a brief note telling my husband that I couldn't live like this any longer, and telling my older sons how much I loved them. You and I drove off towards Lucas' home with the promise of love beckoning.

Upon arriving at the quaint cottage-like house Lucas had told me about, I excitedly stepped from the car and gathered my sleeping baby into my arms. I wanted nothing more than to walk into my love's arms and stay there forever. But his house was dark, no car in the drive, and several days' worth of mail overflowing his mailbox. As I debated what I should do, the older gentleman who lived next door came out. "Isn't it a shame? Nice man like that mugged and shot for a measly few dollars? He would have given anyone the shirt off his back, no reason for him to lose his life like that. Truly is a damn shame."

Not knowing what to do or what to say, I just blinked back my tears and loaded you back into the car. I had only one place to go so I headed back to the loveless house, gathered up the note from the kitchen counter, pretended the day had never happened, and promised to make your life the best it could be in the surrounding circumstances.

Luke, I'm so sorry you never got to know your father, your daddy. He loved me, and he loved you. You two would have been inseparable, best friends.

I never learned of more details about his murder. It was easier to close off my heart and focus on you than to dwell on the hurt of losing him.

Luke, I'm so very tired. Tired of being unloved, tired of fighting this monster inside of my body, tired of being tired. I hold on only for you. You are my reason for fighting, my reason for breathing. I won't give up until I no longer have a breath in me.

Baby boy, I know you struggle with who you are. But know this, you are a truly beautiful person inside and out. My wish for you is to be happy, to find love. Don't give in to the hatred your father and brothers spew. Don't let them win in making you scared and miserable and lonely. When it comes time, don't fight love. No matter who the person is, don't deny your-

self love, sweet boy. Let love in, let love win. Only then will you defeat the hatred that tried so hard to keep you down.

You, my precious boy, are a beautiful miracle, a true gift to this world. I love you so very much.

Love,

Mom

Sawyer was crying by the time he finished the letter, and had to reread the last paragraph several times. "My God, Luke. This is heartbreaking and beautiful at the same time."

Turning to him, Sawyer gathered him in his arms. "I'm so sorry for what you lived through and that you lost your real dad without ever having the privilege of knowing him. I'm sure if he's half the person you are, he was a wonderful man."

He held him close for a while, just breathing him in.

"So, all this time..." Sawyer started.

"Yeah, all these years, I took a broken sentence from my mom and made it my motto, *Don't give in, don't let them win,* when in reality that was the furthest thing from what she was wanting to tell me. And thanks to that jackass who I called a father, I went on living with that misguided promise leading me for several years too long." Luke gently placed his forehead against Sawyer's. "But do you know why I can't be too upset? Why I'm not angry? Why I'm totally okay with the way my entire life has played out?"

Sawyer looked at him in confusion and barely croaked out, "Why?"

Cupping his hands around Sawyer's cheeks, and lifting

gently so their eyes met, Luke spoke solemnly and sincerely, "Because every moment of my life, both the good and the bad, brought me here to Torey Hope, here to *you*. And I don't regret a single thing that had a hand in leading me to you, to us."

Lowering his mouth, Luke let his lips hover mere millimeters from Sawyer's. "Will you help me work through the fear? Help me move on?" When Sawyer could only nod, Luke closed the distance and placed a gentle, loving kiss on his lips.

The kiss quickly morphed from gentle and loving to rough and desperate. Over an hour later, still warm and sated from their joining, Sawyer held Luke in his arms.

Taking a deep breath, Sawyer's gruff voice echoed in Luke's ear. "I guess I was wrong. That story completely changed the way I feel about you."

Luke stiffened and began to pull away.

"Stop, that's not how I mean it." The warmth of Sawyer's arms engulfed Luke once more. "What I meant was I was crazy about you before, but now I'm in awe of you. You are one of the most resilient, strong men I've ever met. What you went through, it was enough to end many people, but you pulled yourself through it. And now you've faced your past, and are working to move on from it completely, not letting it hang over your head, looking over your shoulder any longer." Sawyer kissed Luke's cheek. A finger gently tipped his chin up and turned his face so Sawyer could place a long, lingering kiss on his mouth.

18

———

Sawyer awoke to his body on fire. Reaching down to relieve the sweet ache, his hand found Luke's head. In complete shock, he lifted up on his elbows to stare down at the most beautiful sight he'd ever seen. With his head thrown back he groaned. "I could get used to waking up like this."

As Luke hummed his agreement, Sawyer knew the end was imminent and he worried about it being too much for Luke to handle too soon. "Babe, I'm not going to last much longer with you doing that, so you better stop."

When Luke's head shook in disagreement, Sawyer closed his eyes and savored his release. Never had it meant more to him than to share it with Luke.

When Luke crawled up his body and kissed him roughly, Sawyer could only smile. Chuckling through kisses, he teased, "Well, you certainly got over that fear pretty quickly."

Luke nuzzled their noses together, while two other appendages took a moment to say good morning as well. "I would gladly do that every single morning." He kissed him. "You taste good. You smell delicious. And I know you'd never do that to hurt me."

"You know what else I'd never do to hurt you?" Sawyer smirked.

"Yeah, I know, just give me a little more time on that one." Luke spoke as he eased himself between Sawyer's legs. "Until then, I can never get enough of this." Thrusting slowly, he allowed time for Sawyer's body to stretch against him.

Looking down to where they met, Luke's voice cracked, "Look at us, we are beautiful together."

Pulling him into a hot, toe-curling kiss, Sawyer couldn't have agreed more.

AFTER AN EXTREMELY SENSUAL shower and breakfast, Sawyer walked up slowly behind a bent over Luke as he put the cereal in the bottom cabinet. "Nothing to be afraid of, it's just me," he said softly as he rocked himself against Luke's ass.

Tensing momentarily, but forcing himself to relax, Luke stood up enough to rest his arms on the kitchen counter. Sawyer wrapped his arms around Luke's chest and nuzzled his ear. "Just feel me. Even through clothes you can feel how much I want you, how hot you make me. I won't force it or rush you, but I will take every single chance I can get to make you more comfortable with this." He continued to rock into him, pressing the evidence of his desire firmly against Luke's jean-clad backside.

"Mmmm, well, now that you've got me so worked up I want to spend all day in bed, would you like to hear about my plans for us today?" Luke pressed himself back against Sawyer's steely heat.

"If the plans involve spending all day in bed, I'm totally for it. Let's go!" Sawyer grabbed his hand in jest and pretended to run back to the bedroom.

"So, that's how it is now, huh? Just sex?" Luke laughed as they paused outside the bedroom door.

"No, you know I'm kidding." Kissing his nose, Sawyer got serious. "Tell me all about your plans for today. Leave nothing out."

Luke laughed at Sawyer's silliness.

"Well, I thought I'd cash in my raincheck on the aquarium. Then when we get home, I'll make dinner for you *and* try my hand at making your favorite dessert." Luke was obviously proud of his well-laid plans.

Wrapping his arms around Luke's waist so that their bodies connected from abdomens down, Sawyer leaned back a bit to get a good look at Luke's face. "Wow, you've been all kinds of busy, huh? A date to the aquarium, dinner, *and* dessert? I'm impressed. But, I've got to know, just *how* do you know my favorite dessert is peach pie?"

When Luke's face fell, Sawyer couldn't help but laughing.

"I'm kidding, it's chocolate pie. But seriously, how did you know that?"

Luke rolled his eyes and breathed a sigh of relief. "Don't do that, asshole. I'm already anxious enough about cooking and baking for you, I don't need you throwing me into a panic by introducing a different dessert to the menu. And I *may* have talked to your brother. Well, actually, I talked to Kendrick first, but he kept saying things like, 'Sawyer loves *balls*, melon balls. And anything with *nuts*, Sawyer's crazy about nuts. Hmmm, I seem to remember him saying he really loves cream filled long john donuts.' So, I finally gave up getting a serious answer from him and asked Decker. Luckily he'd heard Kendrick's answers and took pity on me." Luke chuckled and Sawyer couldn't help but laugh at Kendrick's answers.

"Yeah, that's Kendrick for you."

"So, I've told you what happened in my past. You planning on telling me what happened while I was gone?" Luke glanced at Sawyer while they drove through the early morning sunshine.

"Honestly, I'd rather not, but I'm sure you'll hear about it around town." Sawyer rubbed the new scar on his forehead.

Luke sat patiently and waited for the story to be told.

"Some local men interrupted a meeting at The Center+ and basically outed both of us to the town. They didn't use our names, but they threw around some derogatory words and caused a stir among the members and townsfolk. Caused some issues with The Center+, that's why we were having the meeting the night you came back."

"Did they start something physical at the first meeting?" Luke was eyeing the scar on Sawyer's forehead.

"No, they waited to do the physical damage once they caught me alone on a park path." Sawyer's jaw gritted against the memory. "There's no way I could have taken on three grown men at once. Even if I could have, they didn't fight fair. They roughed me up pretty good. Right before I blacked out, I called out to Decker in my mind. We've always had this weird ability to know when the other was in trouble."

"My God, Sawyer. What did they do to you?" Luke reached for his hand and held it tightly.

"Gash in my forehead, broken ribs, bruised kidneys, busted lip and nose, concussion. Those were the main injuries." Sawyer laughed humorlessly. "I was *lucky* they didn't rape or sexually assault me."

"Lucky? Yeah, some luck."

They both knew Sawyer was truly very fortunate his attackers hadn't done worse to him, but the thought of the physical pain he'd endured made it difficult to feel very lucky, especially in light of knowing what Luke had experienced.

"They weren't very bright and left a lot of evidence. They were also on the security cameras, and all three threw each other under the bus in the interrogations. The judge here in town was quick to give them the stiffest sentence he could. They were transferred to separate jails not long ago, and their families traveled with them."

"I'm so sorry that happened to you. I hate I wasn't here to protect you or help in some way." Luke kissed Sawyer's hand.

"It's okay. They are gone, you're home, and I'm doing fine now." Sawyer replied sincerely.

"They may be gone, but there are always more like them, aren't there?" Luke's apprehension was palpable.

"Yeah, there will always be people like them; there are mean people everywhere. We just have to focus on the good: our families, our friends, each other. I'd like to think enough people doing good in this world can overshadow all of the bad."

"You're pretty amazing, you know that?" Luke smiled at him.

"I don't know about that, but thanks."

They arrived at the aquarium just as it was opening. As Sawyer started to throw his car door open, Luke grabbed his hand. Sawyer looked down in surprise. Cocking his head the side he whispered, "You okay?"

"Yeah, I'm good. It's just, um, well..."

"Go ahead, I'm listening." Sawyer caressed a thumb across the back of Luke's hand.

"Wow, are you really this perfect?" Luke smirked and shook his head.

"Perfect? Hardly. But whatever I am is all yours, so tell me what you were thinking."

"I just wanted to say that aside from our library non-date and today, I've never really been on a date with a guy. I've barely been on dates with girls. I'd go a lot of places by myself, which didn't bother me, and I've hung out with some pretty decent groups of people in my travels, but a one-on-one actual date? This is a first."

Luke stopped and looked at Sawyer bashfully.

"You're my first for a lot of things. And I just want to say thank you. It's like I didn't know I was missing out until I find myself doing things for the first time with you. Then I realize I *was* missing out, but I'm not now. And honestly, I'm glad I missed out so that we can do these things together *now* when I can actually appreciate and enjoy them."

He leaned in to kiss Sawyer, and whispered, "It's my promise to my mom, myself, and you. To be happy."

Sawyer got the impression that Luke wanted to talk about

the *let love in, let love win* part of his mother's letter as well, but he seemed to get nervous and stopped before he uttered the L-word.

"Well, let's go be *happy* together. After all, we gays are really good at being happy." Sawyer smiled cheekily.

As they walked toward the ticket booth, Sawyer let his hand brush against Luke's casually. "So, while we're discussing things, where do you stand on public displays of affection?"

"I'd prefer no heavy making out since we're in a family oriented place and it's broad daylight, and that has nothing to do with gay or straight, I just don't like to see tongue and groping in public. Now, if it was a dark nightclub, my expectations would be a bit different." Luke laughed when Sawyer muttered something about getting him in a dark nightclub sometime soon.

"I'm sure the looks and stares will take some getting used to, but I'm okay with some hand holding here and there, and the occasional kiss. I just don't want to make a show of what we have. Whenever I see couples of any pairing making out heavily or hanging on each other, I always feel like they are trying to prove to the world they have something sexy." Luke bumped his hip against Sawyer's as he continued, "I already know I have something sexy, I don't need to prove it to the world."

Sawyer smiled ear-to-ear just as his phone buzzed.

Kendrick: Hey, what's Luke's number?

Sawyer: Why? Don't mess up my date, fucker.

Kendrick: I won't mess it up. Just give me his number. I like the guy, I may want him to be my best bro-friend.

Sawyer: Oh Lord, help us. Be good, please, I like him too. Like REALLY like him. 555-611-1993

Sawyer slid his phone back in his pocket. "So, I may have just given Kendrick your phone number. I'm not sure what he's up to. He says he likes you and wants to be your best bro-friend. Let me know if he gets to be a pain in the ass." Rolling his eyes and laughing, Sawyer clarified, "I mean if he gets to be any *more* of a pain in the ass."

As if on cue, Luke's phone buzzed.

Unknown: Hi sexy, it's Kendrick, Sawyer's much hotter, much sexier cousin.

Luke: Hi Kendrick. I'll add you to my contacts.

Luke laughed as he assigned the name and number to his phone. "That was Kendrick your 'much hotter, much sexier cousin.'" Luke put air quotes up and Sawyer rolled his eyes again. Luke's phone buzzed with another text.

Kendrick: Take him to the prairie dog exhibit. It makes him horny. He loves watching those little dogs go in and out of holes.

Kendrick: Or take him to the elephants. He likes when their trunks get all long and stiff.

Kendrick: Okay, okay, last one. Take him to the dolphin show, he gets really excited when they touch their nose to those low hung balls.

Luke: You realize we're at the new aquarium, right? Not the zoo. But I have to give you an A for effort *and* creativity. Can we enjoy our date now?

Kendrick: Awww, so sweet, my little boy is growing up. Yes, you little love birds, go enjoy your date. All kidding aside...you're good for him, and I'm really glad you came back.

Sawyer returned from purchasing the tickets.

"I still think I should have bought the tickets since this was my plan." Luke protested.

"It was actually my plan to begin with, you just followed through with it on a later date. You can buy next time." Sawyer squeezed Luke's hand briefly. "What's got you so smile-y?"

"Kendrick. He kept sending me messages about which animals make you horny, but he was naming mostly zoo animals. He's a funny guy." Luke showed Sawyer the texts from Kendrick.

"Good Lord, that man is not right. Seriously, I sometimes wonder about him."

They laughed and headed into the aquarium for a day of fun.

"OH MY GOSH, I can't believe you stopped to read every single information plaque in the entire aquarium." Luke threw his head back against the seat and sighed dramatically.

"What? Don't you want to know about the animals you're seeing?" Sawyer chuckled. He had been able to tell pretty early on that his habit of reading every sign was annoying Luke.

"Yes, I'd like to know their name, maybe native country, and something cool like if they can kill me or not." Luke looked at Sawyer incredulously. "I don't need to know their domain, kingdom, phylum, class, order, family, genus, and species like a *certain* someone seemed to be trying to memorize for all 714 animals we saw today." Luke rolled his eyes and shook his head.

"Well, excuse me for wanting to be informed. By the way, could you have walked any faster? I felt like I was with a mall speed walker. The animals must have been a blur to you as you sped on by," Sawyer challenged.

"No worries, I got to see them multiple times as I walked by over and over waiting on you to catch up." Luke shot back.

Reaching a hand out to curl it around the back of Luke's neck, Sawyer pulled him close. "Look at us, our first little spat. We are so stinkin' cute." He kissed Luke softly. "Mmmm, now let's get home so you can fix me some dinner."

Sawyer smiled as Luke fell asleep on the way home. His heart swelled as he watched the man sleep. *Is this what love feels like?* He recalled a conversation in college with Adam about looking for love, longing for it. Had he found it? Wasn't it too soon to call it love? Luke stirred and Sawyer averted his attention back to driving them home.

When they entered Luke's place, Sawyer smiled as Luke immediately started giving him chores to do.

"Turn the oven on, please."

"Go take a shower to wash the animals and humanity filth from your body."

"Go pick up some wine, some whipped cream, and a movie."

Sawyer raised a brow as he questioned the last direction.

"Please, just go so I can get dinner ready without spoiling the surprise," Luke pleaded.

It was so cute that Sawyer had no choice but to comply. He knew Luke was excited to do this for him.

After picking up the wine and movie, he drove to his house knowing they had an unopened can of whipped cream. Grabbing it from the refrigerator, he wandered upstairs to see who was home and what was going on.

Kendrick's door boasted of its signature *do not disturb* sock hanging on the knob. Rolling his eyes and shaking his head, Sawyer popped his head into Decker's room, but it was empty. Zach's truck was gone, so he didn't even bother checking his room.

Bounding down the stairs, he checked in the office and found Decker and Katie pouring over spreadsheets. They both looked up in shock when he came in shaking the whipped cream can.

Raising his eyebrows and fighting a smile, Decker nodded toward the can. "Big night planned there, bro?" Katie giggled and Sawyer blushed.

"No, Luke's making me a surprise dinner. He sent me out for wine, a movie, and whipped cream. I knew we had whipped cream here so I stopped by. I think he plans on putting it on the chocolate pie he's making for me." Sawyer winked.

"Yeah, I'm sure it's only going on the pie. Don't worry about returning that can, we'll get a new one at the store." Decker shook his head and smiled knowingly.

"So, what are you guys looking at?" Sawyer nodded his head at the spreadsheets.

"Enrollment numbers. We wanted to see if that incident with Matt, Joe, and Ben caused enrollment to drop. Initially, it looked like we had about 20 kids and adults drop out of various programs, but the numbers since you talked to the town show those 20 have re-enrolled in the original programs and we've had an influx in several other membership areas. So, it could have been coincidental with the drop outs following the incident, but either way your speech did a whole lot of good. I think it was very beneficial for people to see you and hear from you. You were sincere and personable, the people loved you. Of course, you've had most of this town in the palm of your hand since we were young." Katie smiled at him and winked.

"Can I ask you guys something?" Sawyer shuffled

nervously from foot to foot, absentmindedly shaking the whipped cream.

They looked at him, immediately concerned.

"It's nothing too serious. I was just wondering, how did you guys know you loved each other?" Sawyer blushed as he spoke.

Decker and Katie looked at each other.

"She turned my world upside down, made my perfect control fly out the window, and I didn't even care. All I was concerned about was spending time with her, making her smile, keeping her by my side. I fell hard and fast." Decker winked at his girl over the desk.

"For me it was clear from almost the first moment he ran into me in the hallway. And I mean literally ran into me." Katie laughed as she recalled the moment. "I felt different around him, nothing like I'd ever felt with anyone else. I had truly loved you, Sawyer, but this was different. This was grown up, serious, change your life love, not the young love and best friend love you and I shared. Kendrick and Zach purposely flirted with me to make Decker mad, but I felt nothing for them. None of the men I'd dated throughout college had ever made my heart flutter and swell the way he did. And he wasn't trying to do it, it was just a natural reaction whenever we were together." Katie finished and cocked her head to the side. "Why do you ask? Does this curiosity have anything to do with a certain martial arts instructor?"

"Maybe, maybe not." Sawyer winked and waved good-bye. "You two have fun with those spreadsheets...maybe you should try spreading something on some other sheets sometime tonight."

"Oh my God, Sawyer! That was as bad as Kendrick!" Katie threw a pencil at his retreating back as he laughed out loud.

WALKING INTO LUKE'S PLACE, Sawyer immediately noticed how delicious something smelled. Placing the wine on the counter, he put the whipped cream in the fridge and then surveyed the kitchen. Two huge baked potatoes sat on plates and the entire island was covered with every single baked potato topping imaginable.

"You made me a baked potato bar?" Sawyer was touched.

"Well, you're always talking about how much you love it at your grandma's, so I thought I'd try to recreate it here. I hope I got enough toppings." Luke tried to act like it was no big deal, but Sawyer could tell he was proud of himself.

"Thank you, this is so sweet. No one has ever made dinner for me, unless they are a family member, and they don't count." Sawyer nuzzled his nose along Luke's jaw. "Mmmm, I'm starving. For food now and you later."

They both filled their potatoes until the spud wasn't even visible under all the toppings. "Lucky we can hit the gym tomorrow, it's like we're carb loading tonight." They laughed and shoveled forkfuls in.

"How did the pie baking go?" Sawyer asked. The image of Luke smudged with flour, rolling pin in hand was somehow quite a turn on.

"I followed your grandma's recipe to a T, so I hope it turns out well. I didn't know you could make homemade pie crust; I always thought you just bought it in the store."

When they finished their potatoes and wine, they made their way to the couch.

"Let's start the movie and we can get pie about halfway through." Luke suggested.

"Sounds good to me." Sawyer plopped down on the couch and pulled Luke with him. Showering kisses all over his face, Sawyer thanked him for dinner. "Don't tell my grandma, but your potato bar was just as good if not better than hers." The kiss deepened when Luke grabbed hold of Sawyer's shirt and pulled him close.

It was much, much later when they finally started the movie.

19

The Center+ was good. His family was good. His friendship with Hayden was good. His relationship with Luke was beyond good.

But something was bothering him.

He spoke to Dr. Parks about it during a weekly session.

"I don't even know if I can explain this the way it feels in my head." Sawyer tried to sort his thoughts.

"Try," Dr. Parks encouraged.

"Okay, I know you know about Luke's past." Sawyer had convinced Luke to start seeing Dr. Parks after he'd come back to town. Luke had agreed and seemed to be benefitting from talking about his past with the doctor.

"Don't worry, I won't ask you to break doctor patient confidentiality. But Luke's told me he's told you all about the abuse from the past." Sawyer looked at the doctor, but just continued on because he knew the man would neither confirm nor deny what he'd just said.

"Anyway, I know Luke is emotionally and physically scared to bottom. And this is where it's really hard to explain, I could live the rest of our life being the bottom for him. Our sex life is great, I don't feel short-changed or anything like that." Sawyer glanced at Dr. Parks to see his reaction. As usual, the man had a completely neutral look on his face.

"I think I just feel like Luke isn't completely 'with' me because of this physical and emotional roadblock from his past. I want him to feel completely free. I want him to be able to decide what type of sex we have based on what he wants, not based on his fear of physical pain or the nightmarish memories he still deals with occasionally." Sawyer stopped and waited. "I think I also feel a little hurt that maybe he fears me? Like he's afraid I'd hurt him, even unintentionally?"

"You have the answer in you already, Sawyer. What do you think I'm going to tell you?" Dr. Parks waited patiently.

"You're going to say that I need to share my feelings with Luke. Then you're going to tell me that Luke has to find his way around this roadblock on his own, no one can do it for him." Sawyer sighed deeply. "And to think I'm paying you for this."

Dr. Parks chuckled. "See you next week."

"So, if I can't get over the pain from my past, is that going to be a deal breaker?" Luke asked defensively as he paced the room. "Like if I never let *you* fuck *me,* we're over?"

"No, never. That's not even close to what I'm saying." Sawyer shook his head vehemently. "I can honestly say that I could happily live the rest of my life with things just the way they are. Well, maybe throw in marriage and kids someday, but the sex setup is *not* a problem for me."

Luke relaxed slightly when Sawyer spoke and kissed him. "I just worry that the pain, both emotional and physical, from your past is blocking us from being completely open with each other. I don't want anything keeping us from being the best we can be, but I also never want to push you to do anything you're not ready for. And if I'm being honest and selfish, I'm a little hurt that deep down you could even think I would cause you pain." Sawyer ducked his head sheepishly.

Lifting his chin with the side of knuckle, Luke gazed intently into his eyes. "Sawyer, I have every intention of getting there, hopefully sooner rather than later. And I know you would die before you'd purposely hurt me. I get that in my heart; it's just getting my head to accept it." Luke kissed him softly. "Thank you for being patient with me."

SEVERAL WEEKS HAD PASSED, and Sawyer was happy, except for two things standing in the way of him being blissfully happy. Luke still hadn't worked through his fears completely, but Sawyer was determined to be patient with that issue. They'd get there when they got there. It wasn't like he was missing out on fabulous sex, not at all. He just wanted Luke's defenses to be dropped completely.

The second thing standing in the way of Sawyer being crazy happy was Luke still hadn't agreed to coming to a family dinner. Sawyer had begged and pleaded, but Luke balked or made up excuses every single time.

"We are 100% completely together, right?" Sawyer had asked.

"Of course we are, you know that," Luke huffed.

"You've met every member of my family. You hang out with a lot of them both in and out of work; everyone loves you." Sawyer was beginning to sound exasperated. When Luke didn't answer, he continued on, "I just want to be able to call you my boyfriend and have you by my side at family gatherings. My family is extremely important to me, and so are you. I want, no I *need*, for the two most important things in my life to come together."

Luke smiled sadly. "I know, and I want that too."

"Then what's stopping us? I just want to make things totally, 100%, no-doubt-about-it official. Please? Come to dinner this weekend. I think it's tacos." Sawyer wagged his brows as he wheedled Luke.

"I'll think about it. I don't know what's holding me back. Maybe it's fear of the unknown. I didn't grow up with a fabulous, and very large I might add, family, so this is all very new to me. I'm used to being on my own. I'm not used to big family get-togethers and weekly meals."

Luke wrapped his arms around Sawyer's waist and nuzzled his neck. "But for you, I will try. Just let me work it out on my own, okay?"

Sawyer chuckled and kissed him, "Thank you. And I'll keep waiting, because you're worth it." A kiss to his cheek. "100%." A kiss on the other cheek. "Totally." A peck to the lips. "Worth." Another brief kiss. "It."

When Luke sighed and leaned into him, Sawyer deepened the kiss.

Several heart-pounding moments later, they broke apart breathing heavily when Sawyer's phone buzzed. Looking at the text, Sawyer groaned. "Looks like they can get my car in tomorrow, but they want me to drop it off tonight."

"I'd offer to follow you down there and drive you back home, but I've got that evening class at work tonight. In fact, I'm going to be late if I don't head out right now." Luke grabbed the back of Sawyer's neck and pulled him in for one last kiss. "I...um, I'll see you tonight. Llll...later."

Sawyer's heart swelled at the stumbled words and what Luke had wanted to say. *Yeah, I love you too, babe. We'll get there. Some day.*

Picking up his phone, he called Hayden as he drove his car down to the auto shop.

"Hey man, can you come over to the new auto shop and pick me up?"

Sawyer smiled at Hayden's response.

"Yes, yes, I *could* just walk home. But where's the fun of that? Pick me up, and I'll let you buy me a beer before you take me home."

Chuckling, Sawyer ended the call. Hayden had turned out to be a great friend, and Sawyer was grateful for that.

Sawyer walked the keys into the new shop. It wasn't actually a new shop, but had a new owner. He'd not met the man in charge yet, but his dad and uncles all liked the place and had started bringing their vehicles in.

"Evenin'. What can I do for ya?" A man about his own age came around the corner wiping his hands on a rag. Sawyer quickly appraised the six foot frame, blue eyes, and light brown hair. The man was extremely attractive.

Reaching out a hand to shake, Sawyer smiled. "Hi, Sawyer Morgan. You texted me a bit ago letting me know you could work on my car tomorrow?"

Recognition dawned on the man's face. "Right, right. Glad to meet ya, Sawyer. I have to tell you I really appreciate the business your family has been sending my way."

He shook Sawyer's hand firmly. "I'm Mikael by the way, owner of the shop."

"No kidding? I expected someone older, more my dad's age. Good for you, already owning your own business. It's nice meeting you, Mikael." Sawyer glanced at the man's name tag and noticed the unique spelling of his name. Nodding toward his tag, Sawyer spoke, "Bet that gets misspelled quite a bit."

Mikael laughed. "You have no idea."

Sawyer filled out the paperwork and handed Mikael the keys.

"You need a ride man? I'll be finished here in a bit and can run you home." Mikael asked.

"No, no, I'm good. I've got a friend coming for me. Thanks though."

Making small talk while he waited, Sawyer continued, "So, what brought you to Torey Hope?"

"Long story." Mikael's laugh was a sad and bitter mixture. "Suffice it to say, I was born and raised in a town even smaller than this place. My family never accepted the fact that I was gay. My dad insisted on handing over the family auto shop to my brother and cutting me out completely unless I agreed to 'just be straight.' So, I left and never looked back. Worked for a few shops along the way, saved up a little bit of money, and lucked upon this place a few months back."

Realization snapped in Sawyer's mind; he'd had a sense Mikael was gay, but his senses seemed to have faded a bit since he'd gotten involved with Luke.

Pulling his phone out, he saw a text from Hayden.

Hayden: I'm here.

Sawyer spoke as he typed his reply. "I'm really sorry to hear about your family, that sucks. But you've found a great place here in Torey Hope. And with the previous guy retiring, you've walked into a goldmine of business I'd think. Once you get some customers back who moved when this place closed down, you should be sitting pretty."

Sawyer: Come in. I want you to meet Mikael.

Hayden: You want me to drag my ass into the auto shop to meet an old Russian guy named Mikael? I'll pass.

"Well, I hope those customers come back quickly. Finances are really tight, and I'm probably going to need to talk to the bank to get something set up until money is flowing in a little better." Mikael continued working under the hood of a car.

Sawyer discreetly snapped a picture.

Sawyer: No. I want you to come in to meet a young guy, about our age who happens to be gay with a unique spelling of his name. Check out how good he looks from my angle.

Sawyer stifled a laugh when Hayden appeared at the door in record time. Giving a quick nod in Mikael's direction, Sawyer wagged his brows at Hayden and mouthed, "Niiiice..."

Hayden frowned and cleared his throat before speaking, "You ready, man? The chariot awaits its queen." He smiled good-naturedly at Sawyer.

Recognizing a different voice, Mikael stood up straight and turned around. Wiping his hands on his rag again, he walked toward Hayden.

"Mikael, this is my friend, Hayden. Hayden, this is

Mikael. You two have somewhat similar stories as to why you're in Torey Hope. Maybe you should meet over coffee sometime and swap family disappointment tales." Sawyer teased them, but he noticed that the two men's eyes hadn't left each other the whole time he'd been speaking.

"Actually, Mikael, Hayden is the bank manager at Torey Hope First Financial, you could set up a business meeting with him and then do coffee later. A little business and plea-sure, kill two birds with one stone type thing." Sawyer smiled smugly and looked innocently at Hayden.

Rolling his eyes at his friend, Hayden shook his head. "Sorry about Miss Matchmaker there. He thinks just because he's all cozied up with his man, he can pimp me out to people he's just met."

Mikael laughed. "No worries, man. It's nice you've got a friend willing to look out for you like that. Actually, I *would* love to sit down with you and talk about business. After is optional, but I do love a good cup of coffee."

Sawyer watched in satisfaction as the two men exchanged numbers. *My work here is done,* he thought slyly to himself.

LUKE LEFT the gym after his last class that evening with his head absolutely swirling around his relationship with Sawyer. He wanted to take the next steps. He wanted to be able to bare himself completely with Sawyer, have a completely versatile sex life with him. He knew he just needed to do it and prove to himself that Sawyer would never purposely hurt him.

He also wanted so badly to go to dinner with Sawyer's family, to let them all see them together, in a real relationship once and for all, but he didn't know what was holding him back. It was if he was afraid Sawyer and everything good in his life would go up in smoke if he took that next step.

"Luke?" The captain interrupted Luke's musings.

"Evening, Captain. How are you doing?" Luke instantly felt nervous.

"I'm good, son. Listen do you have a minute?" The captain asked.

As if I'd tell you no, Luke thought. "Sure. Want to sit outside? It's a nice evening."

They walked out to a picnic table. Luke was on pins and needles wondering where the conversation was going to go.

"I've always been a straight shooter, so I'm going to just come right on out with what I want to say." The captain began and Luke nodded to show he was listening.

"Son, I'm not going to pretend to understand what you and my grandson have together. But just because I don't share the feelings or completely understand something doesn't mean it's not real. I've watched you and Sawyer; I don't think either of you *chose* to have these feelings and the struggles and stigmas that come with your sexuality." The captain paused again. Luke wasn't sure if he was waiting on an answer or not, so he just nodded again to show his under-standing.

"Now, something bad happened to me when I was a much younger man. It broke my heart and left me living as a shell of a man. I hid behind the pain, and I covered the pain with the bottle. I missed out on several years of living because I let the fear of moving on stand in my way. People were hurt in devastating ways because of my choices.

"Son, I'm not saying you're hurting others, but I do see you hurting yourself and Sawyer. I know you've had a rough past; I know you two will face some rough times in the future. In all honesty though, we've all got some shitty stuff in our pasts. We can't let the past control our future happiness. And we've all got potentially rough times in our futures. We can either choose to face those rough times with the people we love by our sides or alone. I've done it alone. I think you've had your fair share of alone. I'd much rather face the future with love surrounding me. What about you?" The captain paused and let the question hang in the air.

"Yes, sir, I'd rather have that too." Luke felt the man's words to the very core of his being.

"Well, then. I suggest you stop pussy-footin' around. Come to dinner this weekend; make yourself officially part of our family. We'd love to have you." The captain abruptly stood and nodded his head at Luke.

Such an unexpected, touching, and abrupt talk they'd just had. Luke couldn't help but smile.

As he rode his motorcycle home, a plan began to form in his mind.

IT WAS SATURDAY NIGHT; the next day was the big family dinner at his grandma's house. Would Luke be joining him this week or not?

A sense of dread overtook him when his phone buzzed.

Luke: I need to talk to you. Can you come over, please?

Sawyer: Everything okay?

Luke: Yeah, just some things that need to be said.

Sawyer's heart plummeted to his stomach. Climbing in his newly serviced car, he drove the short distance to Luke's place.

Walking in the door, Sawyer immediately noticed something different about Luke. His body longed to reach for the other man, but his head told him that Luke needed to do this, whatever *this* was, on his own. He let Luke lead him to the bedroom.

"Have you heard the song Take Your Time by Sam Hunt?" Luke's voice was raspy, only his cadence giving away his nervousness.

"No, I don't think so." Sawyer wasn't sure where the conversation was headed, but he knew he wanted to keep Luke talking. Even if nothing ever changed between them sexually, he couldn't bear the thought of not having Luke in his life. If Luke never settled in to Sawyer's family completely, could he live with that? Pushing the thought aside he focused on what Luke was saying.

Watching Luke pace the floor of the room while he rolled a piece of paper in his hands gave Sawyer a flicker of hope. If Luke was going to tell him something bad, wouldn't he have done it quickly to get it over with? With his heart full of half hope and half worry, Sawyer let Luke pace and work his words out in his own time.

Finally, seemingly satisfied with what he'd run through in his head, Luke stopped and walked to face Sawyer. "I want you to listen to this song; when it's over, I have some things I want to say to you. I need to do something on the computer to get ready for my part; put these headphones on and just listen." Luke gently placed the apparatus on Sawyer's head.

"What..." Sawyer started to speak, but Luke shook his head quickly.

"Just listen." Luke handed Sawyer his phone and indicated that Sawyer could push play, then he walked away and settled himself at the computer with his back to the room.

He was glad that Luke wasn't going to watch him listen to the song; he walked over to the bed and sat down, pulling a bent leg up and leaving one hanging over the edge. As he listened to the song's opening lyrics, he was confused: a guy talking to a girl in a bar, promising not to be another sleazy pick-up line, not wanting anything serious, just wanting her time. *Where the hell is Luke going with this song?* As he continued to listen his confusion grew; he could see no connection between their relationship up until that point in time and this song.

As the song ended, Sawyer sat still for a while just listening to the silence which surrounded him. That song wasn't a break up song, but it wasn't a love-filled, hopeful song. He turned cautious, wary eyes toward Luke and waited; his heart pounding.

Luke clicked a few more things on the computer then stood up with the laptop and came over to the bed. He put the computer in front of Sawyer. He settled in behind Sawyer, his legs mimicking the other man's so that his front was flush with Sawyer's back. Leaning in, he whispered, "That song is great, but it doesn't say exactly what I want it to say; I'm no songwriter, but I've changed some of the lyrics and I wanted you to see how I would sing that song to you. Watch."

Luke reached out to click play and a slide show type presentation came on the screen with Sam Hunt's "Take Your Time" song playing in the background. Each slide presented the lyrics as Sawyer had just heard them through the headphones. Still not understanding what was going on, Sawyer took a deep breath and relaxed into Luke's strong arms and solid chest.

As the chorus of the song played, Sawyer watched in breathless fascination as new lyrics of the chorus filled the screen. The original lyrics were played through the speakers while Luke's new lyrics stood out in upper case letters on the screen.

YOU'VE BECOME MY FREEDOM
I WANNA BE ON YOUR MIND
YOU'VE ALREADY MADE ME LOVE YOU
I DON'T WANNA WASTE MORE TIME
I WANNA BE PART OF YOUR FAMILY
WE'VE ALREADY CROSSED THAT LINE
I WANNA SHARE YOUR COVERS
I DON'T WANNA WASTE MORE TIME
I DON'T WANNA GO HOME WITHOUT YOU
I JUST WANNA BE WITH YOU
YOU CAN CALL ME BABY ANYTIME
I WANNA CALL YOU MINE
YOU ALREADY OWN MY HEART
I DON'T WANNA WASTE MORE TIME

Sawyer's body tensed as he read the altered lyrics; he held his breath throughout most of the song until it reached a certain point. Instead of lyrics about blowing your phone up and blowing your mind, Luke had thrown in some light-hearted lyrics about "I want to feel you up" and "I just want to blow...um..." Sawyer's body shook with laughter, and he felt relief flood through his body. He understood this was Luke's way of letting him know he was done letting the past control them.

The song ended, and Sawyer immediately clicked the file to play it again. Luke ran his hands along Sawyer's muscled thighs as the song floated in the air. Sawyer's strong hands came over his; their fingers intertwining.

When the song ended a second time, Sawyer stood abruptly and carried the laptop to the desk. Walking back towards Luke, he sat down hard on the bed and drew in a deep breath. Luke, sensing Sawyer was going to need some clarification on what his words meant for them, knelt on the floor between Sawyer's legs.

"So, like I warned you, I'm not a songwriter, but I hope you heard what I was saying with those words." Luke's eyes beseeched Sawyer to accept the words on the screen, let him off the hook, make this easy.

"I heard what those words were saying, but I'd like to hear it straight from your mouth." Wrapping his fingers among Luke's again, Sawyer longed to dip his head and taste Luke's mouth, but he knew there'd be time for that later.

"Sawyer, I've fought my real feelings since before my mother died. And for years after that, I clung to what I thought were her wishes. I let the pain and humiliation doled out on me rule my heart and my actions. But coming here to Torey Hope, meeting you, it made me start questioning every-thing. Finding that letter from my mom was like a little sign from her that I needed to pull myself together and really start living."

Sawyer ran his hands through Luke's hair, ignoring the desire to fist it and pull the other man's mouth to his own. "You haven't answered all of my questions, Luke."

"Am I ready to take our physical relationship that last step? Yes." Sawyer and Luke both took deep breaths and let their eyes meet over the words. Sawyer let his arms rest on Luke's shoulders, his hands clasped behind his neck. When Luke didn't continue, Sawyer raised an eyebrow and smirked.

Luke's gruff, emotional whisper filled Sawyer's ears, "Am I willing to take the last step and let myself become part of your family? Again, yes."

Sawyer's heart flip-flopped in his chest; in his dreams he'd imagined this happening if he waited patiently enough, but in his reality he'd known that Luke would possibly never be able to move beyond the emotional and physical pain he'd endured. Standing, pulling Luke up with him, Sawyer took in the hard planes of their bodies flush against each other, their almost equal heights putting their heated eyes level with each other, their breathing increasing as anticipation filled the room.

Sexual tension and heartfelt emotion crackled between them. Gripping the back of Luke's head, Sawyer leaned his forehead against the other man's and breathed deeply. "Tell me what you're thinking."

Luke ran his hands up the back of Sawyer's torso, reaching his shoulders and hooking his arms around him to hold him steady. Nipping at Sawyer's bottom lip, he soothed the sting with his tongue; when Sawyer's hips reflexively jerked, causing their hard lengths to grind together, Luke slammed his mouth down on Sawyer's. Each man fought for control of the kiss. Lips, tongues, teeth, Luke muscled Sawyer against the wall, thrusting his hips hard and earning a guttural groan from the other man.

"I'll tell you what I'm thinking, Sawyer. I want you, I need you, I want to be yours." With another punishing kiss against his mouth, Luke whispered again, *"I want to be yours."*

Sawyer sank into the wall, raising his hands above his head in total surrender. "Luke, I belong to you, I am yours completely." When the other man went to his knees, Sawyer almost fell to his. Luke made quick work of Sawyer's pants and boxer briefs. Grasping Sawyer's hard length in his fist, Luke dipped his head to lick the already tightening sac before trailing his tongue up the shaft; when he reached the swollen head, he swirled his tongue around right before he took the entire length in to his warm wet mouth.

Not wanting to finish Sawyer off too quickly, he popped off and stood up to press him hard into the wall with his hips. Their rock hard erections rubbed together almost painfully. Biting at Sawyer's lip, Luke gripped the other man's cock and gruffly whispered, "I know *you* are *mine*, Sawyer, but *I* want to be *completely yours*. I want you, I want *this*." He tightened his fist around Sawyer's erection. "Inside me. Now."

Wanting to believe him, but not wanting to pressure him into anything, Sawyer groaned and threw his head back hard against the wall. Trying to think rationally while his steely cock was caught in the vice grip of Luke's hand, Sawyer gritted his teeth and spoke in pants, "Luke, you need to be sure. I want to sink into your body; I want to be where no one has ever been; I want to own you body, heart, and soul. But I need you 100% on this; once I take you, I don't think I'll be able to give you up."

"Sawyer, my body craves you. I've been inside you, felt your heat and the way your body hugs mine. I want to give that to you; I want you to fill me, take me." He stepped back and waited in front of Sawyer; waited for the other man to accept his offer and make a move.

Sawyer stepped out of his clothes, throwing his shirt to the side. Lifting a rough hand to caress Luke's face, he looked deep into his eyes; his heart swelled when he saw complete surrender in Luke's eyes. "Luke, I love you; I think I've loved you since the night I busted your lip open. I want to take you, own you, love you." Kissing him softly, reverently, Sawyer maneuvered them towards the bed.

"This can't be quick. I'll take my time getting you ready." Kissing Luke quickly on the lips, he removed his shirt and pushed him down on the bed. Landing with a flop, Luke gazed up at Sawyer with such adoration and trust, Sawyer had to take a moment to steady himself. Leaning in to kiss down Luke's torso, he let his tongue trace the Vs which disappeared beneath his waistband. Biting his own lip, Sawyer slowly unfastened Luke's jeans and slid them roughly down his legs. Once his boxers were removed, Sawyer grabbed the lube and began his work. Sliding his mouth around Luke's cock, he massaged the area he most longed to be.

"More, I want more Sawyer," Luke panted from beneath him.

"Kiss me." He wanted to distract the other man from the potential pain. Sawyer smiled when Luke grabbed the back of his neck and pulled him down to devour his mouth. Never letting his finger stop prepping Luke's body, Sawyer gradually added another digit, feeling the muscle spread to accept the intrusion.

"Oh, God, Sawyer..." Luke's voice broke and Sawyer worried it was too much for him; if he couldn't adjust to Sawyer's fingers, he'd need a lot more time before he could take any other part of him.

"Luke, we don't have to do this tonight; I don't want to hurt you." Sawyer kissed the base of Luke's neck and ran his tongue along his collarbone.

"No, it's tight and full, but it doesn't hurt; it just feels...unlike anything I've ever felt." Luke slowly rock his ass against Sawyer's fingers. "But I want more. I want you."

Sawyer continued his work until Luke gritted his teeth and rode out his release.

Several sweaty, breathless moments later, Sawyer took his place between Luke's legs. Leaning in, he kissed the other man thoroughly, hoping to relax him enough that the next moment wouldn't be painful.

"Stop stalling. I'm not going to break. I love you; I've

loved you since the fishing trip I think. I need you." Luke rose on his elbows and grabbed the back of Sawyer's head; crushing their lips together, Luke guided Sawyer to the place where he wanted him the most.

"Relax for me." Sawyer hadn't been the top since before he met Luke, he knew this interaction had the chance to be over much quicker than he wanted it to be. Trying to go slowly, he pushed in gently and stilled when he met resistance. Withdrawing slightly, he meant to inch his way in, but Luke used his legs to press himself against Sawyer.

The searing pain took Luke's breath, but opening his eyes to watch as Sawyer's length invaded his body, Luke felt the pain subside as his body stretched around the throbbing flesh.

Sawyer's hands came down to hold Luke's hips, his heated eyes watching as his length slid in and out of Luke's body. Sawyer felt beads of sweat form on his head as he gritted against the tight heat. He felt the familiar tingle in his spine. Knowing he wasn't going to last long, he reached out and grasped Luke's rock solid length. Luke's second orgasm slammed into him just as Sawyer's barreled through him.

Disposing of the condom, Sawyer gathered Luke in his arms and held him. "You okay? Did it hurt too badly?"

"I'm perfect, Sawyer. That was perfect. I love you. Forever." Luke turned in Sawyer's arms and accepted a lingering kiss.

Proving he could give just as well as he could get, Luke kept Sawyer occupied in bed until neither of them could keep their eyes open. Pressing open mouthed kisses along Sawyer's neck, Luke whispered into his ear, "We should get some sleep, we've got dinner reservations tomorrow."

REALIZING he should have warned Kendrick to keep his mouth shut, Sawyer steeled himself for whatever was getting ready to leave his cousin's mouth.

"Sawyer? Luke? It's Taco Time. Are you two sure you're at the right dinner? I didn't realize you guys enjoyed tacos. Maybe you meant to come to next weekend's dinner? I think we're having coney dogs. You know, the nice long ones? Slap them in a *bun,* cover them in all kinds of tasty toppings and tear into them?" Kendrick howled with laughter as Sawyer shot him a look, but Luke just laughed. He'd never met someone like Kendrick before. The man could tease and laugh, but never made a person feel dirty or wrong.

Before the meal started, Sawyer watched curiously as Libby pulled Luke to the side. Not being able to help himself, Sawyer wandered over to where he could listen to what his mom was saying without being obtrusive.

"Luke, I'm so glad you came tonight, sweetie." Libby pulled Luke into a motherly hug.

"Thank you for having me, Mrs. Morgan." Luke was polite, but Sawyer overheard the nervousness in his voice. He wanted so badly to go save the day, but he didn't expect his mom was going to put Luke in a bad spot, so he held back.

"Luke Hamilton, that is the only time I better ever hear you call me Mrs. Morgan." She smiled mischievously and leaned in to whisper, "That makes me sound much too old and way too much like my mother-in-law." She giggled and put a finger to her lips as Luke laughed quietly.

Grabbing Luke's hands and looking him right in the eyes, Libby spoke sincerely. "You can call me Libby. I'd also be honored if you wanted to call me Mom, but that's entirely up to you. I've not heard the entire story, and I don't need to, but I know your mother was a beautiful woman inside and out, and she loved you very much. I'd never try to replace her. But I want you to know I'm here for you as a mom or a friend at all times. I'm so very happy to see you and Sawyer so very much in love; you two are very good for each other. Even if things don't work out between you and Sawyer, please know that I will *always* be here and willing to step into the mom or friend role if it's ever needed." Libby's eyes shone with tears.

Luke let himself be drawn into another hug, and Sawyer almost lost it. At no time had he felt so much love and adoration for his mother and Luke. His heart broke because he knew Luke needed this acceptance and motherly love so badly, but his heart also swelled with pride because his mom was the perfect woman to show Luke the maternal love and care he'd been missing.

"Thanks so much, Libby. I miss my mom like crazy, but it

means the world to me to know I've got Momma Morgan on my side and loving me." Luke blushed as he used her new nickname.

"Oh! *Momma Morgan*, I love it! It's perfect for the day I become a grandma." Libby winked at Luke, but let him off the hook with just a kiss to the cheek. "Thank you for fighting through the bad to get to the good. I know I'm biased, but I think Sawyer is totally worth it." Libby patted Luke's cheek.

"So totally worth it. Thank you for him, for raising him to be the man he is today, for being so open to who he is and who we are together. Thank you for welcoming me with open arms." Luke leaned in to kiss Libby's cheek.

Sawyer could stand it no longer, he had to join them.

"Hey, you two. It's not nice to whisper and keep secrets." He put his arm around Luke and pulled him close.

"Sawyer Nicholas, don't even try to pretend you didn't listen to that entire conversation. You always have been a bit too nosey for your own good." Libby tweaked his nose and laughed as he tried to appear innocent.

"Fine, you got me. I heard it all." Sawyer smiled sheepishly and pulled his mom into a hug. "Thank you for loving me. And thank you for loving Luke."

Libby smiled at the two of them and walked away to finish preparing lunch.

Sawyer and Luke milled about with the others, laughing and talking. Before long, his grandma called everyone to the table.

Sawyer kept a close eye on Luke during the meal, but he seemed to have settled in nicely and truly appeared to be enjoying himself. Sawyer, on the other hand, was a nervous wreck. He'd called his mom and dad earlier and let them know what he was planning, then he'd popped into Decker's room and filled him in that morning before he went to pick up Luke. Now he just had to get through dinner without puking, get Luke to the backyard, and pray he didn't lose his nerve.

"Oh no, was that thunder? I didn't think it was supposed to rain." Libby's voice was filled with concern and her eyes darted to Sawyer's knowing his plan hinged on outside.

Without thinking his next move through, Sawyer quickly stood. Grabbing Luke's hand, he pulled him up. "I need to show you something outside."

When Luke look confused and paused with a taco halfway to his mouth, Sawyer sputtered, "I mean, please, I need to show you something outside before it rains."

He pulled Luke through the kitchen and out the back door. Under a giant old oak tree, with thunder rolling around them, Sawyer faced Luke and grasped his hands.

"What's going on with you? I'm the one who should be nervous, but you're acting like a crazy person." Luke's eyes held true concern.

From the corner of his eye, Sawyer noticed his entire family spill out to stand on the wraparound porch. He knew they'd been filled in on what was coming next.

"Luke, from the first time I punched you in the nose, to the millions of times you told me we couldn't be together, to our first kiss and everything in between, you've challenged me. You've taught me patience. You showed me what it means to be strong and resilient and courageous. I grew up surrounded by love. I longed to find that same love for myself, but I feared it would never happen. Until that night you stepped into the ring with me and my life has been better ever since."

As huge fat drops of rain began to splat around them, they stayed fairly dry under the tree. Sawyer dropped to his knee and pulled a simple gold ring from his pocket. He watched as Luke's eyes filled with tears.

"We won't rush into things; we'll take all the time we need. But I need to know you'll be by my side until we decide to make that final decision. I love you. I will spend the rest of my life loving you. We'll look for matching rings further down the road, but for now, will you wear this ring to show the world you're mine?" Sawyer turned hope-filled eyes up to Luke and waited on his answer. At the tearful nod of his head, Sawyer smiled broadly and slid the ring onto Luke's shaking hand.

Reaching down and pulling Sawyer to his feet, Luke wrapped him in a warm embrace and kissed him thoroughly. "That was beautiful. *You* are beautiful. I love you so very much." Their lips met tenderly as the heavens opened up and a deluge even the huge oak couldn't protect them from poured down. Soaked to the bone, they broke apart when the sky lit up with lightning.

"Hey you two, you better get those rods in the house! We don't want any lightning strikes!" Kendrick yelled to them over the pouring rain.

Laughing hysterically, they splashed through the rain, and joined their family on the porch.

Pulling him into a wet embrace, Sawyer spoke softly to Luke. "You did it, babe. Your mom and Lucas would be so proud of you."

When Luke cocked his head in question, Sawyer cupped his hands around his cheeks. "Love. You let it in, you let it win. That's all your mom ever wanted for you."

Kissing him gently, Luke whispered, "Thank you for being worth the struggle and pain. I didn't know I had it in me to fight for my happiness until I found you."

"And we will spend the rest of our lives fighting for happiness, because what we've found is completely worth it." Sawyer's sincere words warmed Luke's heart.

ALSO BY A.D. ELLIS

If you'd like to read the other books in the Torey Hope series, please visit A.D. Ellis's website to find out more HERE. The other seven books are male/female romance.

You can find ALL of A.D. Ellis's work (the majority is male/male romance) by checking out adellisauthor.com

The <u>Something About Him</u> series has been revamped with revised stories, updated blurbs, and spiffy new covers.

The series is available on ALL of your favorite book platforms!

Bryan & Jase

Brody & Nick

Barrett & Ivan

Braeton & Drew

Ryker & Gavin

Kade & Cameron

ABOUT THE AUTHOR

A.D. Ellis is an Indiana girl, born and raised. She spends much of her time in central Indiana as an instructional coach/teacher in the inner city of Indianapolis, being a mom to two amazing school-aged children, and wondering how she and her husband of almost two decades have managed to not drive each other insane. A lot of her time is also devoted to phone call avoidance and her hatred of cooking.

She loves chocolate, wine, pizza, and naps along with reading and writing romance. These loves don't leave much time for housework, much to the chagrin of her husband. Who would pick cleaning the house over a nap or a good book? She uses any extra time to increase her fluency in sarcasm.

Sign up at http://www.subscribepage.com/ADEllisNews MMRomance for a FREE male/male romance book.

Find all of my books at https://www.adellisauthor.com/home/

If you prefer to read on other book platforms, I have a series available on ALL book platforms- https://books2read.com/ap/RWrrNx/AD-Ellis

Follow my website http://www.adellisauthor.com or find me on Facebook

http://www.facebook.com/adellisauthor

Check out my TikTok- https://www.tiktok.com/@adel lisauthor

You can also find me on Twitter http://www.twitter.com/ADEllisAuthor

ACKNOWLEDGMENTS

This is always one of the hardest parts of finishing a book, but quite possibly the most important part! It's so hard because I fear I'll miss someone who has helped me out, supported me, been a listening ear, or offered advice and encouragement. If I miss listing your name here, please know it wasn't on purpose, and I love you dearly!

To my READERS!! Without you, there would have never been a third book, let alone a sixth book! Thank you for loving Torey Hope and the characters as much as I do; knowing you are looking forward to another book is a lot of what keeps me writing some days. As long as these stories are in my head, I'll keep sharing them with you.

To the BLOGGERS who read and review and share my books!! You are beyond a shadow of a doubt some of the most dedicated and selfless people I've ever known! Thank you so much for being such a support to those of us who have stories to tell. I love BLOGGERS!

To my author friends! Thank you so much for welcoming me into your crew and sharing your knowledge, experience, advice, and fun with me! Having some real-life authors/friends I can collaborate with is a great feeling. Dance parties, lunches, movies, videos, wine, painting, pizza...the list goes on and on!

I've already mentioned these two people, but they deserve another shout out. Renee, thank you first for reading <u>For Nicky</u> and contacting me to let me know you loved the story. And thank you for introducing me to Brett.

Brett, this book came alive because of your input and feedback. I had the story in my head, but you helped me clear out misconceptions and preconceived notions so that Sawyer's story could be the most honest and realistic possible. Plus, you made me laugh and taught me quite a lot along the way. Thank you for your friendship. My wish for you is hope, happiness, and love. (And don't think you're getting out of our fun and games at a certain convention in a summer or two.)

To my family and friends. I know most of you don't understand my obsession with getting these stories out of my head and on paper, but you're proud of me either way. Some of you get to read my books, some of you get to see cover ideas, some of you have to watch me lose myself in a story, some of you have to hear me vent about the hard parts of all of this; all of you love me and support me and for that, I am truly lucky and grateful.

NOTES

In case you missed my statement earlier in the book, I wanted to be sure it was mentioned again: Sadly, I am very well aware, as I'm sure many readers are, that a large number of lesbian, gay, bisexual, and transgender people are not met with love, support, or acceptance. Sawyer, along with many of his gay friends, deal with discrimination, misconceptions, fear, and hatred throughout the book. The way this story played out came completely from Sawyer and the other characters, I just wrote the story they wanted to tell. It may be a much rougher story than the ones some readers have heard or experienced; it may be a much happier version of what some readers have heard or lived through. But, either way, it's a realistic story focusing on acceptance, hope, and love.

If you or someone you love need information or support in issues surrounding sexuality, please connect with one of the many organizations available to assist. Here are two such organizations:

PFLAG http://community.pflag.org/getsupport

GLBT National Help Center http://www.glbthot line.org/

RECIPE

Sawyer's favorite dessert, chocolate pie. This recipe is from the author's mother. A homemade crust is always best, even though Luke thought all pie crusts came from the store.

Crust:

2 cups sifted all-purpose flour

1 teaspoon salt

2/3 cup leaf lard

5 to 7 tablespoons of ice cold water

Sift flour and salt together. Cut in shortening with pastry blender till pieces are size of small peas. Sprinkle with 1 tablespoon of ice cold water - gently toss with fork - push to side. Repeat until all is moistened. Form a ball. Flatten on lightly floured surface. Roll from center to edge till 1/8 inch thick.

Put into 9 inch pie pan. Prick bottom and sides with fork. Bake at 450- degrees for 10 to 12 minutes. Let cool completely.

Chocolate filling:

 1 cup sugar

 1/3 cup flour

 1/4 teaspoon salt

Two one ounce squares of unsweetened chocolate - chopped fine

 2 cups milk

 3 slightly beaten egg yolks

 2 tablespoons butter

 1 teaspoon vanilla

Combine sugar, flour and salt. Stir in milk gradually. Add chocolate. Cook and stir over medium heat until bubbly. Cook for 2 minutes stirring constantly. Remove from heat. Take small amount of cooked mixture and add it to beaten egg yolks. Stir. Return egg yolk mixture to cooked mixture in pan. Cook for 2 more minutes stirring constantly. Remove from heat. Add butter and vanilla. Stir. Pour into cooled pie shell. Cover with plastic wrap to keep film from forming while filling cools. When cooled top with fresh whipped cream and shavings of chocolate.

Whipped cream:

1 cup heavy whipping cream. 2 tablespoons sugar. *Beat whipping cream until peaks form. Add sugar.*